Praise for

The Rogue and Other Portuguese Stories

"Julieta Rodrigues's short stories are beacons of clarity which signal and propel forward contemporary discourse into Portuguese identity. Her psychologically deep and circumstantially complex characters find themselves thrown into the fires of economic recession. It is not only personal and familial identity which unfurls across the page, but also national identity. The interplay between these two great identity crises, the micro and the macro, ebbs and sways in the great tide of turbulent narrative. The criminal, the victim and the religious rebel are all examples of the marginalized who are here given room to breathe and speak their past and present, always contemplating the possibility that everything will come together in the end. Ultimately, *The Rogue and Other Portuguese Stories* explores the necessity for definition of the 'other'—every rogue has his victim, every mother her daughter and every ideological viewpoint its antithesis. The collection's prose dances through this ample diversity and the waters kicked up elucidate the spectrum of Portuguese attempts at self-definition. However, looming between and within the lines is a deeply embedded and inescapable past—the grip of bygone colonial supremacy, of Catholic oppression, and recent memories of the Carnation Revolution. Broad in scope and psychologically deep, this collection is an invaluable aid in dissecting the current Portuguese condition. Julieta Rodrigues's characters display the optimism of a fresh start, and it is these inner beginnings and brief awakenings that remind us of the current Portuguese and even worldwide context: we exist in an increasingly globalized, post-economic crash and post-colonial world. The characters yearn to solve problems necessarily bigger than themselves—sexism, religious intolerance, familial disintegration, to name but a few—and though they are beaten back, both literally and figuratively, each story ends not with so much a ray of

hope but a guiding light of deeper truth. The sincerity with which each story flows, the economic and class-structure realism, enable a strong empathy with each character and, by the end of the collection, with contemporary Portugal as a whole.

This is an accomplished work which positions its author firmly at the forefront of contemporary Portuguese short fiction."

—Erik Van Achter, Researcher, Center for Portuguese Literature, University of Coimbra and Katholieke Universiteit Leuven, Belgium.

About the Author

Julieta Almeida Rodrigues, Ph.D., has taught courses in sociology, politics, creative writing, literature and culture at the University of Lisbon and Georgetown University. The last story in this collection, "Black on White," was published by the *Interdisciplinary Journal of Portuguese Diaspora Studies,* Vol 2, 2013. Shortly afterwards, a link to the story was created in e-Cultura, Centro Nacional de Cultura (CNC), in Destaques. Dr. Rodrigues is currently a member of the Historical Novel Society, writing a historical novel based on the biographies of three distinguished personalities of the European Enlightenment. The work is based on conference papers presented at Yale University (American-Portuguese Studies Association) in 2008 and the Chawton House Library in 2013. In spring 2014, Dr. Rodrigues was appointed a Visiting Scholar at the New School for Public Engagement, New School University, New York City, as a Consultant on Iberia and Latin America for Project Continua (www.projectcontinua.org). Dr. Rodrigues is a member of the Pen Club of Portugal, the Fulbright Commission Team of Evaluators in Portugal and CLEPUL—Center for Lusophone and European Literatures and Cultures, Faculty of Humanities, the University of Lisbon. Dr. Rodrigues founded the Columbia University Alumni Association of Lisbon.

The Rogue
and
Other Portuguese Stories

Also by the same author

Julieta Almeida Rodrigues, *On the Way to Red Square*
(New Academia Publishing/Scarith Books, 2006)

The Rogue
and
Other Portuguese Stories

Julieta Almeida Rodrigues

Washington, DC

New Academia Publishing 2014

Printed in the United States of America

Library of Congress Control Number: 2014934313

ISBN 978-0-9915047-2-5 paperback (alk. paper)

An imprint of New Academia Publishing

New Academia Publishing
PO Box 27420, Washington, DC 20038-7420
info@newacademia.com - www.newacademia.com

Life is a vexing trap.

Ward No. 6, Chekhov

Em Portugal levo sempre tempo
a reconhecer, outra vez, o cheiro das coisas.

In Portugal, it always takes me time
to recognize the smell of things once again.

Artes e Leilões, Setembro 2007
Paula Rego

Os portugueses não são um povo de sol,
são um povo de sombras.

The Portuguese are not a people of sunshine,
they are a people of shadows.

Time Out, 18/24 April, 2012
Fernando Dacosta

To
Robbie Murphy
my mentor in the craft of writing
and
to my son
Julian
as always

Contents

Foreword

Well-known writers have pointed out negative traits they believe lie at the core of Portuguese identity: wickedness, hypocrisy, envy, pettiness, and revenge. In short, they have addressed problematic concepts that appear to result from a long-lasting lack of national resources. Geographic periphery, chronic poverty, and European isolation might help explain why such unique traits still prevail in our character well into the twenty-first century. They might also help to clarify how this small nation contributed to the era of globalization, using the Atlantic Ocean as point of departure. After centuries of dissemination, the Portuguese nowadays enjoy a considerable Diaspora around the globe. Portuguese live abroad, working and contributing to their communities in myriad ways. It is, therefore, worth illustrating the traits listed above and endeavoring to identify whether they are indeed embedded in our national character. It is a character shaped by our monarchy, the republic, the Salazar years of the Estado Novo, and the democratic regime instituted by the Carnation Revolution in April 25, 1974. Since its foundation, the subtle yet penetrating power of the Catholic Church has constantly underpinned the state.

This is the fertile ground that I explore in my Portuguese short stories. The stories were influenced by Scott Peck, specifically his renowned book, *People of the Lie: The Hope for Healing Human Evil.* Scott Peck is an American psychiatrist who, with the universality of the good essayist, describes the dark side of human nature. This is a notion which, obviously, impacts any society, not Portugal alone.

Two of his theories have remained with me since I read his book. The first one—and a staggering one it is—is that evil in people is not readily visible to the naked eye; in fact, it requires close scrutiny over time. The second is that all great lies are expressed in the deepest of silences.

These are the ways that prevaricators use to trivialize the notion of evil. Their modes of operating preclude a liberating discourse, a creative and open dialogue between human beings. Above all, their behaviors shatter the whole notion of truth.

More than anyone else on the contemporary scene, Paula Rego, the Portuguese artist residing in London, best addresses the issues at hand. Her paintings display a most revealing search for truth—the Portuguese truth. Her works are at the very core of Portuguese identity.

My short stories, in their own way, address some of the same concerns.

I hope the stories will become intellectual vehicles for students in the United States and England who are interested in Portugal. Written from a sociological perspective, my narratives illuminate a wide range of topics in contemporary Portugal. I continue to be surprised by the close interrelation between city and country, by changes in traditional mores stemming from both emigration and immigration, by the lack of quality of our political apparatus, by the poor work done by syndical organizations that pretend to speak in the name of the people, and by the narrow-mindedness of our elites. It goes without saying that my stories are unsettling. They involve impasse, dilemma, ambiguity, and conflict of interest, which I hope will spark lively debate.

As I am currently a Visiting Scholar (Spring 2014) at the New School for Public Engagement, New School University, in New York City, it seems fitting to reiterate that my stories also focus on the banality of evil, a theme so dear to Hannah Arendt, once an outstanding professor of this school.

I know that many readers have lived situations similar to the ones I describe in my stories. This is why I wrote them. The stories are, however, the work of a fictional imagination. Any resemblance to actual facts is purely coincidental.

I would like to thank, once again, a long list of colleagues, institutions and friends that were at my side when I wrote this collection. Their invaluable input was similar to the one I described when I published my first collection of short stories, *On the Way to*

Red Square, SCARITH/New Academia Publishing, LLC, 2006, Second expanded edition. I would like to thank Professor Gina Luria Walker who made possible my stay at New School University. A "learned woman," Professor Walker directs the Female Biography Project and Project Continua with an outstanding group of women, including Koren Whipp, Penelope Whitworth, Kaitlin Sansoucie, and Magdalen Livesey to whom I am forever indebted. Two grants awarded a long time ago shaped this book. In 2003 the National Library of Portugal in conjunction with the Luso-American Foundation allowed me to spend time in Portugal during the summer. In 2005 Instituto Camões awarded me a grant for creative writing. Without these grants I would have never been able to work on Portuguese materials again. Two former Portuguese Ambassadors in Washington, D.C., Dr. Pedro Catarino and Dr. João de Vallera, provided a link to the country and precious discussions about Portugal. Professor Onésimo Almeida from Boston University has been a trusted friend for many years. Doctor Amélia Hutchinson from the University of Georgia is someone who always guides with intelligence what is in my mind. When I lived in Portugal in 2010-2013, Professor José Barreto from Instituto de Ciências Sociais was an academic who made me feel welcome. Dra. Ana Vicente and Dra. Margarida Cardoso provided priceless insights into themes I decided to approach. The artist Celeste Maia has been at my side with the advice of a renowned creator. Anne Christman represents the generosity of heart and the open-mindedness I so much admire in the American people. Teresa and John Greenwald, Patricia Morrill and Edward Riegelhaupt have been compassionate friends on this and the other side of the Atlantic. Gail Spilsbury edited a first draft of these stories and Marian Smith Holmes edited the final draft. Magdalen Livesey kindly did a final proofreading; she is utterly dedicated to her craft. There are others I must recall, in particular Dr. Sérgio Luís de Carvalho, Dra. Maria da Conceição Pita Pestana, Dr. Madalena Homem Cardoso, and Artist Thelma Chambers. Last but not least, friends in Portugal are part of this book by being present in my life: Dinah Azevedo Neves, President of the Associação dos Amigos de Monserrate, Manuela Tuna, Sílvia Chicó and Ana Mantero. I again feel fortunate that Professor Anna Lawton appreciated my stories and offered to publish them.

To conclude, I feel honored that the Portuguese Artist Manuel Pessôa-Lopes granted me permission to reproduce his remarkable photograph intitled "DA BAIXA DE LISBOA, OBTIDA DA MURALHA FERNANDINA NO PALÁCIO DA INDEPENDÊNCIA" on the cover of this collection of stories.

I am solely responsible for the content of this book.

The Rogue

"Any news?" Borges asked Sandra, his secretary, as he abruptly opened the front door of the Lisbon law firm Borges & Mendes. It was past one p.m. and the attorney's day already promised to stretch well into the evening.

"Indeed there are," Sandra replied. She was at the computer with the telephone close by. The silk drapes on the window behind her attested to the status the firm Borges & Mendes had acquired over the years.

"There is a lady waiting for you in the conference room," Sandra continued. "Unfortunately, her face looks like a chocolate cake with sprinkles. She's bruised black and blue with splotches of red."

"Sounds like she needs a medical doctor, not an attorney," Borges said, quickly crossing the hall.

"Her neck and arms are in bad shape, too," Sandra added. "Mr. Nunes called you on her behalf and said the matter is urgent."

"Probably another accident victim." As he uttered these words, Borges entered his office, dropped his briefcase, and grabbed a yellow legal pad. As he headed for the conference room, he contemplated the statistics that showed Portugal having one of the highest road accident rates in the European Union.

At the doorway, Borges saw a woman sitting by the large mahogany table. She was staring at the wall. She wore her coat and could barely open her left eye. Due to the state of her face, he could not determine her age.

"Good afternoon," Borges said. "I'm told a colleague referred you to me. I'm sorry I've kept you waiting." He shook the hand hardly stretched out to him. "I see you need medical attention."

"Perhaps I do," the woman answered in a low-pitched voice. "I hear you are the best attorney to help me."

"Your name, please?"

"I'm Ema Bivar."

"Interesting name. It reminds me, somehow, of the famed Emma Bovary."

"Oh, I hope not. Emma had such tragic destiny!" Ema replied.

As Borges wrote down the name on his yellow pad, he asked, "Ms. Bivar, what can I do for you?"

"Dr. Borges, I'm divorced, no children." As customary in Portugal, Ema addressed the attorney as if he were a medical doctor. She was having difficulty speaking and supported her jaw with her right hand. It seemed she could not open her mouth wide enough to push her words out. Her split lip oozed a tiny rivulet of blood.

"You aren't in good shape. Let me get you some water or coffee before you continue," Borges said. He pressed the intercom button and asked Sandra to bring the drinks.

"I'll get straight to the point," Ema said. "I need legal advice before I go to a hospital." Ema's voice was on the verge of cracking. "My ex-boyfriend wants to kill me; I left him a while ago."

"I assume you are using your words cautiously," Borges interrupted. He wasn't indifferent to human suffering.

"I might be murdered one of these days," Ema said, trying to be concise. "More than a year ago I met a man in Paraíso da Damaia—Damaia Paradise, how ironic! It's a *pastelaria,* a pastry shop, next door to the building where I live. He was a very handsome man, slim, more than a decade younger than I. He worked as a car mechanic before losing his job."

Ema took a deep breath and supported her jaw with her hand again. She was trying to loosen it up so that her words sounded clear.

"One day I sat down at the counter and we struck up a conversation. Nothing serious at first. Before going home after work I often stopped at the *pastelaria* for a break. I'm a manager in an industrial plant. After a while, I realized that Lucas—that's the young man's name—seemed to be waiting for me."

Ema interrupted her phrase, a painful look stamped on her face. Sipping her coffee, she gazed at the pictures hanging from the wall opposite the mahogany table. They were a series of engravings of pillories from the Alentejo region of Portugal, south of Lisbon: stone columns in public squares, surrounded by noteworthy buildings—the city hall, the principal church, the palace. In the far distant past, criminals were punished by hanging from iron bars or rings attached to the columns. Then, for public viewing, they were whipped or mutilated, often causing a slow, torturous death.

Disturbed by the pictures, Ema looked away and continued her story. "Every time I stopped at the *pastelaria,* Lucas's eyes captivated me. He enjoyed looking stylish and dressed in ragged jeans, like a teenager. He had a *cara lavada,* a clean face that exuded reliability. He personified someone yearning for me at the end of the day. How could I resist?"

"Were you obsessed with him?" Borges asked, trying to gather as many details as possible.

"It's possible. While driving home at the end of the day, I started wondering whether Lucas was at the *pastelaria.* I drive a red convertible and I would usually park my car in the square in front. "

"Nothing in your description explains the state you are in," Borges stated, wanting to get to the point.

"You need the whole story. That first day at the counter, we chatted and he said he had been waiting for me for months. After coffee, I asked him over to my place. We kissed by the front door and a few minutes later were in bed."

"I see," Borges replied.

"At the beginning all went well—really well—I was happy to have someone in my life. Saturday mornings we went shopping and in the afternoon we drove around in my car. I didn't mind paying for all our expenses; they weren't excessive."

"What happened next?" Borges was eager to get to where things went awry.

"With time, men can't stand women like me. Lucas wasn't my only failed post-divorce relationship. Men envy the things that women get through hard work: money, a nice home, a convertible. In all, security."

Borges listened to Ema in silence.

"Months passed and Lucas wasn't getting a job. I know that the country, and the world, are in crisis, but Lucas didn't seem to be trying hard enough. He visited the local national employment agency and applied for a few positions; but it seemed he was just letting time pass by."

"Then what happened?" Borges was getting hungry for his midday meal and feared he might not have even five minutes to grab a bite.

"At first I paid for our weekend expenses, including the movies now and then. Then, dinner every night. Soon, Lucas started asking for money for transportation."

"Not good." Borges knew now where the conversation was heading.

"Originally I believed that Lucas wanted to get a job. The sexual relationship was good—really good—so I put up with his unemployment. When he asked, I bought him clothes; I didn't want him poorly dressed in my company. Our age difference was already a striking contrast." Saying this, Ema adjusted her jaw once more. She lifted her right shoulder as if to align neck and spine.

"Once in a while we drove to Madrid for the weekend. Lucas had never left Portugal and he loved travelling. I let him drive my two-seater sports car. It's a Fiat. Often we'd leave on Friday evening and not return until Monday morning. It was fun; we enjoyed flamenco dancing. When we got back Lucas began staying at my house a lot, sleeping all morning. At the beginning I enjoyed thinking of him in my bed."

"I see you enjoyed each other's company," Borges said, fondly remembering his own trips to Spain.

"Lucas loved my sports car. As a good mechanic, he always took care of the Fiat repairs. This was his way to reciprocate my paying his expenses. Once, he offered me a brand new top for the convertible. Black, very classy!"

Borges shaped his next question with utmost tact. "Ms. Bivar, if your ex-boyfriend didn't hold a job, where did he get the cash to offer you such a gift?"

"Frankly, I don't know, Dr. Borges. I asked and got an elusive answer. Lucas said a friend had bought it, and he wanted me to have it."

"As a gift?" Borges displayed a worried expression. Ema Bivar seemed naive.

"I interpreted the Fiat's expensive top as compensation for my financial help. For Lucas, my car was a toy." After another long pause, Ema added, "But, with time, things started to go sour; I needed an older, more responsible man by my side."

For effect, Borges emphasized his words so that Ema had a chance to reflect on something that seemed to have escaped her. "The convertible top had to come from somewhere. The question is where."

Ema ignored the detail. "Lucas is a jealous man. That's why

things were going wrong between us. I often have professional meetings late in the afternoon. Other managers come from branches around Lisbon, and due to heavy traffic, we usually start the discussions behind schedule. If I got home even half an hour later than the usual time, he'd start a fight. Then he cursed. I wasn't used to it, Lucas's origins are humbler than mine."

"Lucas was being possessive," declared Borges, all along taking notes in his yellow pad.

"I explained to him that my job was demanding, that my salary didn't simply fall from the sky. Getting home late was beyond my control. If the plant was launching a new product, the meetings with other branch managers were frequent."

"Of course!" Borges knew the business world very well.

"Lucas spent his days either with his friends or glued to the TV. He frequently made a mess of my place and never offered to clean up. For him, the grand moment was when I got home in the evening."

"Your description is rather indicative of his personality."

Ema moved her right arm and readjusted her position. "I got fed up. In the past I never saw myself as a victim of circumstances. So I told Lucas that things couldn't continue as they were. Either he did something useful with his life…or else."

"What exactly did you mean?" Borges gazed directly at his client.

"I told him we needed to head our separate ways. I was still in love, but a break-up was inevitable. His jealousy made no sense; my home was topsy-turvy every day. I was suspicious that he brought his friends over when I was absent, even if he denied it. Once Lucas introduced me to a friend of his at the *pastelaria;* the fellow looked derelict."

"Yes, that would be very unsettling!" Borges exclaimed.

"But sex with Lucas was satisfying, so I waited a while. On the other hand, what else did I get from the relationship? I got trips—that I paid for—and a sense of adventure. Besides that, there was nothing there."

"I understand your predicament," Borges said in a friendly voice. "Reciprocity is essential in relationships."

"Once we went to Barcelona to see the Gaudi architecture. What Lucas really wanted was to drive the convertible; he didn't give a damn for the buildings. He loved hitting the gas, and my car is very fast."

Borges glanced at his watch; the conversation had already consumed an hour. Here was Ema Bivar in front of him—a woman close to forty with a battered face—and he needed to turn to pressing matters in his agenda.

"You're looking at your watch," Ema said, once again painfully adjusting herself in the chair. "I'll finish quickly. One day I was leaving rather early for work and Lucas was still in bed. I asked him to get up to help me bring in a heavy carton of beer from my car. It was a Monday morning; I remember the day as if it were yesterday. Since it was cold, I asked him to dress and put on his coat. As if in a hurry for work, I said I had his keys with me." Ema took in a deep breath. "Downstairs I told Lucas our relationship was over."

"Ahhh!" murmured Borges, anticipating the consequences.

"Lucas turned into a viper. He grabbed my arms, yanked my hands behind me and started pulling on them as if to rip them off my shoulders. I fell on my back and he began kicking me all over."

"Lucas is dangerous!" Borges declared as he scribbled more notes. "We need to file a police report immediately. "

"Since that day—over six months ago—Lucas has attacked me repeatedly. He follows me everywhere: in the staircase of the building where I live, near the entrance of the plant where I work, even when I visit my relatives. I spent a couple of weeks with a cousin, but he found me there. He knows my routine, so he can predict my whereabouts."

"This is inexcusable!" said Borges.

Ema Bivar felt reassured she had chosen the right attorney. "Lucas has beaten me up, on average, once a month since we broke up. And he's threatened that he won't rest until he is done with me—kills me or cripples me, or destroys me psychologically. " Ema paused. "I can't go on living in fear, something needs to change," she continued. "Otherwise I will disappear from this earth pretty soon."

"I've got all the details necessary for a police report," Borges assured her. "You need to go from here to the hospital so that we can attach a medical report. It's really a pity you didn't come to me earlier."

"I thought Lucas might stop after the first beating. Now I see he is serious about his intentions."

"Where did Lucas find you today? Were there any witnesses?" Borges grabbed the yellow pad again.

"He attacked me on the stairway of my building, I was leaving for work. If he goes around the block where I live and sees my car, he knows I'm at home." Terrified, Ema continued. "As soon as I opened my apartment's front door this morning, he attacked me."

"Did anyone see what happened this morning?"

"I don't think so. When I started screaming—at first I held back—Lucas punched me repeatedly in the face and neck. Afterward, he dashed down the stairs." Ema opened her coat, which she hadn't removed during the interview. Placing her scarf aside, she showed the bruises on her neck and shoulders.

"This is bad. If you screamed, someone in the building should have come in your defense," Borges said.

"I went back into my apartment and lay in bed for a few hours. I felt so ashamed."

"Ms. Bivar, we must stop our conversation now. You need a medical doctor, and I need to file a police report. Please bring back the medical evaluation as soon as you have it. We'll also include all pertinent information about your ex-boyfriend. We'll put this scumbag where he belongs."

"I surely hope so."

"You don't have previous medical reports, correct?"

Ema shook her head.

"Too bad. But we'll state that this complaint refers to repeated acts of violence on the part of your ex-boyfriend." Trying to protect his client, Borges said, "You should consider moving in with your cousin, or a friend, for the next couple of weeks. At least until the police finish the investigation."

"But he finds me wherever I go!"

"I believe he'll change his tune as soon as the police call him in for questioning."

Borges stood up, and as Ema did the same, she was unable to stifle a shriek of pain. Showing concern, Borges led her out of his office.

Ema headed to the crowded hospital in her neighborhood. Examining her face in the car's mirror, she asked herself why had she taken so long to seek legal advice. Was it the recollection of the satisfying sex? A vague loyalty to someone she had felt close to? The memory of the fun trips in the convertible?

Or was it the fear of Lucas's retaliation?

She spent the entire afternoon in the emergency room waiting to be seen. Some other patients—a few had arrived earlier, others came in with strokes—had priority. Ema sat in a corner, willing to wait as long as it took for her turn. At least, there, with loads of people around, Lucas wouldn't be able to get her.

She considered visiting her mother in the South, in the beautiful plains of the Alentejo region. The idea of a few days' rest seemed wonderful. But her mother's side of the family lived with her in a small village: everybody would ask questions. How could she explain what had happened? Ema recalled the engravings on Borges's wall. The pillories were symbols of power and tyranny; for centuries they had represented physical abuse and public condemnation. No, her cousin's apartment was a better option. She didn't feel like opening her wounds to people's scrutiny, an unbearable humiliation.

The female physician who attended Ema was most sympathetic. Had the doctor been a male, an older one, things might have been different. The doctor disinfected and dressed her bruises, then prescribed medication. She wrote and signed a detailed medical report that Ema took to Borges's office.

A couple of weeks later Ema, in better shape, met again with Borges. She was more relaxed, her face and lips were healing. When Borges entered the room, Ema took off her sunglasses and greeted him. Her eyes opened normally now. Borges noticed a petite woman of about forty years with a sculptural figure. He thought of a Portuguese saying comparing women to sardines: the smaller, the better. She had a sensuous look and her eyes bore the intensity of a mature woman, ready for love.

"Your condition has drastically improved!" exclaimed Borges.

"I feel so much better that I expect to be back to work in a few days."

"Things are advancing here as well. A detailed report was sent to the police within twenty-four hours of my office receiving your medical evaluation. Here is a copy for you." He handed Ema the file. "My intention, of course, is to incarcerate your ex-boyfriend."

Ema now knew she should have acted after the first beating. At least she no longer felt ashamed of what Lucas had done, as if it had been her fault. She glanced through the police report. Lucas emerged as the man he was: carefree, unemployed, jealous, vindictive and violent when abandoned. A merciless offender, engrossed with his former lover.

"The police will interrogate Lucas very soon, if they haven't already. I contacted a friend at headquarters who will speed things up." Borges paused, studying Ema's expression. "Ms. Bivar, I need to ask you a delicate question, I hope you don't mind."

"Please, by all means. What is it?"

Borges was now a wolf in sheep's clothing. Breaking the suspense, he inquired: "Does Lucas have anything he can use against you in court?"

"We've gone through this before. I grew tired of the relationship and Lucas was unable to accept the break-up."

"That's clear. But think carefully for a moment. Does he possess any information that the police might use against you?"

"I don't think so." Ema's tone held a note of hesitation. She contemplated once more the terrifying pillory engravings on the walls of the conference room. They sent a shiver down her spine.

"You stating *I don't think so* will not suffice, unfortunately. We need to play it safe with the police." Borges said, shifting uncomfortably in his chair." Could Lucas disclose something to the police in order to harm you?"

"Actually, there might be something," Ema said after a short sigh while still looking at the pillories on the wall.

"Let's hear it." Borges added promptly.

"As I told you, I have a Fiat convertible. However, the engine is from an Alfa Romeo. I let Lucas install the more powerful engine, one of the reasons our trips were so enjoyable."

Borges nodded, as if nothing could surprise him after his many years in practice.

"Where is the Fiat engine?" He asked. "Do you still have it?"

"It's in a box on my balcony."

"Good! Ms. Bivar, as you know, every vehicle's engine has a serial number registered to the vehicle's identification plate. The change introduced to your convertible by your ex-boyfriend is a felony punishable by law."

Ema remained silent and Borges was certain she understood what he was saying. "The situation is easily resolved. You must put back your original engine immediately." Borges said emphatically.

"You mean go back to driving like a snail?" Ema asked, unhappily.

"Absolutely! The police report has been filed, and you'll be called to testify on very short notice. You don't want to be hurt again, do you? You will be, for sure, if the police find out about the Alfa Romeo's engine in your Fiat."

"Okay. I promise I'll change it," she replied.

"Please take the car to a garage far away from your neighborhood. Pay someone—late evening might be safer—to take your Fiat engine to this garage. Then have the engines exchanged. Find a secure place for the Alfa Romeo's engine. Don't keep it at home, don't sell it either. After this, we can relax and wait for the police to do its job."

"This is utterly inconvenient—and expensive," Ema protested, turning red. Her *joie de vivre* seemed vanished forever. "Like Lucas, I enjoy speeding on the road."

"Your engine's number and vehicle's plate must match. It's the law." Borges stood up somewhat abruptly; he had another busy day ahead. "These are precautionary measures, you must follow my advice."

While waiting for the elevator outside the law offices, Ema fumed. She now must part with her treasured Alfa Romeo engine. The celebratory mood of that remarkable day—the day she had agreed to Lucas changing her car's engine—was gone forever.

The following morning at Paraíso da Damaia, Ema asked about Lucas but no one had seen him for weeks. Lucas apparent disappearance was a reason for concern for Ema. She knew only fear of the police might deter him.

Going about the rest of her day, Ema reflected on the vagaries of life. The affair with Lucas had been sheer pleasure at the beginning. He behaved like a cocky adolescent in his late twenties, like a Portuguese James Dean, overflowing with lust. Lucas was ready for adventure and stated so, unabashedly. He hated routine and his youthful excitement was intoxicating. After being long on the road, his sexual vigor lasted for hours on end.

Ema had discovered new aspects of herself in the relationship: Lucas hitting the gas on the road to Spain with the sound of the Gypsy Kings blasting in the background; returning from Madrid at dawn; the unforgettable nights of tangos, castanets, and the sweet, cold, *sangria.* Lucas dancing wildly like a bird trying to reach the sky—his hips like wings viciously undulating. He was filled with mischief—a *gingão,* a rogue—and that captivated her. Together they had discovered the rapture of life.

But reality had hit Ema with an ugly blow. Disillusioned now, she must move on. While being constantly on the lookout for Lucas, she had to get her car's engine changed as she had promised her attorney and return to the never-ending routine of her work. Her schedule began at dawn and lasted the entire day. Only sacrifice after sacrifice—and boredom much of the time—guaranteed her paycheck at the end of the month. Fundamentally a disciplined person, she accepted the fact that she must continue with her long-established habits.

The mirror still reminded Ema of the recent assault. Close

to middle age, how was she going to rebuild her life? Certainly not with her recently divorced colleague who shared her office space—such a wary, bitter ex-husband.

No prospects at work. But returning to the office, she found her desk piled high with papers that required her attention.

Back home after work that first day, Ema opened her mailbox. Afraid of the dark entrance hall to her building, she had avoided getting her mail the past few days. She opened a notification letter stating that she was to testify the following day with the police.

The turnaround had been fast, no doubt due to Borges's friend in the head office. Police cases habitually take months before an investigation gets underway. For a split second it crossed Ema's mind to try to postpone the meeting. But she didn't want to disappoint her sympathetic attorney. Besides, he had mentioned how the police interrogation would affect Lucas and place him instantly on guard.

Ema felt pleased. Finally she would have her day to set the record straight and make sure Lucas never returned to her path. She needed to put the soured affair behind her, once and for all. She experienced a moment of soaring revenge. It would be a short step from her testimony to the police sending the case to trial in court. Lucas would be in jail soon, unable to enjoy the light of day.

For the deposition, Ema wore a brand-new cobalt blue pantsuit. Approaching the police station, she hoped parking wouldn't be a problem. Traffic was as intense as ever and she was already a bit late. Just then, someone pulled away from the curb and Ema slipped into the space. She still had to walk a couple of blocks but didn't mind. The light breeze seemed to kiss her face.

Once inside the police building, Ema walked endless corridors. The edifice was a maze filled with narrow stairways at every turn. She passed various departments with telling names: Fraud, Homicide, Organized Crime. She found Room 27, the office of inspector Possidónio de Sousa.

The room was empty, but almost immediately an officer came in. He pulled out a chair and politely asked Ema to sit down saying that de Sousa would arrive in a few minutes. Ema felt good about the attention thrown on her; her new pantsuit had certainly helped.

Looking around, she realized it wasn't a surprise that the inspector wasn't in his office. If she had a desk like his—so piled up with files, many of them wrapped up twice with twine—she might only enter her office at gunpoint. There was a computer on the desk but it was barely visible. Along the walls stood shelves filled with legal codes. The phones rang nonstop and no one bothered to answer them. Ema had heard that with the financial crisis, crime had increased in the country. It surely appeared to be that way.

Inspector de Sousa arrived a few moments later. "Sorry, my boss called me with a pressing matter," he said kindly as he stepped into the room.

"I've just arrived." Ema extended her hand to greet the inspector but didn't get up from her chair.

"Let's begin, Ms. Bivar," de Sousa said, "Neither you nor I have any time to waste." The inspector brought one of the piles on top of his desk closer to him. "Our department already summoned Mr. Lucas Camacho, and I personally took care of his interrogation. For brevity's sake, please allow me to address Mr. Camacho simply as Lucas. I must admit to you this situation isn't looking good. Lucas has denied all allegations. He only confirmed that he knows you but denies ever laying a finger on you—not even with a flower, he said."

"Jesus Christ!" erupted Ema, a handy expression in a predominantly Catholic country.

"Your medical report helps your case; without it we couldn't even begin to proceed. But Lucas peremptorily denies that he assaulted you."

"It's hard to hear your words," Ema said somberly. "As stated in the report, Lucas didn't assault me just once, but several times. I spoke up only now because I feared for my life."

"Ms. Bivar, we've got a problem. You're a respected manager with a university degree and I have no doubt you're speaking the truth. But Lucas, your former companion, has denied all allegations. He says he never touched you. He says he feels sorry for you. He says one of your co-workers probably beat you up."

Ema couldn't contain herself. "Lucas is messing with me again!"

"Cases of domestic violence are difficult to judge. You and Lucas lived together for a while, you gave him the keys to your home." The inspector paused patiently. "I'm not expressing an opinion. Facts are facts. You don't have witnesses, and without them, I'm afraid there's nothing we can do." Seemingly annoyed with the situation, de Sousa hit his pencil against one of the files on his desk.

"Your former companion also said…let me show you the pages in his deposition…" The inspector leaned toward Ema across the files on his desk to say, "that he is still very fond of you."

"I'm outraged," Ema replied.

"We police officers deal with fact, the truth, and proof. These do the talking, not us." De Sousa used a neutral tone of voice. "Lucas was already here twice, has collaborated with our inquiries, and provided invaluable details about his activities. I'm going to interrogate him one more time, tomorrow. Before that, I'd like you to confirm some of the case's particulars. Your attorney asserts that you had been assaulted earlier but you didn't press charges." After another pause, he inquired, "Do you have, by chance, medical reports documenting the previous aggressions?"

"Unfortunately I don't." Ema felt slightly alarmed now. The pillories in Borges's office came back to her mind. One in particular stayed with her. It was the usual stone column, in the main square of town, but it had on top four crossed iron bars inserted into the stone. The bars were large enough for the criminals to hang with the arms stretched out like Christ on the cross. Ema imagined the bisected bars above her head like a gigantic spider on the attack.

"It's too bad, it is easier to prosecute a repeat offender," de Sousa said. "Perhaps I could confer with the doctors who assisted you."

"That's fine," Ema asserted.

"Please bear with me now. I need to hear in your own words what happened in the ill-fated hours you were last attacked."

Gradually, with difficulty, Ema related the specifics of Lucas's last beating. She described her shock upon seeing Lucas waiting at her doorstep as she opened the front door to leave early for work: his deranged, blood-thirsty eyes as he attacked her. His fists relentlessly pounding her face, neck, and shoulders. How she used all her might to prevent him from entering her apartment. How she tried to reach the stairway lights.

"No neighbor came to your rescue, right? Why didn't you shout?" In a mechanical gesture, the inspector repeatedly tapped a stack of papers with his pencil. "Are you a hundred percent sure that no one in the building heard you?"

"I only shouted when I couldn't take it any longer. I think I heard someone opening a door—an imperceptible sound—but I was under such distress that I can't be sure. I felt ashamed, I only wanted to disappear inside my apartment, shut my door."

"How many tenants are there in your building?"

"There are fourteen apartments, the building has seven floors."

"Conceivably we could interrogate all tenants. Hard work. And people don't talk easily to the police. Names are recorded and folks fear retaliation."

"I'm not sure I want the police to interrogate my neighbors. This is very embarrassing for me," Ema said. "I'm a very private person, I don't want my secrets disclosed to others."

"We also summoned Lucas's mother," de Sousa continued. "She testified that on that day, at that time, her son was at home, asleep. We also called some of Lucas's neighbors; two people came in, a mother and her son. We checked, the two young men worked in the same garage a couple of years ago. The mothers are friends. These two testimonies matched that of Lucas's mother."

"What do you mean?" broke in Ema.

"Both neighbors, the mother and her son, stated that Lucas was sleeping at home that morning."

"Explain something, please. How do they remember the day I was assaulted?"

"Easy. The birthday of another neighbor took place the night before and they were all celebrating together."

"But Lucas was at my doorstep the following morning!"

"The neighbors corroborate Lucas's mother's story, that he was asleep at that time. They said, moreover, that this is a normal pattern with Lucas: he never starts his day before lunchtime," de Sousa asserted.

"How is it possible that you, Inspector, believe these people?" Ema was at the end of her rope.

"I explained earlier. Without witnesses on your side, there is no way to prove this case. The devil here is in the details. For all legal purposes, it's your word against Lucas's."

"And you deem Lucas innocent?" Ema shot out like a lioness.

"No, I don't. But without witnesses, we don't have a basis to press charges. The case will be automatically dismissed in court."

"Oh, please! If it wasn't Lucas, then who attacked me? My colleagues from work, as Lucas suggested? No one ever visited me."

"I think our only recourse is to talk to the people in your building; someone could provide new information." The inspector seemed ready to proceed with the investigation.

"You presume I enjoy mistreatment like the ill-famed Madame Bovary, don't you?"

The inspector stared at Ema, speechless.

"Or you suppose I engaged in self-flagellation, like a martyr in the Catholic Church, don't you? "

Ema was shaken as she pronounced these words. Suddenly she leaned back in the chair and covered her face with her hands. Lucas was still playing tricks with her; he was having the upper hand with the police. The inspector was right, without witnesses on her side there was no case. She felt she had reached a dead end.

"So, it's my word against Lucas's?" Defeat suffused Ema's statement.

"Lucas has witnesses stating where he was at the time of the assault; you seem to have none," the inspector concluded.

"Mark my words, Inspector: if I appear dead in my apartment, it's because Lucas murdered me." Ema's emotions had been chaotic during the interview, but now incredulity set in.

De Sousa spoke in a decisive tone of voice. "I want you to know we care, we're on the alert. We know Dr. Borges well; he has an impeccable reputation. You are naturally upset, but this investigation isn't over yet."

Ema started to feel dizzy and asked the inspector for a glass of water.

"You look pale," he said, handing her a glass. "We're finished here. I'll escort you to your car now, you are obviously not feeling well."

De Sousa helped Ema get up and they headed downstairs together. Ema leaned against the handrail feeling as if the ground was disappearing from under her feet. Her mouth tasted of rubber. She was now convinced the police would never find out the truth about her beatings.

And, on the loose, Lucas might succeed in his ultimate intention.

By the door, the inspector said, "You're white as a ghost. Where did you park?"

Ema mentioned the spot and they walked the two blocks together. She remarked, "Please Inspector, the fresh air is helping. It's not necessary for you to accompany me. I'm sure you're terribly busy."

"It's no bother, the short walk is good exercise."

Seeing her car in the distance, Ema Bivar pointed. "My car is the red convertible Fiat over there, the one with the black top. Thank you for escorting me."

This is when Inspector Possidónio de Sousa said in the most obliging tone: "Ms. Bivar, I hope you won't mind if I look at your engine. I need you to open the hood so I can verify the serial number. This will take only a few minutes."

Bruna

My name is Bruna and I've been locked up for a few months. When I was a drug dealer and my own boss, I had a first-class life. I rented a flat with a sea view, dressed in clothes from exclusive boutiques, and wore designer stilettos. I always ate lunch and dinner at fancy restaurants. Lagos, where I lived—in the southern tip of Portugal—reminded me of my native country, the Cape Verde Islands. Lagos is hot but pleasant, with radiant sunshine. It also has plenty of tourists. The locals don't need to migrate to faraway lands in Europe or the Americas. The Cape Verde Islands, on the other hand, are poor, small, isolated bits in the Atlantic Ocean, off the coast of Africa. We Cape Verdeans have been robbed and colonized for centuries. The Portuguese, of course, are the ones to blame. Since the Atlantic slave trade, our national identity has been in permanent jeopardy.

I need to confess, for starters, that I have a vice: an indescribable attraction for the smell of money. Looking at euros gives me a high. Thank God, I was disciplined when I was dealing. I sold my goods—heroin, cocaine, hash, whatever I could lay my hands on—to strangers, but I never used. I didn't shoot up, I didn't snort, and I didn't smoke. The shit arrived by sea at night, and even if I was always bad with numbers, I paid off my suppliers as soon as my clients paid me. It didn't even take me a week. I lived in style: I earned money and I spent money.

The credit card business was my downfall. A real pity! Gervásio, my boyfriend, says it was my own fault, that if I hadn't gotten lazy we would be fine today. The Lagos court gave me eight years; he got five. My best shot is to get used to my new life and stay calm. Life inside prison could be worse. Much worse. The bad part is the food: the fish is always frozen, the stew has potato but no beef, and the meat smells like cat food. We only get to eat yogurt in the evening, just before the guards lock us up in the dens we call cells. Sometimes we have fruit, but the fruit is, as I say, only good for pigs. Drug dealers make a lot of money and get used to the best life has to offer. Unlike me—I used to spend carelessly all the money I made—many of the inmates in here have large bank accounts. We are what we are.

Better to remain silent about the guards who take care of us. Silence is gold in here.

Last Wednesday I attended a yoga session on the upper floor near my cell. I got curious when the loudspeaker announced that a new instructor had arrived. This broad has no clue whatsoever about life. She can't imagine what it is like to live without a roof over your head, or without a husband, or no salary at the end of the month. Or to have no food to quiet your children's hunger. She doesn't know the fear tied to the possibility of being shot in the street by someone who happens to pass by. Hours are long inside this gridiron of a prison. So I decided that when I have nothing else to do, I'd join the yoga group.

Today, I was the only Portuguese-speaking prisoner in the class. The others come from all over the world, from Russia, Latin America, Spain, and Morocco. This place is like an international airport, or a tourist resort. I'm friendly with everybody except the Eastern Europeans—they're all racists. They think they're better because they're white. Even the Portuguese, our colonizers, are more tolerant of color.

The teacher started the class with meditation. I already forgot her name, but she explained that introspection was good for the soul, not only ours but hers as well. We sat in the lotus position and she spoke softly, slowly. She asked us to close our eyes and concentrate. Then she mentioned nature, plants growing, trees that bear strong roots and support thick trunks. Yolanda, Natasha, and Clementina came in together—late. They made all the noise they wanted before settling down. What's-her-name opened her eyes and calmly asked for silence. Then she said we needed to listen to ourselves, to listen inside. She told us that we can gain self-knowledge, build a new life, and have a future.

That chick can say what she wants, but I'm unable to enjoy nature through bars. Besides, no one in the class understood her idea of making an existence for ourselves.

When she mentioned the trees, my childhood in Cape Verde came back to me. I remembered the splendor of the sea and the coconut trees by the side of my grammy's hut. Those were trees! What's-her-name said that, like a tree, we could grow, develop. Imagine your body divided in two, she said. Above the waist, your arms could reach for the sky; below, your legs anchor to the earth. She said the center of the earth was the center of our gravity. I kept still, quiet as a mouse. What this woman says has nothing to do with me. If she had described the flames of hell then maybe I could have understood. But never mind. Either I go to yoga or I walk the corridors like a ghost with a lost gaze, looking at the clock, waiting out the hours.

When Gervásio called me on the public phone in the corridor, I told him about the yoga sessions. But he wasn't interested. He is also from Cape Verde, but I'm more educated than he is. I finished sixth grade. After my grammy died, I joined my dad in Chelas, a suburb of Lisbon. Unlike my father's second wife, my Portuguese language teacher liked me; she said I wrote very well. This teacher hinted that I should give up my Cape Verde dialect, my native *Creole,* to better integrate in Portugal. Gervásio never studied. From the day I met him, he has said that he doesn't want to do construction work like his friends. He says that carrying buckets of sand back and forth all day long for a lifetime is not his trade. This is why he got me into the credit card scam. When his wife—who was a cashier at a supermarket and supported the whole family—figured out what he was doing, she immediately left him. She said that she wasn't interested in *chulos,* men who live off their wives. She took the two kids and the furniture with her. By the end of the month, he was out of the apartment as well; there was no way he could afford the rent.

I took Gervásio in my bed the night his wife left, and before we were busted, he never left it. My cousin Nilza had pointed him out to me since they were neighbors. She said that he and his wife fought all the time; she could hear them through the walls. I had seen him before, and I liked his face.

Gervásio is the reason I'm locked up in here. He stole credit cards and passed them on to me. Then I went to the mall and bought this, that, and the other item. This was hard work; I had only a few hours to learn to copy the signatures. But, like my language teacher, he said my writing was perfect. Yes, I've always been good with my letters. I still can't figure out exactly what happened that fateful afternoon. I got excited; that's what happened. We had decided a few weeks earlier to move our operation from the large malls on the outskirts of the city into the smaller shops in the center of Lagos. This area is closer to the five-star hotels where the well-off foreigners stay by the sea. I had set my eyes on a fancy jewelry shop. It had only two employees; the older one must have been the owner. That day I took a long bath with salts and got ready for the job. I used a provocative mini skirt and fancy shoes, decided on a good perfume. I entered the shop like a lady and chose two beautiful diamond rings. I paid with the American Express card Gervásio had stolen at lunchtime. The rings were the best I had ever seen. I even thought I would keep one, a present from Gervásio.

I had parked my small Citroen close by and, when I left the shop, the younger shopkeeper saw me entering the car. And I stupidly thought he was admiring my ass. Or appreciating the way I rolled my hips.

I never had a chance to wear the brand new ring. A week later, early morning, the cops knocked at our door. In court, to protect my Gervásio, I even gave sworn testimony that the idea had been mine. But it was no use; the police had already discovered that Gervásio had stolen the credit card. Not only that one, but all the others that we had used in the previous months. We were both convicted. Bad luck! We had started a family business; we could have gone far. The police also found a few bags of hash under our bed. Gervásio hinted—he didn't state it openly—that I traded. So I got the heavier sentence.

I don't mind. I love Gervásio.

I'm mulatto, and I'm told the best translation of Bruna, my name, is Brownie. I've got green eyes. But I could've been white. My father is as white as the yoga teacher. My skin is chocolate, like my grammy's. I've always loved my body as much as the land where I was born. When I had tons of euros I used to send a stipend to grammy in Cape Verde. She thought I was a cook in Lagos. I still recall when she would make fish soup with *mandioca* root. She sang the *mornas,* our beautiful folk melodies, while she cooked. In between, we heard only the sound of the pans clanking together. There was no need for words between the two of us.

I sang my grammy's *mornas* while waiting for my clients in Lagos. Many times they asked that I repeat a tune they had heard before.

Portuguese men like the combination that God gave me: skin the color of a brownie, eyes the color of the sea. My eyes change with the light of the day—or the direction of the wind. Once, I was talking with an older man at a shop near the marina. It was winter and pouring. This guy said to my face that if I stayed in the rain long enough, I might turn white one day. Then he looked at me from top to bottom, stopping his eye at my crotch. He offered me dinner and I accepted. He paid for sex—and he paid well.

But that was before I met Gervásio.

I exercise in the yoga class to calm my desires. Being locked up is hard on the body. If the guards say I am well behaved, Gervásio might be allowed to visit me at the end of next month. We've got a sort of prison exchange program. Inmates of the opposite sex are allowed to get together once in a while. But intimate life inside a prison is occasional at best. It's better, however, than to go hungry between the legs. Gervásio and I will be alone. I'll give myself all naked to him. He will run his hands over my body, getting, as usual, to the very center of me.

We'll see if I get the visit. Doroteia, the bitch, was taking down the names of the participants in the rebellion last month. Detainees started banging on the doors in unison; we couldn't stop. Yelling that the food was lousy, we created quite a stir. There were more than a hundred women making the fuss. The guards appeared, a dozen of them, their pads and pencils in hand. As soon as I saw Doroteia at the end of the corridor, I hid in the depths of my cell. This guard is like the devil; she frightens me. I abandoned Esperancinha, my cell companion, to her own fate.

It was a mistake to rebel the day Doroteia was on duty. That slut likes women—and she prefers darker women, like me. I knew she had her eyes set on my body. Someone told me that she returned from Angola in 1974, after the Carnation Revolution in Portugal. She has her favorites among us, but please do not ask me to speak out. If I do, I might not leave this place alive. Good behavior has a price in here, and keeping one's mouth shut is worth a ton of euros. The day after our protest, Doroteia told me she had taken down my name. She was measuring me up. Now, when I see her, I try to make myself invisible. I see what she wants, but I won't give it to her. Doroteia is like a construction worker, heavy built and broad shouldered. Not to my taste; I like only men. But I'm not sure for how long I will be able to resist her.

And I would die for my Gervásio.

Doroteia is fully in charge in this jail. She prefers black women, but, depending on availability, she also sleeps with mulatto and white convicts. And she is ready to exchange favors. Inmates under her control are on the first floor, near the pavilion's entrance. A huge gridiron block, the height of the five-floor complex, separates the guard's office from the first-floor cells. But the distance is a mere few steps. I'm told Doroteia pursues her prey at night. And she isn't the only one conducting these activities. I notice her admiring my body whenever she has a chance. Let me state again: I do not want to be part of her circle.

When the light is dim—and I feel like a rag.

I might or might not see my Gervásio next month. Without a clean sheet and with a name on the guard's list, sex in here is only between women—guards and inmates or inmates and inmates. Cells for four women have two empty beds most nights. The guards know this and come in to stay with us when they want. How could drugs enter these walls every single day without their knowledge? Everybody knows the guards are our accomplices. How could so much cash circulate around here? The guards instigate, participate, and take advantage of us; they must bring home a double salary every month. I'm sure that working here is very lucrative.

I feel sorry for Esperancinha; we shared a cell before. But, after the door-slamming episode, she was transferred downstairs. I see her at yoga once in a while, but we don't speak to each other anymore. Outside, Esperancinha was a street prostitute; inside, she turned into a prison whore. Outside, she had her pimps; inside, she has her madams. They must pay her well. Everything has a price in here, and the hierarchies are clear for those who can afford them. The other day, Esperancinha was happy and wearing new clothes. Who did she hook up with? Was it Doroteia? Or her new cellmate?

In addition to huge salaries, many guards get also paid with services. When I walked into the slammer, I saw what was going on. Many prisoners showed me pictures of their large houses, their fancy cars, their expensive laptops. I'm told that the guards do not need to spend weekends or vacations at resort hotels. It's much cheaper to use prisoners' empty houses. There is always a reason to visit, whether to make sure rain isn't coming through the roof or a thief hasn't broken a window. The prisoners thank the guards; and the guards, those hoes, have a hell of a vacation.

I'm afraid Esperancinha will go back to snorting coke. Well, if she does, it's none of my business. Loyalty is a well-measured commodity here. If that weren't the case, I wouldn't have left her by herself under Doroteia's eyes. Stunning as this Brazilian is, desirable as she is, she will not last long in prison. In our cell, she never used. And I can testify that no one ever touched her. If Doroteia thinks I'll be jealous, she can suck it. Esperancinha is from Rio de Janeiro, a kid from the *favela,* the spawn of a slut. But she is hot. I'm sure the public doesn't know that women have OD'ed inside these prison walls. The poor souls gave up on living; they didn't know who they were anymore. If I had warned Esperancinha, she wouldn't give a damn.

Rain or shine, I'm going to yoga on Wednesdays. When I'm busy my problems seem smaller. I don't even worry about Esperancinha. The teacher does quite a variety of poses. We wear tights and stand, sit, crouch, invert. She transmits a will that shows that maybe change is possible, even for us. The other day, some chicks were sitting on a sofa watching us. They didn't want to hop on the mats. First, we're sitting in the floor with our legs together. The second pose was to spread our legs apart, little by little. The third pose was to touch our toes with our fingertips. When we were in the second movement with our legs far apart, the women comfortably sitting down on the sofa started to laugh.

A deep laugh, boorish and vile.

What's-her-face didn't think the scene was funny. She confronted the hyenas saying that either they got on the mats or had to leave the room. And they all ran out like a cheetah was chasing them.

During this exercise I thought of Gervásio, when he says he's my Tarzan.

The tension inside the room cleared when those whores left. Dália was exercising but took the opportunity to leave the room as well. She was laughing with the others from her mat. Dália, the poor wreck, constantly covers her mouth with her hand. Her husband knocked all her teeth out, and she is embarrassed by the spaces between her teeth. But Dália is no good. When she found out her husband had a girlfriend, she cooked up some acid that ruined the slut's face forever.

The instructor says that the yoga poses are a way to exercise not only our body but our soul as well. I don't get it. She says the body is the guardian of our spirit, that we must respect it. I agree on that one, I always took good care of what my mama gave me. When summer comes, my eyes change color with the heat. Sometimes they reflect the sunlight, it's pretty amazing. My clients usually noticed the change, and I always got compliments. The men would ask me for more than drugs. But I was always careful; those guys couldn't be trusted.

Prostitution in prison is different from outside. We're here against our will. What can you buy by selling your body? Here's the list: drugs, cell phones, sleeping pills, liquor, French cheeses, perfumes, chocolates, cigarettes. This is when sex doesn't pay for simpler things like washing and ironing your clothes. If we get along with the guards, we can avoid trouble. For instance, we can go to the dentist in less than 24 hours if we have an abscess. If we're bleeding, we might be able to save our lives with an emergency visit to the gynecologist.

No one fools around from inside the gridiron. Tasks either get accomplished or not—there are no half measures.

Once in a while I sit in the hallway, talking. The chatter is always the same, boring. Women talk about how good life was on the outside; they forget what they went through. Sometimes they complain that the family has stopped visiting them. Or talk about leaving the prison and having to start all over again. The gossip is only useful when I learn new tricks like how to carry pot in unusual places or pass unnoticed at international airports.

I try not to go near the gridiron, the prison's spot of choice for gossip. The women yak all day long, and that makes me uncomfortable. Guards and prisoners make the perfect confidantes. The only difference between the groups is that some are inside and the others out. But the two groups need each other. When we go to work in the surrounding factories, the inmates, happy to get out for a few hours, help the guards count the prisoners. Everybody knows who's sick, who has their period that day, who was able or unable to talk to their mother or boyfriend. During sewing classes, the prisoners know who steals the materials or threads. If stuff that a guard wanted for herself happens to disappear, there is always a hullabaloo.

I prefer to stay upstairs. It's not only the height and the sunshine, but I can think more clearly up here. The other day I was thinking it would be a good idea to continue with my accounting course. Gervásio agrees. But the course is tedious. It's all about credit and debit and more debit and more credit. But Gervásio said these classes might help me one day.

I want to stay in the upper floor, but I miss the things the inmates near the gridiron have access to. The luxury of a cell phone, for instance. Inmates hide them in their own bodies or inside the beds. I spend my afternoons waiting in line to talk to Gervásio on the public phone located in the corridor. We only talk once in a while, and sometimes I lose my place in line. The other women know that I've spent all my cash, that I've nothing now to give in exchange for a favor. So, no one bothers to hold my place when I need to use the bathroom. There is always fuss in the line, it makes me nervous. Thus, when I return from the bathroom, I have to go to the end. To mess with me, Natasha—she is Russian—calls me a "mulatto." I reply that she can go fuck herself and, trying to offend her, I say that she's a "white." I call her white instead of "broad"—or "slob."

Come to think of it, Doroteia could be my ticket. But I don't like her body, and I don't sleep with women.

The other day the yoga class didn't start well. It happens often, we take some time to settle down. When Natasha started talking, what's-her-name asked for silence. I knew that Natasha had just arrived from detox, where they give her methadone pills. She came in because she desperately needed to talk and she couldn't bear the silence. When the instructor asked her to quiet down a second time, she screamed. This was the only way she felt the teacher would hear her. She seemed a lost wolf in the prairie. She howled long and hard until her voice was gone. The instructor stopped the class, gave us a few minutes.

After this interval, Yolanda came in crying like crazy. She said that when a guard called her to the office downstairs, someone stole her place in the phone line. She explained that now she would not be able to talk to her sister until next week. Her tears were like a waterfall. She cleaned her nose with her sleeve and created a racket. I know how it feels. We go nuts if we can't use the phone; it's our only connection with the outside world. We did wrong, but the outside world is like heaven from within these walls. I saw that what's-her-name was getting impatient; she wanted to proceed with the exercises. She told Yolanda that what had happened might be upsetting, but it was not the end of the world. She could call her sister tomorrow; it would be a new day. Goodness gracious! Yolanda got furious and told the teacher it was clear she had never been locked up, that in two hours she would be outside, on a different planet, that she would have erased us from her memory. I think Yolanda got lucky. What's-her-name could have answered that if Yolanda hadn't transgressed society's rules, she would also be out.

But the instructor didn't answer; I noticed, even, that she paid attention.

Yolanda is from Latin America, a loud mouth. And she went on saying that the instructor didn't have the slightest idea of the difficulty in reaching Colombia from a public phone. The instructor wanted to continue with the class. But Yolanda wouldn't let her; she needed to justify her behavior. She explained that she always had to get psychologically ready for the call, be in a good mood. The reason for that was that everything she told her sister was made up. She would invent what she bought that week for her home, this and that place she visited, her work at the factory. When she called, she always told her sister it was during her work break from the shoe factory where she had been employed for a few years now.

What's-her-face stared at Yolanda but didn't respond. Instead she said she had decided to change the lesson plan. She said that we needed more relaxation than exercises. So we did only deep breathing for the whole hour and a half. At the end, the teacher asked if someone wanted to say something. I felt like saying that I felt better; some of the others stated it. But Yolanda kept silent. The teacher spoke last. She said that she also felt different after the class. She gave Yolanda a long, steady look and said that, with us, she had understood the power of words in more depth. As she heard this, Yolanda got up slowly, moved near the instructor and leaning down, embraced her. It was a long embrace, an encounter. And Yolanda's eyes were not a muddy swamp anymore. This time they were crystal clear.

The next week, the yoga session was calmer. If I get the nerve, I'm going to ask the teacher if we can watch TV while we exercise. Silence is heavy and we would avoid all the thinking. We could watch the Brazilian soaps. I love those! They show the rich people, the husbands and lovers with the best cars, the country houses facing the sea. The women are all dressed up. They obviously use expensive perfumes. No one works, and everybody has time for this, that and the other. It's not clear where all the luxuries come from. But it's not important, either.

Life would also be easier inside the gridiron if we could use the Internet. Gervásio and I could make virtual love. Not only that, I would be able to get in touch with my hook-ups, advise them that eight years will go fast. Natasha could ask her macho Italian business partner why he stopped answering the phone; it's been three months now. The partner has all their money in his own name only so Natasha is, naturally, concerned. A blonde with blue eyes, she could find a good marriage in Portugal.

With Internet use, all conflicts would disappear. The other day

I lost my cool with the gypsy who currently shares my cell. That bitch gets up early and makes a hell of a fuss. Telling her to be quiet didn't produce any results. She pretended she didn't hear me. I threw our only chair at her head. This time she got the message. She fought back with her long nails, left me covered with scratches. My face, neck, and shoulders were bleeding for hours. But she went to the hospital for a scan to check if her bones were all still there.

If I could make love to Gervásio, even if only virtual love, I wouldn't have done what I did. The guard on duty punished me, locked me up in cell 111 for the week. The cell is dirty, dark, and humid. I could only get out one hour a day. When my nerves got the better of me, the guard outside the cell gave me a sleeping pill the first night. Earlier in the afternoon, she had offered me a cigarette butt. This was Vanessa, the prison guard who was hired last month. I wonder what she wanted in exchange; I had already heard that she is a roach. One inmate gave her a stack of bills as soon as she saw her, and Vanessa already repaid the favor. That slut got her own individual cell with a shower and everything.

Like in a first class hotel.

Vanessa is different from the other guards here. She stands out. She is sexy and slender, and acts like a punk rocker. She is always moving around the complex as if she's busy. She must need quite a sum to keep up that appearance of hers. It's like we are watching a magazine model every morning, wearing a tightly fitted uniform. Sometimes she wears her long hair down; other times she wears a ponytail. She always wears dark glasses and makes herself unique.

The two of us talked as she passed on to me the little that was left of her cigarette. She told me that she loves heavy metal music. Next time we talk, I'll ask if she has heard Cesária Évora and if she enjoys the music of my islands. I like "Miss Perfumado;" the lyrics are tender and sweet. She's gonna enjoy the reference. After all, the song is about a cool, gentle young woman whose body is bathed in perfume.

Today is Wednesday and I already went to the yoga session. We have a small group that always shows up these days. Clementina didn't want to remove her socks; she is into being clean and said the floor was dirty. She is studying Buddhism in the library and doesn't want anything to do with Catholic advice anymore. What's-her-name told her that without socks we are closer to our center of gravity. I'm sure Clementina doesn't give a shit about gravity, but she removed her socks when she heard that. She always states that she is innocent and was jailed by mistake. She must have thought that gravity will help her leave sooner. She got a heavy sentence, apparently twenty years.

I didn't mind the dirty floor. Now dead, Cesária Évora always sang barefooted.

This morning I saw Doroteia when we went for lunch. She was in the guard's office talking on her cell phone. She looked at me provocatively. Vanessa was in the room as well. The sleeping pill Vanessa gave me was a bad sign, a warning of sorts. Like the colonizer giving alms to the colonized.

When Doroteia is in command the guards behave differently. She has power and uses it. It's when she's around that prison favors are distributed—or not. For now, I'm outside of her circuit. But I'm still not sure how long I'll be able to resist.

The prison inspections take place when Doroteia is on duty. Guards say that the officials' arrival is random. What a fucking joke! These visits are carefully planned. When the loudspeakers announce that the inspectors are about to turn up, we don't need a second warning. We've more or less two hours to prepare. No crisis, no reason to panic. When the party arrives, we are ready to greet them. The clowns come regularly to see how we're faring—to see if there's liquor under the beds, if we hid drugs in the bathrooms, and where to find the cell phones. Well, is there a safer place to put the stuff than the guards' office?

When the circus arrives, we're ready. When the circus departs, everything goes back to normal.

Today, the yoga teacher arrived with a bird's nest that she found inside the compound on the street leading to our complex. When the guard at the gridiron said that she couldn't admit her, the instructor insisted that she was bringing in something that was already inside the prison grounds. It was a cute bird's nest, all tangled up. What's-her-name passed it around and asked us to admire the masterpiece. She said that people, like animals, can do the right thing—instinctively. We need willpower, she added. Then, she offered the nest to one of us. I felt groovy and said I would take it. The nest is a miniature crib. I placed it on my night table.

During class, what's-her-name spoke about the connection between yoga and the paths of life. I immediately thought about Gervásio. She said that there are many paths, and that we must choose among them all the time. She evoked small country roads—and at once I recalled the entrance to my grammy's hut. Then she mentioned routes, courses, tracks, trails, bridges, and rivers flowing into the sea. She said it is up to us to settle on the options available.

I didn't get it.

Then, reflecting, I was about to ask if the teacher thought the convicts had the same choices as the prison guards. Or if we should follow the advice of a few, the prisoners who handle their fat bank accounts from inside. But I bit my tongue. I swear, however, if the woman bothers us again with stories about the many ways, the new paths, I must address the question. I want to see how she reacts. I'll ask: who shall I make myself available to? Doroteia, the worthless piece of shit who controls everything in here? Or Vanessa, the new butterfly with the tight uniform, her eyes forever hidden behind those disturbing shades?

At the end of the class, what's-her-face asked us to share a feeling. She wanted something positive. Does she talk! Esperancinha said she admired the solidarity inside the prison. She said that she had made friends who will stay with her forever. I looked at her in disbelief. Yolanda said that she hopes her sister will believe the explanation that the euros that she earned in Portugal, for years, were all stolen at the airport on the day of her departure. Clementina is inside because she killed her husband. She spoke assertively, loudly, with the rhythm of a cathedral belfry. She said that if given the chance she would stab her husband in the liver again. But she would do it when he was awake, not the way it happened, with him drunk and asleep.

Not everybody wanted to speak and I was the last one. I said it felt good to express the thinking I've been developing since I crossed the gridiron. The yoga teacher said we can build our lives, incorporate the good, and hold it close to our hearts. I come from a people who are softhearted by nature and also due to centuries of submission to the Portuguese. This being the case, I would like my eight years to go fast—as if I were only in a bad dream. I want to return to my hangout in Lagos, have my regular clients appear, as before, in the early morning. But I've changed inside this prison. My accounting will be up-to-the-minute. In one single page there will be a column for credit, another for debit.

Free, I'll carry my nest wherever I go. And it will be only me and my Gervásio: he will be ready for me, at the tip of my fingers.

In Bairro Alto

Bairro Alto is a picturesque area of Lisbon that attracts newcomers by day and night while still retaining a traditional way of life. Since the early 1980s, when Gaspar was born, the so-called hilltop High District has been filling up with a diverse population. Expensive antique dealers, fashionable bars with refined wine labels, and clothing stores for socialites have moved in. Fado houses where local celebrities sing and drug dealers who openly sell in the streets appeal to affluent tourists. Immigrants from around the world pile up in small, airless cubicles where entire families share one bedroom. While strolling the cobbled streets of his neighborhood, Gaspar enjoys the contrast between the old and the new that is visible everywhere.

Now in his early thirties, Gaspar has the same emotions about his neighborhood he had as a child. From the time his mother transported him in a Snugli baby carrier—which allowed him to observe the world while dangling from her torso—Gaspar has taken special delight in the close-knit community. It pleased his mother when neighbors stopped to chat, caress her son's cheeks, and admire his brown hair and inquiring eyes. Walking to and from home by himself during elementary school, Gaspar got to know the neighbors he passed along the way. He would wave goodbye to Edite, the policeman's wife on her way to the fish market; keeping a distance, he would glance at Hildeberto, the corner drunkard whose girlfriend kicked him out when he couldn't stand on his feet. And Gaspar always ran away from Alda, the heavy-breasted black woman wandering aimlessly through the streets. His mother had told him to stay away, that the woman was no good.

Gaspar also watched Vanessa from afar: short pleated skirt, bottom swaying as she walked up the alley ahead of him. Both attended the same school. Years later Vanessa would become, unquestionably, Gaspar's first love. Unfortunately the affair ended abruptly, the disappointment of his life and something that left a permanent scar.

Nowadays Gaspar is a branch bank clerk, a job he cherishes during the country's current financial crisis. His stuttering, a speech impediment that manifests itself when he feels under particular duress, didn't prevent him from finding well-paid work. He takes longer than others to express himself, but there isn't a single sentence that he won't complete. Hardworking and responsible, he has earned his manager's trust. Gaspar remains calm if a rude customer, usually his age, mimics his stutter. Gaspar might blush but he answers politely, leaving the fellow to deal with his own behavior problem. He thrives in his job, adores the tall lines of figures, the signed checks, and the downloading of spreadsheets. These are business matters that touch his heart, details that give him satisfaction.

Every day Gaspar descends the narrow Bairro Alto streets he has known since he was born. He delights when passing the music conservatory with the dissonant sounds of students playing their instruments. He savors the spicy aromas drifting from tapas bars at the end of dark alleys. Even the trash that drug users leave behind at night feels familiar to him. These are the hallmarks of a fashionable, bohemian neighborhood, he reflects. On his way to work, he turns right at Caixa Geral de Depósitos, a state bank in Calçada do Combro, and continues down Santa Catarina in the direction of Estrela.

After the heartbreak with Vanessa, marrying is not an option. Gaspar lives with his mother, a widow who likes having her son close by. Mother and son are comfortable still living together in the same apartment he was born in. As a special gesture to his mother, he always buys freshly baked bread rolls on Saturday mornings.

The young man begins his Saturday by talking to the neighborhood paralytic. Janota is an *agiota,* a shark pawnbroker, who spends his days in a wheelchair on the sidewalk outside his apartment. To search Internet sites for his business most of the day, he has strung an electrical cord from his apartment through the window to his computer. Passersby don't mind changing their route to accommodate the *agiota's* well-established habits. He is old and physically broken from the colonial war he fought for Portugal against the Angolan liberation movements in the early seventies. A military truck ran over him, breaking his spine. But Janota makes good money from his makeshift office on the sidewalk. For breaks, he goes next door to the café and watches video games or television shows. He is particularly interested in the ones in which participants compete for money. These small maneuvers comprise his entire daily routine, probably 200 feet per day.

Janota's profession as moneylender makes him well known in the area. The fact that people obligingly navigate his wheelchair on the sidewalk every day shows the respect he has acquired over the years. And in these difficult times of widespread unemployment, many are in dire need of cash. Bank loans, however small, are nearly impossible to get, which explains why Janota charges exorbitant interest rates.

Gaspar learns something new from Janota every Saturday while the two animatedly discuss the week's most memorable events. The nickname, Janota, can be roughly translated as "dandy." It dates from the time the veteran arrived in Bairro Alto from the hospital, paralyzed but proudly wearing his military uniform. His nickname might also refer to the old man's manner and articulate speaking style. The data he studies and the astute knowledge he has of his business—which includes mortgage rates, lending for starting small businesses, and loans for students—are most relevant to the neighborhood.

Gaspar thinks often how appropriate Janota's nickname is for the character seated before him. His flamboyant style of operating shows how his brain works a thousand times better than the branch bank's calculators.

Following the chat with Janota, Gaspar enters the café next door to enjoy a double espresso. Afterward, he walks down the streets, moving with an ease that attests his enjoyment for the weekend. When he reaches his favorite bakery, the scent wafting out its front door permeates the entire block. Gaspar's mother loves the *carcaças*, the elongated traditional rolls. Many local bakeries employ Romanian workers, and the bakery where Gaspar is a habitué hired Lena last year. She is about fifty-five years old, wears a white coat with a matching cap and is a pleasure to look at. With a bold, proud look on her flushed face, she meticulously fulfills the clients' orders.

Now and then, Lena uses her passable Portuguese to engage in conversation with Gaspar. The young man answers with a humming intonation to avoid drawing attention to his stutter. Lena tells him about the heartbreaking poverty of her own country, past and present. In Ceausescu's time, parents were allowed one full year to register their newborn children. The reason for this was that if a child died during this period, not yet registered, he or she wouldn't be counted as an infant mortality. The law successfully altered the mortality statistics, as hundreds of newborns died every year of starvation and freezing temperatures. It was as if these suffering children had never existed. Lena learned Russian using the Cyrillic alphabet in primary school, when the Soviets occupied Romania and declared their language would be the future of communication worldwide.

When Lena moved from Romania to Portugal to join relatives, she first worked in the Bread Museum in Seia in the northeastern part of the country. And she still feels nostalgia for her former workplace; bread is honored there as a food with spiritual qualities. For Lena, like many Orthodox Christian Romanians, bread that is consumed daily is a never-ending source of sacred symbolism that emanates blessings and joy.

Gaspar's father died when he was two. To this day, his mother blames his stutter on the fright he took when his father suddenly keeled over with a heart attack. Some Sundays Gaspar gets into the small Honda with his mother and drives to Uncle Isidro's, his father's older brother. Isidro lives alone in a small house with a vegetable garden in Caldas da Rainha. He is rather fond of Gaspar and has helped with his nephew's education from the beginning. An attentive presence in Gaspar's life, Isidro has always given him presents at the end of the school year, birthdays and Christmas. When Gaspar was a child, Uncle Isidro would let him step inside the aviary where he housed a dozen parakeets. The birds seemed to recognize the boy because they perched expectantly on his head or came to eat from his hand. To further show his affection, Isidro took Gaspar and his mother to the beach in Nazaré for summer vacations.

Gaspar, his mother, and Uncle Isidro are Jehovah's Witnesses. It was Uncle Isidro's devoted daughter, Manelita, who initiated her father and later on Gaspar's mother to the religion. Gaspar prefers traveling to Caldas da Rainha to go from door to door on Sundays to proselytize. He tells his mother that his stutter is an obstacle to the mission. It's difficult, however, to refuse his mother, so now and then he accompanies her.

Vanessa, Gaspar's ex-girlfriend, hated everything connected

with the sect. The "love thy neighbor" motto as a sign of genuine Christianity wasn't for her.

The family members, including Manelita's husband, André, often get together on Sunday afternoons for a snack at Isidro's house. As soon as Manelita enters her father's living room in the middle of the afternoon, she takes off her shoes and lies down on the couch. She is childless, with intense eyes, like an eagle's. She dresses like a maid of a bygone era and is very prickly. Gaspar attributes her bad temper to the old-fashioned girdle she wears to slim down; the constriction hinders her movements.

Stretched out on the couch, Manelita starts rambling as if her door-to-door Sunday mission isn't over yet. Isidro listens carefully and willingly accepts his daughter's pontifications. She mentions the Bible as the only moral authority and the need to preach the "good news of the kingdom;" then she dwells on the difficulties of her work. Sometimes, she says, she and André manage to read the scriptures to one or two old ladies. Young people state outright that they aren't interested in religious matters. The men they approach half-smile and say the newspaper awaits them. The women are too busy in the kitchen cooking. Not infrequently, the couple faces rude or angry individuals who scream or rant at them.

Manelita enjoys asking Gaspar whether he has been attending the Bible study group in the *salões do reino,* the so-called kingdom halls, the sect's meeting rooms. She is so forceful that Gaspar compares her manner to that of the first-in-line *forcado,* the man who takes the bull by the horns in *touradas,* the bullfights. She inquires about the hours Gaspar spends in religious work in the streets of Lisbon; then she asks about the bank and the number of colleagues he's managed to attract.

After much thought, and soon after his break-up with Vanessa, Gaspar found a strategy to deal with Manelita: he simply nods while she's speaking. This way, he somehow manages to give Manelita the feeling that he's listening attentively. But what he really wants is for Manelita to shut up and leave him alone. He also thinks that without her girdle, Manelita might need to proselytize less. Privately Gaspar doesn't take the Jehovah's Witnesses religion or his cousin seriously, but he goes along with both for his mother's sake.

Gaspar is bothered by Manelita's belief in religion's role in medicine. But confronting her openly would only cause family conflict. Manelita once told Gaspar and Vanessa that the Bible prohibited blood transfusions. Gaspar doesn't like to remember the moment of realization that devoted Jehovah's Witnesses let their children die rather than allow them to receive someone else's blood. Gaspar bitterly believes that a horrified Vanessa abandoned him shortly after she began to understand his family's religious circle.

As a boy, Gaspar liked Manelita. But not anymore. He can't understand why she speaks only about one subject. He also hears her on the phone with the people who attend the same meetings he goes to in Lisbon. She's nosy, always asking questions—and he resents that. On the other hand, trying to be the nice guy, he informs her of recent events. He mentions that a new sister recently joined the congregation. The young woman happens to be, like Lena, from Romania; he describes her as blond, tall, and very pretty. Gaspar speaks factually, deliberately omitting his feelings, feelings he didn't even know still existed after Vanessa's departure. Unluckily, the Jehovah's cult is an easy way to find out about Gaspar's private life in Lisbon.

Gaspar fears that Manelita is jealous of his and his mother's relationship with Isidro. The fact that Uncle Isidro has always been so generous with his sister-in-law and her son is unusual. Manelita may be worried that her aging father will leave something to the two of them in his will. Gaspar believes this is the reason Manelita is constantly trying to show her supremacy.

Isidro enjoys partying with the family and recently proposed a visit to the Bread Museum to celebrate Gaspar's upcoming thirty-third birthday. Gaspar had hoped that Manelita and André wouldn't go. As devoted members of the congregation, they might not want to celebrate his birthday, a form of idolatry for many. But, at the last minute, the couple decided to join the weekend outing.

During the visit to the Bread Museum, Gaspar, his mother, and Isidro walked together; Manelita and André toured on their own. The threesome was intrigued by the history of bread-making, the cereals used in various parts of the country, and the diversified construction of ovens and mills. The descriptions of bread as nourishment that had political, social, and religious meaning deeply touched Gaspar.

When the family sat together for lunch expecting to enjoy a lavish meal in the museum's restaurant, Gaspar felt, once again, Manelita's argumentative manner.

"I don't know why we had to come this far to visit the museum. I didn't like it," she said.

"Why not?" asked Isidro.

"It was a waste of time," Manelita replied.

"Didn't you enjoy seeing how the museum honors bread, such a basic food?" Isidro insisted.

"Not really. Jehovah's Witnesses use matzo in the annual communion and the museum doesn't address the issue."

"But they address many others." Isidro didn't seem ready to let go.

Seeing where the conversation was heading, André intervened to say that the codfish they had ordered was delicious. But Manelita told him to shut up.

Gaspar tried to redirect the conversation using his interest in accounting. "The museum's number of annual visitors is very high. I'm surprised, this is a private institution."

"So what?" Manelita was contentious.

"I like the idea of a self-supporting cultural entity independent from the government," Gaspar added politely.

"What difference does it make to you?"

"Quite a bit," Gaspar started to stammer heavily now. "The museum is supported with money that doesn't come out of my pocket."

"You and your ideas!"

"Self-supporting institutions are good for the country," Gaspar continued as slowly as he could. And maybe his birthday made him daring, for he added, "with or without a reference to the matzo we use in celebrations."

This was a direct allusion to the fact that Jehovah's Witnesses use unleavened bread, considered sacred, the body of Christ.

"You think so?" And looking at his mother, Manelita said, "If I were you, I'd watch closely who Gaspar is associating with in Lisbon."

Gaspar's mother exchanged a quick glance with Isidro and continued enjoying the meal. Manelita had made a remark; it didn't need an answer. But Manelita insisted on advising her aunt to accompany Gaspar to the weekly Bible meetings.

Seeing his mother frustrated on his birthday, Gaspar had the courage to address Manelita openly. He took forever to finish his phrase. "Allow me to add a detail. You don't need to be a Jehovah's Witness to worship bread. The Romanians, for instance, do the same. And it can be leavened or not; it doesn't matter."

Manelita wasn't ready to answer Gaspar with reasoning and therefore resorted to insult. "Romanians in our country are a bunch of idiots running away from downright misery."

Gaspar answered forcefully, " I'm sorry, Manelita, but I don't agree with you."

"That's irrelevant. The fact is that Romanians bring nothing to this country except cheap labor. Moreover, they take jobs away from us all."

Despite the good food, lunch didn't end peacefully as Isidro had expected. On the trip back to Lisbon the following day, Gaspar was still upset and wondered if he should bother going to the Friday Bible study group. But he was curious to see if the young Romanian woman would be there. She was so pretty! A bit broken by life, yes, but still very desirable. Gaspar already knew about her country; now he wanted to know about her.

When Gaspar arrived at the meeting and saw the young woman already sitting there, he forced his shyness aside and sat next to her. The woman's smile astounded him. As she greeted him in broken Portuguese, Gaspar thought about the joy of the language equalizer. He was a stutterer, and the young woman had to communicate in a language that wasn't her own. The short dialogue between them started precisely there, with language. She apologized for her poor Portuguese; he replied that he also had difficulties with communication.

The woman's name was Xana; she had been in Portugal three years and had recently joined the Jehovah's Witnesses. The financial crisis made her life difficult, so she was currently between jobs. She felt disappointed that this country wasn't the El Dorado she had imagined.

When the seemingly interminable meeting ended, Gaspar offered to escort Xana home. She agreed and said she lived in Praça da Alegria between the Hot Club and the Pensão Iberia, the Iberian Hostal. As they walked, Xana mentioned the wireless Internet as something positive about the room she was renting. Gaspar didn't feel like sharing the thought that Xana was bragging about something so insignificant.

At the shabby front door, Xana asked Gaspar if he was attending, as she was, the annual convention that was taking place the following week. Gaspar babbled a yes, and feeling passionate, asked Xana if she was free to have dinner with him afterward. When Xana replied it would be a pleasure, Gaspar felt that he wasn't the only one feeling lonely. Who knew, maybe his romantic past could be redeemed.

The Jehovah's Witnesses caucus was, in Gaspar's opinion, worse than he had expected. From the stage, the congregation's brothers quoted Bible verses as they asked for offerings. Multitudes of devotees directed their steps to the stage. Some threw bills and coins into strategically placed wooden chests; others threw bracelets and earrings, even wedding rings, into tin receptacles. Jewels tinkled as they landed. In the heart of the mass confusion, people fainted after going into a trance. A few threw themselves on the floor, saliva or blood trickling from their mouths. Fat security guards spread around the room, slapping the fallen to revive them. The whole scene was outlandish, Gaspar concluded.

The caucus behind them, Xana and Gaspar headed back to Bairro Alto to have dinner. They decided on one of the *tascas*, small, cheap restaurants with very appetizing food. Xana was wearing very high heels and thus stood a full head taller than Gaspar. She wore a leather jacket and a short, pleated skirt. If someone were listening from the next table, he or she would have been entertained. Xana spoke in disjointed Portuguese, and Gaspar, acutely nervous, took several minutes to finish each sentence. Facial tics typical of stutterers accompanied his labored words.

Xana told Gaspar that as she approached thirty she was starting life all over again. She was currently working as a domestic for an affluent family who lived in Santa Catarina. Gaspar was surprised: Xana dressed well, seemed educated, and had gracious table manners. When she chose her entrée, she wanted *guisado à portuguesa,* a tasty stew, and told Gaspar she would like to order Barca Velha. Caught off guard, he replied that since that was a reserve wine, he had never tried it. Xana replied it was one of her favorites, as if she drank it every night. Then, as if reading Gaspar's mind, she said she was just kidding and that it would be best to order a bottle of water.

During dinner, Xana confessed that she had never worked as a cleaning lady before. While quoting from the Bible, she told Gaspar that she believed the kingdom of heaven would one day favor innocents like her. She added that recently she had gone through something that had broken her heart. Gaspar, being a bank clerk, would certainly understand.

Her precarious situation had to do with a large sum of money that had been taken away from her bank account through the Internet. Everything that she had managed to save in the last three years in Portugal was gone. Up until that catastrophe, she had been sending an allowance to her mother and siblings in Romania. With her new cleaning job, she couldn't help her family in Romania any longer.

The desire to overcome her depression had been a major reason for her to join the Jehovah's Witnesses. She needed to erase the past, start all over, and regain hope for the future. As an active member of the new religion, she wanted to memorize the Bible by heart. She also wished to be baptized. She wanted to submerge her body in holy water—a notion she found sensual—in a public ceremony with an affectionate audience surrounding her for support. She said that she had already bought the white dress she wanted to wear that day. It was simple and not transparent.

Gaspar felt taken in by Xana's proclaimed innocence. But thinking about numbers, as was usual for him, he asked with difficulty, "But according to what you said, you make more than the minimum wage in the house you currently work in."

"Yes, I do," answered Xana in her Romanian accent, stressing the last syllables. "But I'm used to having certain kinds of things."

"What do you need that you can't have?" Gaspar asked.

"Look, like every Portuguese," answered Xana, "I enjoy drinking '*uns bons travos*.'"

"You enjoy good flavors in wine? Here is a typical Portuguese expression!" said Gaspar. And he added tenderly: "You know more Portuguese than I thought."

"I already discussed the matter with Brother Paulino from our congregation," said Xana. "Since I want to be baptized, I must stop drinking."

Gaspar went along. He liked the idea of Xana's baptism, the crowd witnessing it, and the white dress.

"Do Romanians drink as much as the Portuguese?" Gaspar asked, hiding his thoughts.

"Yes, they do. I've got a lot of experience in that," Xana tucked her hair behind her ears and exposed the earlobes. After a brief moment of silence she added, "I worked in a hotel bar in Bucharest when I was a teenager."

"I thought hotel bars in Eastern Europe, even for work, were only for the well-to-do," Gaspar muttered fearful of his ignorance.

"They are!" said Xana.

"Didn't you say earlier that your family was very poor?" Gaspar hummed.

"There was a hotel for foreigners with a bar in our village. My mom knew the state construction magnate. He offered me the job."

"Why?" asked Gaspar wishing his tongue would unravel.

"The man convinced my mother that I was pretty and could make good money. My dad had left the family; we had nothing to eat."

"How sad!"

"But now my mother can't help me," Xana said, feeling suddenly sorry for herself.

"Why not?" asked Gaspar. "If I were in trouble my mother would do anything to help me."

"My mom can't produce the kind of money stolen from me."

"Tell me the details of the Internet withdrawal," Gaspar tried to get involved. Xana's earlobe left him breathless and she knew his fascination. Gaspar purposely did not touch Xana; he thought it better to give the relationship time to develop.

"I'll tell you the story out of friendship. But I don't want any of the Jehovah's Witnesses to know about it."

"I swear to keep the secret," Gaspar said.

"In one day 50,000 euros disappeared from my account," Xana replied, again accenting the last syllables.

"That's a lot of money. It would take me more than a decade to save that much." Gaspar's stutter intensified as he tried to finish his sentence. And after a long pause, he added "Please don't get me wrong, Xana, but how did you manage to save so much in only three years?"

Feeling defenseless, Xana pondered whether to end her confidences for the day. However, looking into Gaspar's puzzled face, she saw his genuine concern and realized that she could either tell Gaspar the truth or risk losing a new friend. "The facts are that in Portugal I've been working all along for the construction magnate from my Romanian village," Xana confessed quietly. "His name is Vladimir. I continue serving the man who helped our family by giving me a job."

"That's some news!" Gaspar exclaimed.

"We hired young Romanian women to come and work in Portugal."

"Doing what?" As if to postpone finding out the inevitable, Gaspar waved the waiter to bring two coffees.

"I've nothing to be ashamed of. Vladimir and I are partners in a cleaning service business," replied Xana. After a brief moment of silence she added, "The company was in his name."

"Were you married to Vladimir?" Gaspar asked, his tension deflating somewhat.

"No way! He wanted to tie the knot but, in the end, accepted that I didn't want to marry someone so much older." Xana noticed Gaspar's flushed face and continued, "The girls we brought to Portugal were good people: primary school teachers, nurses, accountants for state organizations and so on. Some were from showbiz, the music world. They all wanted to escape utter poverty, just like me."

" Why would they accept working as domestics?" Gaspar was baffled.

"They're all starving back home."

Gaspar felt drawn into another world that stood on the abyss, an abyss into which he himself might fall through his connection to Xana.

"My work as domestic in Santa Catarina," Xana looked innocent, her habit of stressing last syllables always present, "is only a temporary thing."

"I want to know how 50,000 euros were stolen from your bank account," Gaspar said.

Xana explained how Vladimir had committed a virtual crime. The cleaning business's transactions were made through a bank in Seville, Spain. She and her boss had two bank accounts: one for daily business, the other for Xana's savings. They used the same password for both accounts.

In time, Xana had grown tired of travelling to Romania by car to recruit staff. Moreover, after getting her Portuguese work permit, she wanted to start her own business. She had continuously paid her dues to the Portuguese social security administration and her immigration process was advancing. Her partner wasn't too happy about her wish for independence, and she had agreed to work for him one more year. It was at the end of that year that he stole her savings.

"I trusted Vladimir. He had helped my family when we didn't have anything to eat. And he used me. Now I'm alone in a foreign country." After a long pause Xana added, "And this happened because I wanted to change my life."

Gaspar remained silent, pondering all and each of Xana's words.

"A person in my situation, Gaspar, doesn't get out of the mud," Xana continued after the silence. "I spoke to the bank manager in Seville and he said that I should have been more careful."

"Why didn't you notify the police?" Gaspar wanted to know.

"About what? Are the police interested in two bank accounts in Seville, Spain, that I shared with a business partner I met in Romania as an adolescent? "

"Still. The account was in your name only and your partner

used a common password to void it."

"I let Vladimir have the password because I didn't want him to think I didn't trust him."

"I understand."

"You know the meaning of the name Vladimir? It's a composed word. Vlad means to rule, to master; mir means world, universe."

"You see Vladimir as more powerful than you."

"He is. The bank manager in Seville told me that this kind of crime is most prevalent between couples, a revenge from jealous husbands."

Disconcerted, Gaspar nodded a yes.

After a few more minutes of silence, Xana, looking distressed, said she wanted to go back to her room in Praça da Alegria. She didn't want Gaspar to take her home. Gaspar warned Xana that she shouldn't walk home by herself wearing such a short skirt. But Xana insisted that she needed to be alone to relieve her thoughts.

Gaspar was left with questions he couldn't answer. Xana's story was farfetched; it could even be a complete lie. How was it possible that a cleaning company had such high profits during times of increased financial hardship? Yes, the Portuguese enjoy clean homes and are willing to pay for the service. But could the sum that Xana said belonged exclusively to her actually be company's money? Or could she be hiding that she had married Vladimir in Spain? Thus, he could have had access to the password of the account in her name only. If she hadn't registered the marriage here, then she wasn't lying; she wasn't married in Portugal. Lastly, was it possible that some men were so spiteful that they used such schemes to destroy a woman?

Unable to sleep that night, Gaspar decided that if he could help Xana get out of her mess, he would. Somehow she resembled Vanessa, his teenage dream. Was it the long hair? The short skirt? Maybe there was still time in his life to get married, be happy. Whatever it was, he wanted to be at Xana's side. She accepted his stutter with kindness, something Vanessa had never done. Vanessa had the habit of finishing his sentences, something he hated. When he took longer to express himself, she threw piercing glances at him. Maybe the fact that Xana's Portuguese was as imperfect as his own speech patterns placed both of them on equal footing.

Gaspar felt true to himself.

A few days later, Gaspar met Xana after work and the two headed to the weekly Jehovah's Witnesses gathering. He told her that he wanted to give her a proof of fraternal love, something their religion cherished above all. Gaspar was willing to introduce Xana to his old neighbor Janota; he would give Xana the financial help she needed. She would immediately have additional funds to help her family in Romania. As soon as Gaspar managed to finish his sentence, Xana softly kissed Gaspar on his lips without uttering a reply. Right there, in the middle of the street. The young man remained speechless until the two entered the Jehovah's building.

Fueled by the fire she sensed in Gaspar, Xana added details of her dream. Not only did she need to help her family back home. She also wanted to resurrect her own cleaning business and expand it by recruiting from countries bordering Romania. She would be able to pay Janota back in installments. There was no shortage of young women dying to live in sunny Portugal. The immigration laws were restrictive and the country in financial duress, but the large educated class in Lisbon could still afford household help. With Janota's help, Xana could start flying to Central Europe very soon, thus avoiding the tiring journeys by car.

Gaspar's mother was surprised to see her son suddenly so distracted, so busy in the evening. When she spoke with Isidro, she told him about it. She knew that Manelita was in her father's house and listened to the entire conversation. So what? Gaspar's mother thought. She wasn't complaining about her son; she was just pouring out her heart. Isidro advised her not to fuss. At thirty-three, Gaspar had the right to his own life; it was about time he stopped hiding behind his mother's skirts. Had he found a girlfriend?

Gaspar's mother had no information on that subject. On the other hand, a few days ago Gaspar had told her that he now realized that people enjoyed diverse pursuits and had different dreams. He had talked about the people in Bairro Alto—foreigners or Portuguese—and their common humanity. He had also mentioned that being a Jehovah's Witness meant salvation for many. And that was a good thing.

Gaspar's mother asked Isidro to pass her news about Gaspar on to Manelita. Her son had also recently complimented Manelita, she said. Gaspar now saw Manelita as a woman who, instead of getting her much needed rest, went to work for the church because she believed in it. Gaspar had himself discovered the golden rule: Help thy neighbor. Following Manelita's example, he wished to get closer to those in need. Gaspar's mother ended by saying that Gaspar now seemed more mature. He had recently acknowledged that sometimes in order to survive difficult moments, people had to hold fast to religion.

Meanwhile Gaspar, Xana, and Janota met the following Saturday morning. When Gaspar introduced Xana, Janota whistled with his fingers and told Gaspar he didn't know his friend had such stunning female friends. Gaspar blushed with pure joy. After a two-hour conversation, Janota lent Xana a large sum. Xana thought the interest rate too high. But Janota was unyielding, so she signed the pre-arranged monthly installment plan. Gaspar was caught by surprise when Janota asked him to be Xana's guarantor. Gaspar immediately signed, even though it was his first time. What did it matter? Wasn't Janota a longtime friend? When Xana expressed excitement in her new company, Janota hinted that he didn't care how people used the money he lent them.

Looking at Xana, however, reminded Janota that beauty still existed in this world.

The deal closed, Gaspar suggested that they stop by Lena's bakery. He wanted to buy some *carcaças* to take home to his mother, and Xana might enjoy meeting Lena, a native of her own country. But Xana said that she was in a hurry; her boss in Santa Catarina was expecting guests and she must hurry to work.

When Gaspar got home he heard the phone ringing as soon as he stepped in. It was Manelita on the line needing to talk to him. She had unpleasant news, regrettably, and needed to talk to Gaspar not only as a family member but also as a Jehovah's brother. She had recently been informed of Gaspar's involvement with a young Romanian woman named Xana. Was this true? It would be best if Gaspar admitted the truth, she cautioned.

Gaspar started stammering and Manelita's suspicions were confirmed—he was in love. But she had information: Xana was a stripper in a hotel bar not far from Praça da Alegria. She was a whore who slept with anyone, a prostitute who survived by selling her body. More than that, she was notorious for recruiting young women, all of them Romanian, to work in bars and hotels all over the country. And, finally, she was known and praised for allowing men to touch her body when performing in white, transparent dresses.

Doomsday was coming, and fast, Manelita warned. Gaspar didn't need to trouble himself: she had taken it upon herself to inform Brother Paulino of her findings. The Jehovah's Witnesses sect was about to oust both of them. Manelita said she knew better than anyone else that religious practice was a way of life, something that must be preserved.

And the sect had no place for people like Gaspar and Xana.

Salò, National Version

Bianca is a character worthy of *Salò, or The 120 Days of Sodom,* Pasolini's film based on the book by the Marquis de Sade. Of average stature and just over forty, Bianca is neither pretty nor ugly, neither fat nor slim. Her skin has the olive complexion characteristic of people in the Mediterranean; smooth and ageless, it is a source of attraction. Another distinctive feature is her conservative attire. In autumn, she enjoys wearing shades of blue with a dark-brown suede belt, slightly loose. An Yves Saint Laurent scarf stylishly wrapped around her neck provides the finishing touch. She accessorizes with rings and earrings of gold inlaid with silver. With the pretensions of Imelda Marcos, she has innumerable pairs of shoes that always match the dominant color of her outfit.

For years Bianca has been under intense social pressure. Her mother sells plastic toys from a portable gazebo in the Lisbon Zoo, which she sets up every day before sunrise. The seventy-five year old woman has labored her entire life and the daily hardship hasn't changed her; she is who she is, a street vendor. As for Bianca's father, no one has ever heard from him. Belief has it that he either died at an early age, perhaps the consequence of a fall from a construction site, or that he's serving a lengthy prison sentence and has been forgotten by his family. Bianca comes from the lowest echelon of Portugal's social strata. To get ahead, she assiduously exercised an iron grip to hide her origins from the hypocrites that abound in our Portugalinho, our small Portugal.

To fully understand Bianca, one needs to visualize a few details that she still clings to in her social decline. She imitates the tone of voice of Lisbon's upper class as if everyone she addresses is inferior. She exudes hauteur as she bosses her housekeeper in an aproned uniform. But, above all, she drives through Lisbon, head held high, in the back of her vintage Volvo still driven by a chauffeur, an immigrant from Guinea-Bissau who was briefly her lover. When she arrives at her destination, she waits for Adriano, the black driver, to come around and open her door, his cap in hand. Only then does she slide herself smoothly to the sidewalk.

Downtown pedestrians stop and stare as a restaurant's doorman rushes to greet the supposedly affluent customer. In Lisbon, the easily impressed poor curse their fate; middle class residents show their envy through tight lips; and the rich abhor Bianca's disdain.

We need to go back in time to understand Bianca's current situation. She grew up with her mother and sisters in Alhandra, a poor and dilapidated Lisbon suburb. She yearned for a better life, a future far away from the dirty and smelly outskirts of town. She considered herself better off than her cousins whose mother sold fish in the open market. The children had to help her aunt unload the fish truck every morning despite the bitter winter cold. There was nothing unusual or exceptional about Bianca's ambition to escape poverty, except that in Portugal the possibility of changing one's social status is as problematic as climbing Mount Everest—even with the proper gear.

Between watching soap operas and small talk with high school friends, Bianca realized prostitution was the quickest way to climb the social ladder. Her school friends managed to create an escort group for men, and Bianca joined them the year before getting her high-school diploma. With "good girls" saving their virginity for marriage and priests advising couples to eschew divorce despite conjugal unhappiness, a steady clientele was easy to find. Young and old, the men were locals as well as visitors from the provinces. Some paid huge sums; others, being steady clients, could pay in installments. The mother of one of the girls, a connoisseur of the seedier side of life, became the club's madam. Assignations took place in a rented flat in Campo d'Ourique, a well-chosen Lisbon district where commercial activity camouflaged the young women's business.

Not being a virgin when she started out, Bianca's exploits proceeded without any major surprises. A mixture of innocence, intuition, and physical voraciousness took care of the rest. She felt lucky. One of her first sexual partners, an experienced middle-aged kindred spirit, enhanced Bianca's versatility.

The young women confided among themselves, nevertheless, on the difficulty of their lives. Their purpose was to pleasure men whose ages varied but in some cases were fairly advanced. Some clients were provincial and without manners; others arrived drunk and turned violent. Many enjoyed describing the way they mistreated the wives that they now ignored. The madam, aware of her young charges' sensibilities, offered advice: this kind of life, she told the girls, would need to last only as long as it took to save enough money for new and better paths.

One day, one of the young prostitutes announced an invitation to visit the house of one of the group's clients. The young man's parents were vacationing abroad, and his house was open. He was a college student with erectile problems and he hoped that if he had the chance to freely choose a partner among the young women, his problem might be resolved.

And that was how Bianca and Eduardo met. Eduardo liked the way Bianca presented herself; she was simply yet tastefully dressed. Her skin tone pleased him. He also liked the distance he sensed between her and the other women of the group, as if she had more depth or class. Within weeks, Eduardo had become Bianca's 'regular' at the Campo d'Ourique apartment. Sometimes he brought along one or two college friends to share the pleasures; the young men paired up with girls and went to separate bedrooms.

Over time the Campo d'Ourique group grew happy and successful. By selecting patrons one at a time, the madam had succeeded in establishing a refined clientele for the young women. Many customers turned out to be college students with ages comparable to the young prostitutes. The students marketed the service by spreading word of their love nests. Quite a few of the young men came from families who had money or social standing, or both. Some had cars and occasionally invited the girls on outings.

Months passed by in a sweet dreamland between Bianca and Eduardo until the inevitable happened. Eduardo confessed to his friends that he was in love with Bianca. And he added that from that moment on Bianca belonged solely to him. If any of his friends or even acquaintances dared to try to touch her, he wouldn't vouch for his reaction. No matter how innocent it might appear, no flirting was allowed with Bianca. Eduardo soon went to Bianca and confessed his love. He told her he wanted to help her change her life. He would ask his father to find her a job in one of the newspaper and television chains he owned.

Bianca had, to her credit, achieved a remarkable success. Eduardo now had a balanced sexual life; he was capable of giving and receiving pleasure.

The young woman hesitated at Eduardo's offer and said she needed time to think matters over. For Bianca knew she wasn't in love. Prostitution had taught her about herself and the power of her feminine charms. She wasn't in a hurry to change her life. But she was aware, on the other hand, that the opportunity Eduardo was offering involved huge social significance and might never be repeated.

Unlike her friends, Bianca had an enormous capacity to learn, not just in matters of sex but social skills as well. She felt totally comfortable in the circle that Eduardo moved in. She quickly learned how to order food in a chic restaurant, how to use and set aside fork and knife, and how to greet Eduardo's family and friends who might be sitting at the nearby table. She felt confident as nobody asked indiscreet questions. And she felt deliriously happy whenever Eduardo took her for a drive in his convertible.

With alarm, the club's madam noticed that she might be on the verge of losing one of her most valuable girls. And if Bianca left, other girls might follow; her livelihood was, therefore, at risk. The girls, in turn, were divided about Bianca. Some were glad about her future prospects, a good fortune that might one day also happen to them. Others resented her, feeling sorry for themselves. For comfort, many slept together after a client left.

With considerable vision of the future and after much thought, Bianca decided to give herself another chance in life. One Saturday she told Eduardo she was ready to make a commitment to him once the new job became available.

Soon Bianca started to work for one of Eduardo's father's publications, a magazine of celebrity gossip that nurtured the sweet dreams of people unable to act on their own fantasies. At the office, Bianca was a gal Friday, handling the phone, running messages, and doing odds and ends of secretarial work. Having returned to her former home in Alhandra, she had to commute by train to work, something she viewed as a total waste of time. From the very beginning, things didn't go the way she expected at work. The job required attention and skill, but she earned less than she had before. The tasks never ended; someone was always shouting for her help. The only moment of the day she enjoyed was her lunch break with colleagues, women who did similar tasks to hers.

At odds with her new situation, Bianca secretly visited her friends in Campo d'Ourique regularly. From the very start, Eduardo had insisted on complete separation from her old group. But the old vixen in charge whispered in Bianca's ear that whatever happened at her place was none of his business. She added that Bianca wasn't married to Eduardo yet; the future remained unknown. Bianca, on the other hand, was relieved to have a place to stay in Lisbon whenever she felt like it.

Because her co-workers at the cheap magazine were bohemian types, Bianca discovered it was easy to conceal her unsavory past. And it was even easier to *épater les bourgeois*—to dupe her associates. No one questioned her when she stated that she hadn't gone to college because studying was a nuisance. No one proposed to visit her at home when she said she lived outside Lisbon. And no one seemed to care about her whereabouts at night or after work; they all went to discotheques and bars. Staying at the Campo d'Ourique apartment at night while Eduardo studied for exams, Bianca became accustomed to lying to him, saying that she was with her mother in Alhandra.

Eduardo took his studies seriously and he was in love with Bianca. Therefore it never crossed his mind to question her veracity. All Eduardo wanted was to continue dating Bianca; he was waiting to see how the relationship evolved. One of his friend's apartments was always available, when needed, for lovemaking.

Months later, on a spring day, Eduardo took Bianca out for lunch at Guincho, on Lisbon's coastal outskirts. There, by the roaring sea, he proposed a future for them. He wanted to marry her and start a life together. He had already spoken to his father who was willing to help financially, providing Eduardo finished his degree. Bianca used the opportunity to let Eduardo know she didn't like the magazine work and viewed it only as a transitional occupation. Her real ambition was to open a shop in Lisbon. She had a passion for home decoration and loved the idea of owning a business in Estrela, Lisbon's posh district. She wanted an address people would remember. Eduardo replied that that was fine with him. On the verge of finishing his degree in economics, he would be able to turn Bianca's dream into reality. Hearing his plan, Bianca readily accepted the marriage proposal.

A simple ceremony with only family and close friends took place soon afterward.

As the months went by, the couple seemed adjusted and happy. Eduardo's inner circle knew that Bianca had been born and raised in Alhandra, but nobody seemed to care. The town was no Babylon and therefore none had acquaintances in the area capable of providing information. Besides, they all liked Bianca. The former Campo d'Ourique prostitute had now risen through marriage to a position in society. The possibility of being recognized by an old client was remote. Moreover, it wasn't as if Eduardo's friends and their girlfriends didn't harbor secrets of their own, their own *telhados de vidro,* their own glass houses. Bianca was charming with Eduardo's father; oblivious, the old man reciprocated. And if Eduardo's mother, a member of Lisbon's stuffy high society, didn't like her daughter-in-law, well then, too bad. The grande dame had always been hard to please.

A few months after marriage, Bianca and Eduardo opened the home decoration establishment financed by a bank loan. Located in Estrela, the space glittered with imported goods that could certainly attract affluent customers, in particular friends of Eduardo and his parents. Bianca spent her days at the boutique tending to her clientele. Eduardo was the store's *ponta de lança,* the buyer, and from the beginning the business provided the couple's main source of income. Eduardo travelled abroad almost every week to buy merchandise. From the outset, the posh shop seemed to hold a lucky star, its sales flourishing. At the beginning the couple sold imported exotic fabrics, classy English furnishings and contemporary paintings. Someone was always getting married who wanted a gift registry in the shop; or another was renovating an old house that required exclusive pieces; yet another wanted to invest in a new painting for the living room.

The clientele soon became more and more demanding, asking for antique pieces of furniture, oriental art, export porcelain, and Persian rugs. More and more often the boutique displayed beautiful objects of an increasingly higher value. The luxury items were well beyond the shop's original scope but delighted the enthusiastic costumers. Even Bianca's old friends from Campo d'Ourique visited during off-hours to admire the opulence. They came without Eduardo's knowledge as he had warned Bianca that the grounds were off limits to them. One day, when Eduardo returned earlier than expected from abroad and found his wife's former madam on site, chatting away happily as only old vixens seem able to do, he immediately pointed her to the doorway. Closing the door, he looked Bianca in the eye and said that if he ever found that woman there again, Bianca would see her dream collapse; he would close the establishment that same day.

Although Eduardo spoke sternly, his excitement about the shop's success was evident. He also enjoyed its clientele and the purchases made in foreign European capitals. His work was free of dull routine and the buying trips opened up a new world. For her part, Bianca knew instinctively how to engage and entice customers. She let them take pieces home, on speculation, to see if they fit the décor of a prospective room. If they wished, clients could pay in installments. Bianca also continuously perfected the subtle art of manipulating her customers' weaknesses, making mental notes to herself about their idiosyncrasies.

As business partners, each member of the couple had his or her own *métier*: Bianca knew how to insinuate herself and how to persuade clients to buy. In particular she knew how to address the regulars, the ones with greater buying power. Eduardo, on the other hand, was experienced on how and where to purchase items. He was now a habitué at international art auction houses. While traveling, he and Bianca spoke daily by phone. As soon as Eduardo arrived back in Lisbon, Bianca placed the new pieces in the store's front window; many of the items sold the very same day. The couple was delighted to see their bank loan decreasing every month.

Bianca was especially alluring with male customers, particularly if they visited the shop without their wives. If Eduardo got jealous, he didn't show it either to Bianca or the clients. Maybe because, like his wife, he enjoyed the sums coming in. Bianca was developing a mind of her own; defying her husband's authority was therefore becoming a possibility. Maybe she didn't respect Eduardo enough to pay attention to his feelings. And since Bianca had never loved Eduardo and saw him only as a step to her personal advancement, his ultimate opinion of her didn't matter. The Campo d'Ourique girls knew about the madam's incident with Eduardo and kept to Bianca's strict instructions to visit only when Eduardo was abroad. Bianca would make a quick call to signal them that he had boarded a plane. Long conversations ensued, sex being a major topic. The prostitutes openly discussed their interest in each other's bodies, as if a form of protection against the brutish advances of male clients.

Within only a few years, the owners of the new decoration business had undergone a significant transformation. Similarly, the establishment changed from its original conception as well. Renowned people now came to the shop to meet each other: journalists who spread the latest news; politicians who looked for help in the corridors of power; top-echelon lawyers and doctors with money to spend. Eager to satisfy the desires of such an elite group, Eduardo now traveled most of the time, a courier between Lisbon and major European cities. Sometimes he bought on special request to earn substantial returns.

Then, suddenly, without an obvious reason, the moneyed and influential clientele of Estrela boutique who usually entered the front door started to sneak out the back. Bianca was now in charge of another parallel operation: she had turned herself into a madam. Not only that, she herself was one of the most sought-after women on the circuit; of course she only engaged when she felt like it or when the financial prospects were enticing. If a client came in to exchange an item purchased the previous week, he usually stayed a while to chat. But, since the afternoon was sunny and warm, wouldn't Bianca like to go out for a drink at a nearby hotel? And if she were unable to leave the shop, wouldn't one of her friends like to join him?

Unnoticed by most, the merchandise sold at the shop began to include flesh and bone.

The new business appealed to older men who wanted to enjoy a relaxing afternoon, in particular those with fat bank accounts. The transformation was gradual, imperceptible and unplanned, as if by accident. Bianca continued to dress conservatively, always taking good care of her luminous skin.

One of the clients with whom Bianca left through the shop's back door was an international arms dealer who inhabited Quinta da Marinha, the elite's preferred neighborhood outside of Lisbon. He was a friend of Eduardo's parents and very wealthy. Another regular client was a parliamentarian with eccentric tastes: he had a fetish for vases decorated with nude mythological figures and a commensurate love of sacred art, particularly black Madonnas. The pieces he bought at the store went straight to the chapel at his country estate to delight his wife during Sunday mass. Another client was a high-ranking military officer, an adventurer of sorts during the Portuguese colonial wars in Africa. He was rumored to have invaded a country in the Gulf of Guinea known to harbor enemies of the Portuguese.

Indeed, Bianca had a diverse clientele!

She continued to rise, fully aware of her newfound power. To give the business even more momentum, she occasionally spread big lies. She let it be known that she had inherited some valuable land near a recently built soccer stadium, an area on the verge of commercial development. The gullible believed it; it bore the scent of money.

Bianca's leap from lucrative businesswoman to globalized sex queen was subtle. And the people who might have discerned the situation, in particular Eduardo, failed to realize what was happening.

Sex was like food for her: get satisfied, move on. Eventually, Bianca's sexual exclusivity ended; she started sleeping not only with men but with women as well. She particularly enjoyed the company of her old friends from Campo d'Ourique. The more time she spent with these women, the more efficiently she hid them from her husband.

Inevitably, all hell broke loose one day. Tamara, a friend of Bianca and Eduardo, asked if her teenage son could stay with them for two weeks. Tamara's mother, who lived abroad, was dying of cancer, and Tamara needed to look after her. At age fourteen, her son was clean at the moment but already had a drug and criminal record. His father had left the family some years before, and the boy was needy.

Fertile ground for some crazy nights arose from this unexpected situation, and Eduardo's absence on one of his business trips undoubtedly facilitated events. Miguel was an attractive young man with an innocent appearance. On his first night at Bianca's, he told her that he was afraid of sleeping in the dark. Bianca, seizing another opportunity for her voracious appetite, offered to sleep next to him. As soon as she turned off the lamp, she drew Miguel's hand over her smooth face. It took little effort from this initial touch to Bianca's full seduction of the adolescent.

She had plunged irrevocably into the abyss.

What took place over the following months wasn't pretty. Tamara returned home after her mother's funeral with a full load of estate business to handle and, as usual, her son wasn't a top priority. But she did notice with alarm that Miguel was doing drugs once more. Was he also stealing again? His rapid mood swings left her uneasy. Feeling unable to have an honest conversation with her son, Tamara sent Miguel to a psychologist and discussed her worries with Bianca. Bianca, afraid that Miguel would reveal their affair, suggested that Tamara send him to a rehab clinic. In fact, Bianca had been financing Miguel's new addiction to heroin; it was the easiest way to play with him in bed whenever she wanted.

Everything imploded when Miguel, eager to avoid the rehab clinic, told his psychologist about his relationship with Bianca. Because he was a minor, the psychologist felt it her duty to inform his mother. The boy needed a safe haven and the perpetrator needed to be punished. But Miguel's mother didn't prosecute the case; what judge would believe a kid with a drug problem?

Tamara instead took another kind of action. She went straight to Eduardo and told him what Bianca had done. Eduardo was so shocked that he left the house that same night and a few months later filed for divorce—but not without conflict and sorrow. One of the biggest questions was, of course, what to do with the decorating boutique that had brought the couple such huge financial success. Using her own secret stash of client money, Bianca bought out Eduardo's share.

In the years that followed the couple's calamity, Eduardo struggled to sleep, eat, and hold his head above water. He even struggled to see his closest friends. Some spared him but others told him about the whole Campo d'Ourique affair at the shop. Eduardo was lost. If the person he had married could betray him so thoroughly, what might other women do in the future?

Inspired by a friend, Bianca had been devouring the entire works of the Marquis de Sade and enjoying the sadomasochistic stories. She had also watched Pasolini's film *Salò,* inspired by Sade's writing. In her thirties at that time, she took the opportunity to view it several times to memorize the unsavory practices depicted. She then began to indulge in the most perverse ones in the company of her partners.

With Sade's protagonists as her models and inspiration, she engaged in lewd practices characteristic of sexual deviants. Her freedom was absolute and her lack of morality total. Like the Marquis de Sade, Bianca's sexual habits were a form of tyranny imposed on her prey. She practiced Sade's evil seduction, setting her own standards for her base fantasies; the cruel, wanton practices victimized her sexual partners. She trained her fingers skillfully, the same instruments with which she accepted and signed checks.

Bianca mixed sex with rosaries and debauchery with humiliation. In the midst of her promiscuous exploits she often hid her face behind a black tulle veil. Her partners never knew if she was experiencing pleasure or pain, if she suffered or rejoiced, or if she was willful or compulsive. During such encounters, she demanded to be called Clara—as if Clara, which means bright in Portuguese, would wash out the darkness of her soul.

At the end of these sessions, Bianca pulled off the black tulle veil and laughed like a madwoman to show her disregard for her cohorts. Her sexuality became a hand grenade, poised to blow up in the face of her chosen guinea pig. Sexual partners were a symbol of her personal accomplishments, her career trophies. Love didn't exist for Bianca; it repulsed her. Only exploitation was conceivable.

It was at this juncture that Bianca, like an acrobat, executed yet another somersault. She took as a lover an older banker whose prestige came from a combination of art-collecting and soccer sponsorship. Everybody in the Lisbon art world now knew the reason behind Eduardo and Bianca's divorce. As for her financial life, she was in trouble not only for her lack of liquidity but also for her ignorance about buying merchandise. Eduardo had been an irreplaceable partner in this regard. He was a refined man who could walk with confidence into any art show around the world. Moreover, he had an eye for an outstanding piece and knew how to negotiate prices to his advantage. In Eduardo, Bianca had lost a most dependable associate.

Aware that she was adrift in her business endeavors, the banker was willing to support Bianca. He thus became the ideal partner to give his companion the credibility she needed. Bianca assumed that she possessed the business skills to fool customers in the same way she had fooled Eduardo. But she did not. Counting on some of her clients' lack of connoisseurship, she had begun to sell fake art. When acquiring merchandise, she wrote post-dated checks and on occasion bad checks. The police discovered that long-distance bidders for art she placed at Lisbon auction houses were phonies, their only role to drive up prices. Clients began to place Internet comments denouncing Bianca.

The old banker helped as much as he could. He brought in a relative to work with Bianca and keep an eye on her. To lend her credibility, the new lover placed pieces from his private collection for sale in Bianca's boutique. His ploy raised the eyebrows of people who had seen the pieces in his house just a week or two before. As a financier who was not in the least naive, the lover was well aware of Bianca's past and her diverse exploits. He figured out, however, that this was the only way to hold on to Bianca. She had enchanted him the same way she had enchanted Eduardo. Also, he enjoyed her sado-masochistic delights in the bedroom. To keep her at his side, he even bought her a Brazilian love nest in Bahia, Brazil. After his death, he reasoned, she might need to leave Lisbon.

Bianca had no friends, only acquaintances who expected a form of payback for expensive purchases made at her boutique in years past. Women in Lisbon gossiped, keeping the memory of Bianca's past fully alive. As if the shop's vulgar transactions had occurred only yesterday, they chattered about their husbands, fathers, and friends sneaking out of the shop's back door in undignified company.

Thus, it was no surprise that within twenty-four hours of the banker's death at the end of one summer season, his heirs fell upon Bianca. Only powerful *Lisboetas,* citizens of Lisbon, could have deployed such a clean operation. Judicial officers entered Bianca's store and confiscated everything they deemed worthy: furniture, sculptures, vases, and paintings. Humiliated as never before, Bianca begged on her knees, pleading that the objects belonged to her, that they were gifts from her lover. Her groveling didn't help, even though she also offered her body. The agents had instructions to start and finish quickly.

Some people, however, never give up; the abyss seems almost irresistible. A new ambition soon filled Bianca's days; she now wanted to be a mother. So she found herself another man. The new conquest was about her age, on the verge of getting divorced, and from a low-income background similar to her own. Tói couldn't claim that he had not been warned about the person he was coupling with. Tamara, as Bianca's sworn enemy, had called Tói and warned him of the danger. Tói must have mulled over the matter when his only child, a boy, moved in with him and Bianca. But fascination is blind; besides Bianca was now pregnant with his child. Did Tói have any clue that once his procreative function had concluded, he would become disposable merchandise?

That was exactly what happened. A few months later, driven insane by Bianca's cruel behavior, Tói took his own life with a gun he had hidden in their home. Rumors flew in Lisbon that Tói had bought the gun from his wife's former lover, the arms dealer. At the time of the suicide, Tói's son from his first marriage was with Bianca and her infant daughter, vacationing in Bahia in the house the old banker had given her. People gossiped that of all of Bianca's partners, Tói had been the most gullible; they wished that he had killed her instead of himself.

Suspicious of Bianca's wickedness, Tamara spread word that Tói didn't commit suicide. She accused Bianca of hiring an assassin in Bahia to come to Lisbon to kill Tói. Suicide, however, remained the official cause of the death. Still, Tamara wondered, if Bianca had molested Miguel, what would stop her from doing the same to Tói's son, also a teenager?

In half-whispers, the Estrela elite used various epitaphs to describe Bianca: sexual sorceress able to delight those who feel inadequate; abject woman, clever instigator of the most absolute devastation; social climber, eagerly able to delude Lisbon's dupes as she mounted Portugal's Via Sacra of society.

In a detail worthy of a book written by a present-day Lusophone author, it is reflective to mention Eduardo's sympathy for Tói. He says he cried inconsolably when he found out that Tói had committed suicide. A childhood friend called to inform Eduardo of the tragedy. But Eduardo says he didn't cry for Tói; he cried for himself. Apparently Tói returned to Lisbon after a trip to Bahia, certain his son was now sleeping with Bianca. Tói poured his heart out to a relative and several hours later pulled the trigger. Eduardo understood that Tói believed he had lost all dignity—and that nothing, absolutely nothing, remained.

The Living Dead

I remember Isabella's father fondly. Dr. Monjardim was a medical doctor, an elegant man, and a gentleman of the old school of living. People like him are distinguished *Lisboetas,* illustrious citizens of the city of Lisbon. Isabella's father was a man of the world well before Portugal's entrance into the European Union in 1986. Dr. Monjardim wore perfectly tailored suits with an elegant pin positioned in the middle of his silk tie and a matching scarf in his jacket's breast pocket. His shoes invariably shone with fresh polish. In his waistcoat pocket, he kept a gold watch on a beautiful chain that he consulted now and then for the time. In those brief moments, Dr. Monjardim was not only checking the hour of the day but also observing the effect the jewel produced on those around him. If I happened to be present, I ran over to get a closer look. The gold filigree hands, the Roman numerals, and the mother-of-pearl face were all extraordinary. Dr. Monjardim also possessed a unique way of blowing his nose into an impeccably ironed Egyptian cotton handkerchief. As he blew, he emitted a hilarious sound, like the horn of a ferryboat crossing the Tejo River on foggy days.

I wasn't the only one to admire Isabella's father. His daughter was always referring to women's fascination with Dr. Monjardim—her mother's friends, various female relatives, and even the mothers of our schoolmates. Alas, an entourage of well-dressed desirable women wearing expensive French perfume. Speechless, I could well understand the reason for such high esteem: Dr. Monjardim had class. The illustrious look, the reserved smile opening to white teeth and the first-rate apparel all conveyed a sense of distinction.

Dr. Monjardim earned all he wanted or needed as a heart surgeon. He also had the honor of being a professor at the University's Faculty of Medicine. The family lived in a house in one of Lisbon's principal districts, Restelo. The street faced the emblematic Torre de Belém, a jewel of Portuguese architecture, a reminder of our collective greatness. The family's summer residence was close to Ericeira, right at the end of a small bay in a row of wealthy houses. Local fish auctions took place at the adjacent pier at the end of the day when sunset started. Dr. Monjardim attended those sales on weekends and enjoyed bidding for just-caught fish. The interiors of both residences showed an unpretentious style despite the family's enjoyment of a battalion of servants. The staff moved around the house unnoticed, as if tiptoeing. Isabella's father drove a Chrysler, polished daily by someone unknown to me.

I always had the feeling that Dr. Monjardim knew the spectrum of human nature, the labyrinths of the heart. It wasn't just his profession that provided such knowledge. It was also his circle of acquaintances in Lisbon's high society: professional colleagues, the Portuguese aristocracy, and the elite banking and finance executives. I recall with nostalgia his office located in Lisbon's downtown area, Rossio, a place I visited whenever Isabella invited me. As a properly raised young girl whom Isabella's parents considered beneficial to their daughter, I visited often. Those were the best Saturday afternoons of my early adolescence, well before Isabella and I parted ways.

Our afternoons started in the old Ramiro Leão, a clothing shop in upper Chiado, the city's upscale district. Chiado was familiar territory, and we started our jaunt in this spot for the fun of it. The mega department store had a golden baroque elevator that we went up and down many times with immense pleasure. The elevator's operator knew Isabella's mother and invited us in as soon as he spotted us. We then occupied the cushioned seats and busied ourselves making comical faces in the gold-framed mirrors that covered the walls. From this glitzy private carousel, we took notice of shoppers, and just to be irreverent sometimes asked to see the items acquired.

Afterward we stopped at Benárd, perhaps the most fashionable coffee shop of the day, for a snack. We sat comfortably at one of the tables and ordered hot cocoa; Lisbon's winter afternoons, although sunny, were rather cold. The pastries at the marble counter were to die for, the choices virtually endless. Our favorites were the large madeleines and the famous palmiers doubled with chocolate. Before leaving, we bought colorful lollipops for the walk and set out down the street.

Dr. Monjardim's office was not far from an extraordinary symbol of Lisbon, the Santa Justa Tower, constructed by an apprentice to Alexandre G. Eiffel, the man who designed the Paris tower. Santa Justa is still today an eccentric structure made of iron and embellished with filigree. Two wood-paneled elevators with brass fittings are located inside the tower and provide regular service to pedestrians between the lower and the upper part of the city. I cannot explain what possessed us whenever we approached it. Without exchanging a word or look, we ran zigzag headlong past the long queue of pedestrians waiting to get in. They were either amused or upset, but we didn't care; we played hide and seek as soon as we saw the steps surrounding the elevator. Being the first to reach Dr. Monjardim's front door was our only concern. The winner stood breathless by the large wooden structure while intoning a hymn of glory. Isabella and I were good friends; we always took turns being champion.

Once inside the office, the first person to suffer our intrusion was the nurse. She usually indulged us with a conspiratorial smile. In between her regular tasks as the afternoon progressed, the woman gave us lessons in first-aid, mouth-to-mouth resuscitation, and the uses of various medical instruments. Isabella enjoyed talking to her father's clientele in the waiting room as if, instinctively, she was already taking mental notes about her future in medicine. Familiar with us, the patients enjoyed the diversion that Isabella's conversation provided. She was utterly polite. When she sat down she always took pride in adjusting her skirt, as if ironing it a second time. If Dr. Monjardim took longer than usual to see his last patient of the day, we settled down on the couch and flipped through the fashion magazines on display.

Isabella adored her father. This meant that sometimes, my role of companion accomplished for the afternoon, she tried, with empathy but determination, to get rid of me before Dr. Monjardim finished his work. She longed at this point to have her father only to herself. And who could blame her? She always had an excuse for her request to dismiss me. For instance, she needed to be alone to ask her father for an increase to her weekly allowance; this way, her mother wouldn't know. But I was clever in finding a better reason to stay: my parents weren't home yet and I didn't have the keys. Having gotten that far, I also wanted to share Dr. Monjardim's company walking up Chiado.

At the Santa Justa tower, a special smile always stole over Dr. Monjardim's lips. He would raise his right hand and lift his gray felt hat with its round brim and grosgrain ribbon. Isabella's father was now greeting all those he knew, people who happened to stroll up and down Chiado on those Saturday afternoons. If he happened to glimpse one of his wife's friends coming out of a shop, he quickened or slowed his pace accordingly. If he met the widow of an already deceased patient coming out of a pastry shop, someone he wished to talk to, he held his hat in his hand and followed the traditional hand-kissing greeting that conveyed proper breeding. Dr. Monjardim's public display was a way to show the world how good his life was.

The convent school that Isabella and I attended in the district of Lapa was Lisbon's most exclusive school for girls and was subtly but highly segregated according to each family's social standing. I knew Isabella regretted that her surname wasn't more prominent. Monjardim, though hardly objectionable, didn't adequately convey the splendor that made up her life. She was aware that she didn't belong to a noble family with a name dating back centuries; nothing associated her with shipyards generating huge profits in the southern banks of the Tejo River, nor with vineyards in the Douro River near Oporto. But her father's prestige as a medical doctor somehow made up for those shortfalls. A good marriage would solve that small, underlying ripple in her pedigree.

Besides, Isabella had plenty of other attributes: she was well bred, really good-looking, and a born extrovert. With her boundless high spirits, the smallest occurrence turned into high drama. Stories lasted for weeks wherever she told them. Once we were in a taxi with the radio on, and a reporter was interviewing a poor devil from the street about a recent soccer game between the main Lisbon opposing factions, Benfica and Sporting. And the fellow, a true *benfiquista,* defended fiercely his defeated Benfica team. Dr. Monjardim was a member of the Sporting team, so Isabella instantly found a few weeks of recreation. To every question he was asked, the man answered by introducing the word *prontos*—in rough translation, "y' understand?" Isabella made *prontos* such a hit in school, with all of us constantly mimicking the word and using the same lower-class inflection that the teacher in charge of the Portuguese language demanded to know the origin of the utterly inappropriate trend.

True pals, Isabella and I enjoyed each other's company without reservation. Of course Isabella knew that there was no competition from me; she would always be the star in any social situation. The unspoken social registry in our school was much larger than surnames. It involved country homes' locations, political high connections, and plenty of cash to spend at leisure. And our friendship went far beyond our visits to Isabella's father's office on Saturday afternoons. We looked at life the same way, we laughed at the same jokes. We understood that the financial differences weren't worth losing sleep over. Our parents had comparable lifestyles to our higher-class schoolmates. All the girls dressed in the same English kilts and attended the same hairdressing salons. Only the *nouveaux riches*, and there were a few at the school, spoke aloud about their ski trips to Chamonix.

Isabella and I had something priceless in common despite the innumerable social conventions that restrained us. We shared an unspoken inner world with plenty of room to maneuver. Having freedom of movement in a city that felt most safe, we took public transportation to stroll in parks and to visit other girls at home; we also went by ourselves to the afternoon matinee. I felt lucky that she nurtured our friendship the same way I did.

Isabella once told me that her her father hid a complex personality beneath his outward friendliness. Apparently, the relationship between her parents wasn't easy because her mother constantly complained about the doctor. Berta shared with her teenage daughter that he wanted to keep his lofty lifestyle and thus practiced *coitus interruptus;* he never stayed inside her for fear of conceiving more children. Isabella had a brother called Alexandre, three or four years her senior, so Dr. Monjardim considered himself lucky to have a child of each sex. Isabella also disclosed that her mother suffered from a psychological disorder called neurasthenia, which I didn't understand at the time. Symptoms included chronic fatigue, which resulted in Berta lying in bed, the bedroom curtains closed to prevent sunlight from entering the space. She also suffered from a stomach ailment.

Isabella's brother, Alex, attended a Jesuit school, but he was a poor student with a reputation for bad behavior. Overall, the situation was a source of profound unhappiness for Dr. Monjardim. Alex had an open smile, and like his sister enjoyed cracking jokes. Once in a while he granted us the favor of accompanying him to the Tivoli movie theater. But, generally, he stuck to his own group of friends, playing cards or going to soccer matches on the weekends. They particularly enjoyed driving around the Arrábida Casino, outside of Lisbon, in cars borrowed from their parents. The full scope of Alex's friends' activities was a mystery to us, but Isabella suspected that her brother was up to no good. There were rumors of dinner parties rife with debauchery, of consorting with prostitutes, and of seducing the maids at the homes of his friends.

I had Alex under my eye for many years. My understanding of Dr. Monjardim's worry about his son was intuitive: if Alex didn't shape up soon, how would he become a respected man like his father? How would he handle the responsibilities that life inevitably brings? Were the Jesuits capable of helping young men like Alex, the future elite of the country?

Alex drove me crazy with lust; he was so handsome. His tiny waves of golden brown hair filled me with *frisson.* At that time I already saw myself married to him, the mother of his children and his rock of support. I wanted to help Alex become a man, the man Dr. Monjardim hoped his son would be. I had a clear understanding that marrying or, more precisely, taking care of Alex wouldn't be easy, but it was a mission I yearned to fulfill. I kept my dreams to myself, but it was crucial that Berta, his mother, liked me so that one day she would give the union her blessing.

Isabella was always complaining that her mother overprotected Alex. Berta considered her son weak and therefore in need of constant supervision. Despairing, Berta once blamed her own heredity for her son's behavior. Were her own delicate genes to blame, she asked herself? She feared her DNA had cast a shadow on him, something he seemed unable to shake off.

In Isabella's family, emotional empathy followed traditional lines, running deep between Isabella and Dr. Monjardim and between Alex and Berta. Isabella loved her mother, but their relationship was somewhat distant. Berta often went to spas for treatment of her stomach condition. Alex always accompanied his mother; Isabella stayed with her father. A housekeeper accompanied Berta and Alex even if they stayed at an exclusive hotel with plenty of staff. Each had a private room, and the housekeeper, considered a member of the family, tended to both mother and son. Alex often stayed in his pajamas all day long in his room; meals were brought to him. He wasn't sick; he simply enjoyed being pampered. He listened to music, read comics, and slept whenever he wanted. When the three convened, they played checkers or dominoes for hours on end.

It was most annoying to see Berta whisking Alex away to those spas during the crucial summer months when I was tanned and cute. I was losing the opportunity to throw myself into Alex's arms and show him that I existed, to reveal that I saw him as the father of my children. I constantly pictured myself with a future at his side. Some of his jokes didn't sit well with me, such as his tales about female conquests. However, these were added reasons for me to be close to provide emotional balance, to make him the man he resisted becoming.

I dreamed of freeing Alex from himself.

Our high school years passed quickly, too quickly, and Isabella and I ended up taking different university degrees, in different cities. Naturally, Isabella chose medicine like her father. I didn't think her choice fit her character, but her father was a larger than life figure for her. Thus, following his career path took precedence over any other consideration. I moved to Aveiro when my father was transferred due to a promotion in the public sector. Aveiro happened to be his hometown and my grandparents still lived there. I studied English and became a secondary school teacher. Isabella went abroad to pursue a medical specialty after finishing her degree in Lisbon.

Overtime, Isabella and I lost touch with each other. In those days communication wasn't what it is today. Cell phones and Internet networks didn't exist, and Aveiro was considered a distant planet to Lisbon. Every so often I would hear from friends that Isabella had paid a hurried visit to the city. Later, she married a Swiss doctor named Karl and moved to Geneva. Isabella invited me to her wedding in Lisbon, but unfortunately I couldn't attend. I was expecting my first child and my husband, also a schoolteacher, thought the huge expense unnecessary. So I sent Isabella a piece of jewelry I had gotten from my grandmother; I knew it would remain in good hands. Isabel acknowledged the gift with great appreciation, all the while regretting our absence.

Our mutual friends from school continued to provide me with news from Isabel. And our own annual Christmas cards with portraits of the children together with postcards from her exotic vacations sustained our relationship for more than ten years.

Alex apparently continued the same lifestyle as before. He didn't have a girlfriend; he had many. In the meantime, he had vanished from my radar, his former attraction gone. I had settled down, was interested in my profession, and wanted to do something with my life.

The news of Berta's death from cancer came as a total surprise.

And even more astonishing was the next piece of news: Isabella's father had remarried only a few months after his wife's death. I wasn't as shocked by his relationship—what female would resist his charms—as I was by his marrying a foreigner, a Belgian whose late husband had been one of Dr. Monjardim's patients. According to rumor, Nicole, the new wife, had recently been in trouble.

The problem had to do with international finance, a case in which Nicole's son-in-law had played an important role. He was a Brazilian scoundrel and had squandered almost everything that belonged to Nicole and her daughter. The young couple had invested enormous funds in real estate ventures in São Paulo, but all of them bombed. Nicole, as a result, now lived in more stringent circumstances than during her first marriage. This wasn't, however, something that worried Dr. Monjardim for he continued to earn lavishly. Apparently Nicole, still pretty and vivacious, had loved her first Portuguese husband. Unlike many Portuguese widows who welcome their new freedom and independent lifestyle, she wanted a new relationship.

From Aveiro I enjoyed the juicy gossip. But the matter didn't remain in my mind more than a few minutes, so caught up was I in my family life and schoolwork. I didn't regret my quieter life: I cared about my students, my two healthy children, and my devoted husband. The years flew by with me enjoying the tranquility of my life and, in rare moments of leisure, fondly recalling the fun times Isabella and I had shared.

One day Isabella showed up in Aveiro, as if by magic, in front of my school's gate. Seeing her, I wondered if I was having a hallucination. But my dearest Isabella was there in the flesh, smiling at me from a distance. She walked with the confident step of a woman in the prime of life, her long camel-hair coat matching the leather shoulder strap of her purse. And with eyes dancing, she asked with a British accent, "How are you, my darling?" We fell into each other's arms like the good old friends we had always been; quite a few years older, but filled with the same old joy.

As soon as our hug ended, Isabella announced that she had urgent business to discuss with me. She was in Portugal alone, having left her husband and children in Geneva for a month. Not surprisingly, she had quit medicine some time ago, and had taken up writing. She had already published a play, a British comedy of manners. She pulled a copy of her book from her purse; the cover featured two men in a lovers' pose. I glimpsed my old friend's conniving smile: as in the past always irreverent, cool, and up-to-date.

We walked into the nearest pastry shop and found a nice table by the window. As soon as we sat down Isabella said that she was writing a new play, this one based on family matters. But the going wasn't as easy as she had expected, and now she needed a break to deal with matters she barely knew how to handle.

As she spoke, Isabella's expression became grave and this threw me off balance. Suddenly, an Isabella I didn't know was sitting in front of me. She went on to say her new play was for an audience with Portuguese characteristics: Machiavellian in nature, shadowy instead of sunny, and devious, sharp, ironic. She felt lucky she didn't need to work. Since her husband made enough to provide for the family, she had the necessary time to dedicate to her new venture.

"Oh, Isabella, you haven't changed, " I exclaimed. "I agree, it's writing, not medicine, that's right for you." I immediately added, "But a play based on family matters? What's going on?"

She nodded, determination coming over her features. "I came to see you because I need your help."

"Sure, what can I do?"

"It seems you haven't heard the news," she said.

"I know your mom passed away, I'm so sorry. And I heard your father remarried." When she didn't answer, alarm stole me over. "Is there something else?"

"You obviously haven't heard that my dad passed away a few weeks ago."

I wasn't in the habit of reading the newspaper's obituaries; my heart quickened in shock. I instinctively held Isabella's hand.

"Alex and Nicole, my father's second wife, handled the details of the funeral. Karl, the children, and I flew to Lisbon for a few days but had to rush back. Karl needed to attend to his practice, the children needed to return to school." Isabella's eyes filled with tears as she spoke.

We stood in silence, hand in hand. And Isabella was the first to break it.

"My father died suddenly with a heart attack. And his death changed everything for me. I started thinking about my family as never before. Karl has, actually, been very supportive."

"You're very fortunate, Isabella," I replied.

"But it's not my father's dying that brought me here." And, tentatively, Isabella added softly, "Only a few people know what I'm about to tell you. Alex is in jail."

If I weren't seated at table, I would have fainted. "What did he do?" I asked, astounded.

"You have no idea how down I have been lately," Isabella said gloomily. "My trip here is like going down memory lane, something you're a part of."

"Tell me."

"Alex was arrested a few days after my father died."

"Why?" I asked louder than I wished.

"He embezzled thousands of euros from his company. And this was a job my father had gotten him."

"Jesus!" I blurted. "I find it unconceivable that my adolescent idol is in prison!"

"There's more," Isabella said.

"What?" My eyes widened expectantly.

"First, let me backtrack. Alex's wife wanted her consumer appetites fulfilled, and with three kids, Alex simply couldn't do it."

"How did she take Alex's arrest?"

"She moved with the boys to Madrid to live with her parents. She doesn't want the kids to know their father's is in jail."

"Is she from the Arrábida jet-set?"

"Of course she is! First she wanted to get married because she was pregnant. And, then, when the boat rocked, she abandoned her husband."

"Who can blame her?"

"I can!" Isabella said righteously, her old self emerging. "Alex is unable to see his children now, and God knows for how long. Her voice leaden, Isabella asked, "Do you know who visits him every day? Nicole, the Belgian woman."

To console Isabella I said, "I'm glad someone is there for him."

"Yes and no," replied Isabella slowly.

"It mustn't be easy to be a widow twice in such a short period of time. Nicole must feel close to Alex."

"That's one possible explanation."

I wished Isabella would provide details faster than she seemed willing. She proceeded unhurriedly. "My father and Nicole had joint bank accounts and she withdrew everything the day after the funeral. And now she says that the Restelo house—the place where we grew up and that my father had bought—is hers. She also says that she's entitled to the house in Ericeira."

"Now, I see your apprehension," I said. "Nicole wants what belongs to you—and to steal your memories."

"Look, Karl earns enough for our family, that's not the problem. The story, however, gets more complicated. Nicole's daughter, picture this, has already moved into our Restelo house with her Brazilian husband."

"What a nightmare!"

"To be honest, and coming back to what I was saying earlier," Isabella said with her old mischievous look, "there are things that I'm more concerned with than my father's money."

"Like what?"

"I want to spend a few days in the new hotel that replaced my father's old office."

"Why?"

"I need to imagine my father there engaged in dialogue with the characters in my play."

"That's a great idea."

"I must relive the past," she continued. "I came to Aveiro to invite you to come with me. Carnival is next week. You could take a few days off, get out of this hole. I desperately need a friend like you. This will be good for you, too."

"Be careful. If you tell Paulo, my husband, that Aveiro is a hole, you'll make an enemy. He was born and raised here."

"Please find a way to come with me. I need a week in Lisbon at that hotel with you by my side." I felt Isabella's old self returning. "My treat."

"It's really tempting," I replied, my mind already dreaming scenes of the escape. "How enticing to be back and enjoy our long lost memories."

"Think about it. You don't need to get up early or cook for the family an entire week!"

"You don't need to convince me."

"So I trust Paulo will be persuaded that you join me," said Isabella with excitement glowing in her eyes. "Can you imagine calling on the spirit of my beloved father from that hotel's bed?"

"It's almost intimidating," I stated.

"Not at all," Isabella replied. "I just want to hear my father's voice as if through the walls. The way we used to talk when he was alive."

"Is that so?"

"I need to feel his presence; we always had a special connection."

"I remember," I replied with a smile.

"I am inside a labyrinth and I need to see more clearly. For example, what do Alex and Nicole talk about when she visits him in jail?"

"I guess you have to find out." I looked at my watch; it was time for me to pick up the children at school. Isabella had already checked into a downtown hotel and I invited her to join our family for dinner at eight.

When I made my plea to Paulo that evening for a trip to Lisbon with Isabella, he was surprisingly agreeable. Having heard plenty about Isabella throughout our marriage, he understood she was an important friend to me. At the end of the evening when Paulo said he was more than happy to take charge of the children, Isabella planted an exuberant kiss on his cheek. Paulo blushed; he wasn't used to women with such self-assurance.

And this is how Isabella and I landed at the Four Seasons Hotel in downtown Lisbon the following week. We stood in awe looking at the building's new façade, not to mention the completely new interior. I was keeping company with my dearest old schoolmate—everything paid for—my sole purpose to help her figure out her current family situation. As difficult as Isabella's position was, we were still going to have fun. Isabella had taken care of relevant details, in particular booking the room where she imagined her father's office had been located.

The room had twin beds and a bathroom en-suite. The drapes matched the bedspreads and were made of *moiré* silk, champagne-colored on top and golden brown below. The wood floor was the same as in Dr. Monjardim's time, though it had been freshly waxed. The mini bar was filled with liquor. Everything around us had a refined, intimate elegance.

The next day breakfast arrived shortly after Isabella ordered it. Each tray was covered with a linen cloth and matching serviettes. We had coffee and tea, croissants and rolls with butter and jam as well as a variety of fruit and yogurt. Music played from hidden speakers while we showered. Then we slipped into Turkish bathrobes provided by the hotel. Isabella said that if her father could see the surroundings, he would certainly approve of the hotel's luxurious décor and services. She loved the blue-and-white bathroom tiles and claimed she never wanted to leave.

In the afternoons, we sat at the Four Seasons urbane bar next to the grand lobby on the ground floor. The hotel's entrance was in the same place as the original door, the one that Isabella's father had walked through every workday of his life. The two of us sat in comfortable velvet armchairs next to a window with a coffee table before us where we placed our drinks. The velvet armchairs had sophisticated geometrical designs in shades of green and light brown.

There weren't many costumers around in the middle of the afternoon, so we talked without fear of being overheard. Nevertheless we communicated as in a code, no names mentioned.

I asked casually, as if Alex were on vacation, "So, are you planning to visit your brother soon?"

"I haven't decided yet."

"I can go with you if you like."

"Don't even think of it. There are things one must do alone." She paused for a moment and then added, "Nicole says my brother refuses to see his old friends and that he only wants to see her."

"Why?"

"I don't know. She could be lying, but I don't think that's the case. Do you know what she told me? That she visits my brother every day to bring him clean clothes and real food."

"Were they close when your father was alive?"

"I don't know. I wasn't there to see what was going on. She also told me something that apparently *toute Lisbonne* is talking about. I wanted to tell you this earlier, I just didn't know how." Isabella again had the unusual expression I had only seen at the pastry shop in Aveiro. "Besides the embezzlement, *that* person was also in the habit of stealing stuff when invited for dinner at friends' houses."

"I can't believe it," I said with disgust.

"Apparently he always left with his pockets filled." Isabella went for full disclosure. "A couple of years went by before friends realized that he was stealing from them. You know, when something's missing you usually blame the help, not the guests."

"What was he taking?"

"Not a silver teaspoon for the private collection," Isabella added, mortified. "He was pocketing valuable items such as small pieces of Chinese export porcelain or carved jade. Things that fitted into his pockets."

"Incredible, he stole like a real thief." And I added, "His house must resemble Bluebeard's, a pirate's booty."

"He kept everything hidden in Ericeira, far from Lisbon. I want to return the pieces, but Nicole says I shouldn't. It would be the same as admitting he stole them."

"But he did."

"She says I should take everything to Sotheby's in Geneva. And keep the cash from any sales."

"She is mixed up," I said with a nervous laugh, but then sobered with a new thought. "Is it possible that Nicole lied to your father about her family's loss in the São Paulo investments when she became a widow the first time around?"

"Funny you should ask; the same thing crossed my mind!" Isabella said, taken aback by apprehension. "The thought that she might have married my father for money is appalling."

"The public exposure of all these stories must be unbearable to you," I said.

"My father must be turning in his grave."

"I'm sure he would want those artifacts returned to their proper owners."

"Yes, except that Nicole says—not without reason—that between rumor and truth there's a gap. And no one ever caught *that person* with something inside his pockets."

Soon after, we returned to our room for a rest. Isabella took a steamy bath, which she embellished with salt crystals. Afterward she went to the exercise room to do some yoga. I picked up a book and felt in heaven.

When Isabella returned an hour later, she said that after the yoga she had a revelation while meditating. It was about the puzzling relationship between Alex and Nicole.

"Well?" I said putting down my book.

"I've been mulling this over." Isabella sat down on the end of the bed near my chair. "Nicole always told me that she loved Portuguese men. There's no doubt that she likes Alex. The question is how does he respond."

"What do you think?"

"The few occasions we were ever together, Alex always treated her gallantly. If my father came to visit in Geneva, Alex took her out for dinner in Lisbon. My father always mentioned Nicole didn't mind his absences; she was delighted to have dinner with Alex."

"How did Alex react?"

"I don't know. He was already married, but with my mother dead he missed, for sure, the abiding affection of an older woman, someone more maternal than his wife. All of his relationships before he married were ephemeral. He wasn't a serial killer, he was a serial lover."

"Guess what? You haven't told me your revelation while meditating," I reminded Isabella.

"I know. Unfortunately, I must wait before telling you." Isabella said with trepidation filling her voice. "Let me just tell you for now that I've decided to visit Alex in jail."

I was intrigued, but I knew Isabella was entitled to her privacy. My role had always been that of friend, companion and confidante. It wasn't that I was ready now to damage her trust in me. I told Isabella only that I expected her to set the record straight before returning to Geneva.

I returned to Aveiro at the end of the week with Isabella's promise to call me immediately after seeing Alex. She was intimidated by the visit to her brother, but she wasn't someone to back off from a hard decision. She needed directions to the prison, which was outside of Lisbon, and Nicole offered to drive her in the family car. When she said she wanted to see Alex in private, Nicole agreed to remain in the car while brother and sister talked. At our parting, Isabella's eyes seemed lost in more shadows than I could either enumerate or decipher.

When Isabella saw Alex through the mesh window that separated them, he confessed that he and Nicole were in love and had been for a while. No, of course their father had never had a clue. Now that Nicole was claiming that the family fortune belonged to her, she wasn't just fighting for herself, she was fighting for him as well. They were planning to get married soon, even while he was still in prison. In a few years he would be out and able to return to the family home that held such loving memories for him. The age difference between the couple didn't matter much. Yes, she could be his mother, so much the better. Alex said that his own children would surely remain in Madrid. That didn't matter either; he had never loved their mother. And if the kids later wished to reunite with him, his doors were open. Alex then quoted the saying, o *que não se pode remendar, remendado está,* what cannot be mended is, thus, mended already. He meant that he couldn't undo his past. To conclude their visit, Alex advised Isabella to return to her family in Geneva, the family she had built with loving care and which was now her own. Alex had hired a team of attorneys to make sure that their father's estate remained solely with Nicole.

The Temptations of Saint Anthony

The dark truth from the past emerged the day Dolores's granddaughter opened her heart and confessed with tears in her eyes and an adolescent pout that living with Uncle Rudolf and Aunt Frieda in Germany had been a disaster. For years Uncle Rudolf had been rubbing himself against Gisela. Whenever Aunt Frieda went out, Rudolf slipped into her bedroom while she was doing her homework. Sitting by her side, eyes filled with lust, he told her often that he was in love. The locks to various rooms, including the bathroom, which Aunt Frieda had changed frequently at Gisela's request, didn't help; the keys always disappeared without trace.

That school year, about two months before her confession, the inevitable had regrettably happened: Uncle Rudolf had fulfilled his wishes, Gisela disclosed, and stolen the fourteen-year-old's virginity.

Portuguese by birth and upbringing, Dolores had noticed a new seriousness in her granddaughter's eyes when she arrived for holidays. Every year Gisela was part of the tourist crowd circulating throughout Portugal, but that summer she seemed more contrite than was usual for an adolescent about to enjoy a beach vacation. At first, Dolores attributed the transformation to her daughter Eva's imminent third marriage. Eva, Gisela's mother, was marrying a German, a new colleague at the science laboratory in Berlin where she worked, someone she hardly knew. It was evident that the couple had no intention of asking Gisela to move in with them.

Dolores and Gisela shared a long, painful conversation in quiet tones. Gisela, subdued, was able to describe in depth the loss of her innocence with heartbreaking details. How she had shouted when she heard her aunt close the front door and leave the small apartment at the precise moment her huge uncle was beginning his assault. Gisela's disclosure of the brutal rape struck Dolores's heart like lightning. In some families, it seemed, the past always comes back to haunt its members, like a buoy in a deep well that insists on floating.

Dolores listened attentively to her granddaughter but showed reserve. The moment wasn't appropriate for sharing the secrets of her own life, events she had buried within herself from the earliest age; maybe the opportunity would never present itself for her own disclosure. What mattered most at the moment was to listen to Gisela and show her that her grandmother was unconditionally on her side—capable of holding her and expressing tender support.

Dolores and her granddaughter got along particularly well, despite the long-distance nature of their relationship. Gisela had been living in Germany with Uncle Rudolf and Aunt Frieda for several years now; she spent only her summers in Portugal. The long shared holidays ever since Gisela could barely walk had become for both women the climax of the year. Eva was a chemistry researcher, a professional woman—and she had decided long ago that she wanted little to do with her mother. Dolores's Christmas present to Eva, a fat check, took care of their relationship. Under such circumstances, Dolores saw in Gisela an opportunity for some intimacy with a loved blood relative.

Gisela lived in one of those horrible northern industrial German cities where it either drizzled or snowed constantly during the winter; at three o'clock in the afternoon it was already dark. Thus, Dolores's house in southern Portugal's resort area, Algarve, became a balmy comfort for Gisela. It was a source of nurturing that, unmistakably, gave the young woman the strength to continue a life already scarred. Gisela had a Portuguese mother—now a naturalized German—who was unable to take care of her; and a German father who, excluding the monthly allowance given to his retired brother for Gisela's sustenance, showed little or no affection.

In recent years—already fearful of her uncle's unwanted advances and aware of her aunt's conniving silence—Gisela had asked her parents to let her decide for herself where to live. She wanted to go to school in Lisbon and live with her grandmother. She had hoped her father would consent in the future. But her mother, Eva, was adamant: Germany was a better place for her daughter to be brought up. Unable to detect a warning sign in her daughter's request, Eva stated that her daughter was already bilingual and the German education system of significant advantage to her future. But, deep down, Eva didn't want her only daughter to live with Dolores. It wasn't jealousy—far from it. It was the belief that Uncle Rudolf and Aunt Frieda were better equipped to look after Gisela. Besides, Eva wanted easy access to her daughter without the daily responsibility of caring for her.

Gisela knew that her mother had a mountain-high list of grievances piled up against her grandmother. A colossal psychological distance clearly stood between them. When Eva visited Gisela and Dolores during the summer, she wouldn't even stay an entire week, even though Dolores's house had a swimming pool offering Eva, an accomplished swimmer, a chance to enjoy herself.

Eva declared that her name was Eve, not Eva, which Gisela interpreted as her mother's rejection of her homeland. Moreover, it made no sense to Gisela that her mother insisted she live in Germany, thus denying her a splendid relationship with her grandmother. Gisela felt happy that her own name was the same in both Portugal and Germany, even if pronounced differently. Smiling affectionately at her grandmother, Gisela would add that her name was, in fact, Gisela *querida*, Gisela darling, as if *darling* were her middle name.

Perhaps it was the blood of her forebears that made Gisela, though born and raised in Germany, love her mother's country so completely. Perhaps. It could also be her grandmother's unconditional love, which did wonders for her self-esteem. Or it could even be a genetic predisposition for the mild climate, the good cuisine, and the friendly atmosphere. Dolores, who had studied at a German university, appreciated the discipline of the northern country; even the harsh climate suited her character well enough. When her granddaughter described school adventures, Dolores had cultural references to place the narrative into context. It was good to have a Portuguese grandmother who understood both Germany and the language. The same couldn't be said of Gisela's German relatives. Although they took care of her because of her father's generous allowance to them—an arrangement that allowed the retired couple to live well above their meager means—they were rather reserved. Worse, Uncle Rudolf and Aunt Frieda were sad people with few friends and no hobbies. They didn't even attempt to appreciate their niece's second country: for them the Portuguese were anarchic aliens from southern Europe, endowed with an exoticism that meant nothing to them. Gisela, who greatly appreciated Portugal, was but a thorn in their German sides.

Dolores, on the contrary, was well traveled. She had visited many European countries, Latin America, Asia, the United States and other places. She only stopped traveling regularly when Gisela began spending summers with her. There was never, therefore, a shortage of stories with which to entertain her granddaughter, adventures told in the dim light of warm Algarve nights. Dolores always had a funny tale or joke to share that offered insight on the diversity of human nature. One such story was legendary, and Gisela loved that her grandmother repeated it every summer, adding embellishments as the narrative expanded.

Years earlier Dolores had travelled from Zagreb to Belgrade, in the former Yugoslavia, crossing the Balkans by train as a passenger on the Orient Express. At that time the two cities belonged to the same country, unified by Tito. Not only did Dolores love to travel by train, she also was curious to witness, firsthand, how communist regimes supposedly improved the lifestyle of their citizens. One of Dolores's stories took place on the Orient Express with exciting details that both she and Gisela loved to dissect.

One late night Dolores had boarded the train in Zagreb with a first-class *wagon-lit* ticket that allowed her to get a few hours of sleep before reaching her destination. She was in the final stages of a long journey and was due to catch a flight from Belgrade to Lisbon in two days. She had tried to get a different daytime connection, but the tickets were sold out. One advantage to traveling at night was the chance to have breakfast in the dining car, something that she had never done before.

When she entered her compartment, she noticed that the upper couchette was occupied. A man was lying face up on it, his eyes half-open and staring. She had been warned that due to a shortage of *wagon-lits* on the Zagreb-Belgrade line, opposite sexes sometimes had to share compartments. For an experienced traveler like Dolores, the situation came as no surprise. After depositing her luggage, she used the small en-suite bathroom to change into a comfortable tracksuit for sleep.

As she turned off the wall light next to the couchette's headboard, she wished her travel companion goodnight in English. He replied but in a gruff voice, which for some undefined reason intimidated her. A shiver passed through her spine as the man babbled something unintelligible in a language she didn't know.

As a precaution, to make sure the train attendant would come immediately if she needed help, she rang the bell next to the night light. Not even two minutes passed before the valet came by asking her kindly how he could help. Dolores asked for tea, comforted that her couchette companion witnessed how fast the valet showed up. The tea was served in a glass placed inside an imitation silver holder with a handle. *Comme il faut* service, thought Dolores.

The neighbor above kept his light on, but Dolores assumed he would turn it off soon. She wanted to close her eyes and feel the darkness. Thus, she placed her hand close to the bell so that she could easily ring for the attendant if necessary. The sound of the train gliding along rails with a syncopated pace rocked her to sleep. However, her neighbor's light stayed on and this bothered her. Unable to fall asleep for more than ten minutes at a time, Dolores was now tossing and turning in the couchette.

During one of her restless turns, she thought she heard an agonizing moan coming from above. Nothing to worry about, she thought, her cabin companion must be suffering from insomnia as well. But the fellow kept his light on all night. And Dolores kept hearing—or imagining she heard—grumbles coming from his bed. When the light of dawn finally arrived, she was happy that Belgrade was close. The only thing left to do was have breakfast in the dining car. The sound of a bell from across the corridor was a welcome sign.

Getting up quickly, Dolores started brushing her hair, viewing herself in the mirror across from her bed. While doing this, she saw that the passenger on the upper couchette still had his eyes half-open, unmoved, the same way they were when she had first entered the compartment. Strange, she thought, my companion didn't shut his eyes the entire night. Was his destination close or a far away land, perhaps Istanbul?

In the corridor, the staff was collecting passports for inspection and Dolores handed hers to one of the valets. The coffee she drank a few minutes later was good, brewed the Turkish way; it awoke her senses. The bread was delicious, served with butter and honey.

The movement in the corridors indicated that the arrival in Belgrade was imminent. After her passport was returned and the train was about to stop, two policemen approached Dolores's compartment. In English, they asked her permission to enter but didn't wait for an answer. Crowded into the small space, the agents looked at the passenger in the upper couchette and spoke in a loud, peremptory foreign language. The man raised his head a little and Dolores saw his empty stare. Another volley of words issued. Then the police unceremoniously lifted the man from his couchette.

Only then did Dolores realize that she had spent the night in the company of a blind person! A blind man who apparently had problems with the authorities. The policemen rather roughly moved the passenger out of the compartment—a difficult task because the man's body was so rigid that he couldn't follow the command of the agents. Cumbersomely, step-by-step, they managed to drag the man out, wobbly and disconcerted.

The story was so intriguing that Dolores and Gisela revisited it every summer. Who had put this passenger on the train with a ticket for an upper couchette? To what end? The blind man's body resembled a broomstick. He was like a hermit, lost in the world. Only in books did Gisela find suggestive characters of this nature. Did the man hold a passport?

The previous summer, Dolores had added an interesting possibility. The passenger was carrying gold coins across international borders thinking that the authorities wouldn't suspect someone who was visually impaired. He wore a black suit and an old black tie, not ironed. From the shoes, also black, peeked red woolen socks, bright red, the color of blood. Using her fertile imagination, Gisela said that the red socks suggested that the man was a courier. At a prearranged destination the color of his socks would identify him to his collaborators.

That same summer, while walking at the beach, Dolores told her granddaughter that the time had come for her, Gisela, to add fresh details to the story. As Gisela enjoyed bizarre events she was happy to take up the challenge. She was also an expert in J. K. Rowling's Harry Potter tales.

For Gisela the blind man was, after all, a professor in the Hogwarts School of Witchcraft and Wizardry, a specialist in the magic of transportation. He had wanted the Hogwarts Express, a train that regularly transported students from London to the Hogwarts School, but had boarded the Orient Express by mistake. When the policemen managed to get the blind man down from the upper couchette, diverse objects emerged from several net pouches hanging from a rope belt around his waist. There was a colored eye, a jelly thing that could easily have belonged to a bison. Another pouch contained a large yellow bat with a long beak and black wings, like those of a vampire. Another sack held a vial with a rusty dagger inside a blue liquid. Inside another was an ornate miniature chest of drawers: from one of the drawers an object resembling a finger bone stuck out; from a lower one emerged a small plastic box filled with dried leaves. A dark, flat rounded stone covered with spikes was tucked in one bag, and in another was a small creature inside a glass jar, maybe an embalmed frog.

Gisela recounted that the policemen allowed the mysterious passenger to continue his trip in the Orient Express after a head-to-toe inspection. Bearing in mind that the blind man was a professor in the Hogwarts School of Witchcraft and Wizardry, Gisela inserted an exciting detail. The train's ceiling above the upper couchette had a trapdoor. Minutes after the train left Belgrade, the professor used one of his magic tricks and exited the train. Later, he landed on Platform Nine and Three Quarters in King's Cross Station in London, the same as depicted in J. K. Rowling's books.

To the magicians their magic! Gisela then informed Dolores that the objects inside the net pouches were, in fact, magical portal keys—noteworthy tricks and devices that allowed the professor to reach London. Upon his arrival, the Hogwarts Express students noted the occult meaning of the red woolen socks. The *Daily Prophet,* a widely circulating newspaper dedicated to magicians and wizards throughout the world, covered the professor's return.

Such was the bond between Dolores and Gisela: intimate, adventurous, and filled with humor. Since Gisela couldn't attend the fictional Hogwarts School, she was determined to become an illusionist. Dolores approved of the idea and felt it advantageous for her granddaughter to continue school abroad. The school system there offered wider horizons.

In the Algarve house, there was a deck of cards that Dolores had once bought in an astrology shop in the former Yugoslavia. Grandmother and granddaughter entertained themselves for hours dealing the elaborated, colorful images. The cards illustrated Catholic saints; even St. Anthony, appearing inside a gloomy cave, had been honored in the deck.

Dolores had the means to travel the world because she was the owner of a real estate agency. She had inherited the business from her father who had received it, in turn, from his family. It was a small company that Dolores, with perseverance, had managed to develop over the years. By Portuguese standards, she was a wealthy woman. She had two spacious homes, traveled whenever she wanted, and at Christmas time stayed for a week with Gisela at a five-star hotel in Berlin. The two went to the movies, visited museums, parks, and shops. Well in advance, Dolores would consult catalogs and buy tickets. The previous Christmas season Dolores and Gisela had seen *The Vagina Monologues,* a play that had stimulated many hours of conversation. The play had been Gisela's idea; she could well have been thinking of her uncle's unwanted advances. Dolores had bought three expensive tickets hoping that Eva would have the courtesy to join them but, as usual, she declined at the last minute.

Dolores's renowned establishment provided for the affluence the family enjoyed due to steady incoming revenue. The company had remained secure in good and bad financial times. Essentially, Dolores's talent had to do with her love for money. She could only see her image and power reflected in the shiny metal. Barely able to recall her ex-husband's name due to her hatred of him, she was able to remember, in an instant, exactly how much she had made in her first month of work at the agency when her father was still the manager. She remembered, like a walking calculator, all the apartments and houses she had sold since then as well as the commissions made. She enjoyed taking Gisela for rides around Lisbon and showing her, one by one, the places she had sold. One time Gisela brought along a notebook and jotted down the prices as Dolores recited them. Later on, to amuse her grandmother, she asked the figures again and checked their accuracy.

Dolores entertained the idea that Gisela might take over the family business one day. She was even willing to open an Algarve branch for Gisela to develop a network of clients within the foreign community. Real estate management wasn't incompatible with illusionism, she explained; actually they had a lot in common. It required a third sense, almost supernatural, to locate a property that a rich client had wanted for a long time.

Dolores's company had over twenty employees, the sales people earning only commissions. With a workforce that was easily replaceable, Dolores managed the business with few scruples: mistrust, low blows and personal attacks were the soul of her managerial style. She had that mean ability to pit one employee against another, of saying something one day and doing the opposite the next; also, of turning rival agencies into enemies for life. If money was the sole master—with its own set of dynamics—then there was no choice but to play tough.

Except for her relationship with her granddaughter, Dolores wasn't, as the Portuguese say, a flower worth smelling, *não era flor que se cheirasse.* The vast contacts she had acquired through a lifetime of work terminated inevitably with each deed of sale. She was never invited for the inauguration of a luxury home bought through her agency by wealthy clients. The clientele must have guessed that beneath all that efficiency hid a vulture ready to use its claws.

Eva harbored an absolute disdain for her mother's business skills for she knew Dolores was capable of destroying anyone she targeted. Eva had found out that the rumors spread by Dolores's employees were true. The only employee her mother had kept throughout the years was Candida, the agency's accountant since her father's time and as faithful as a dog. However, Candida had lost her sole possession because Dolores had refused to help her. Candida had bought a small apartment for a good price through the agency and had been paying the mortgage for years. Nevertheless, during the financial crisis that required the European Central Bank to intervene in Portugal, the agency didn't have enough cash to pay the few employees on a fixed salary, such as Candida. Dolores refused to back Candida when the bank threatened foreclosure on her apartment. The former refused to give Candida a loan—a matter of principle, she said, even though the sum needed was small, a few months' salary. Candida, without means, saw the bank take her apartment away. She was lucky to have a sister, single like her, to move in with.

Not only did Dolores refuse to help Candida, but soon after she fired the bookkeeper on a flimsy excuse. Dolores couldn't bear seeing the pain in Candida's face, a reminder of her own lack of compassion.

The incident, needless to say, didn't deprive Dolores of any sleep. Her business hadn't been affected and that's what counted. Small people like Candida had to learn to watch out for themselves. Dolores was proud to keep her independence at all times. She felt professionally accomplished and nothing could take away that feeling.

Although sometimes that inner voice of hers whispered that her given name, Dolores—a Spanish name commonly used in Portugal that means pains, regrets, complaints—was a symbolic allusion. It resembled a karma hovering like the halo of a saint over her head. Her bank account, no matter how large, was unable to make up for the void inside.

And now Dolores had to deal with Gisela's devastating confession, a revelation that touched her own most private wound. Not even *The Vagina Monologues* indicated a clear way to proceed. How could Dolores handle the fact that in Gisela's confession lay a reverberating echo, traces of a traumatic experience she herself had endured more than half a century ago? Something she herself had been unable to bury no matter how hard she tried.

To tell Gisela about *fado*—the word for destiny that gave birth to a unique way of singing in Portugal—wouldn't be constructive. She must do more and help free her granddaughter from the abuse to which she had been subjected. And, by freeing Gisela, free her own traumatic memories.

Thus, Dolores decided that a trip to the national museum in Lisbon was imperative; she must show Gisela one of the most famous canvases in the collection. Its images kept coming to her mind after hearing of her granddaughter's rape. The painting had taken her breath away many, many times before and, in fact, she knew it virtually by heart. The painting was the *Temptations of Saint Anthony*, the famous triptych by Hieronymus Bosch.

Only a few days after Gisela's revelation, the two women left the Algarve for Lisbon one early morning. They traveled in Dolores's speedy sports car and reached Lisbon in barely two and a half hours. In Rua das Janelas Verdes, the Street of the Green Windows, where the museum was located, they passed an old woman crossing the street at a slow pace; she was poor and crippled. Dolores reminded Gisela, as if introducing the painting they were about to examine, that the wretchedness of inhabiting one's body is, sometimes, oppressive beyond redemption.

Inside the museum, Dolores and Gisela sat on a wood bench in front of the incomparable canvas. It was a weekday, and the room was virtually empty. Dolores described the images facing them. Here, Saint Anthony, she indicated pointing with her index finger, appears as a hermit being tempted by demons that had taken over the earth. A chimera of monsters, grotesque gods, and gargoyles crossed paths tempting his tormented soul. They emerged where least expected, leaving an acrid smell of alchemy at their passage. The saint's enchantments were all perverse, the deeds of demoniac creatures; they released inner desires, blurred memories, and called for rites of black magic. Torture, fire and chaos dominated the universe.

The most hallucinatory images depicted Saint Anthony's highest ambition, the possibility of transcending one's body and becoming someone else. The saint's humanity, so to speak, was fearful of seduction, wrongdoing, and entanglement. It was as if his body, a cosmos inhabited by a thousand ravenous beasts, was permeated by abject desires, most of them vengeful.

The picture's background scenery evoked infernal tales that attempted to convince Saint Anthony that what he was seeing was neither fantasy nor delirium but truth. The difference between lying, illusion, reality, and memory had abandoned the saint's world. Animals and vegetables could no longer be distinguished; plants and stones merged, becoming one.

Shortly after interpreting these images, Dolores got up from the bench and led Gisela to a detail in the central panel, in the lower right corner. The scene depicted the Holy Family, supposedly the Bible's account of the escape to Egypt. The mother-demon could be seen riding a giant mouse while carrying in her lap a boy covered in rags, her body bent over the child in a protective gesture of affection. Behind her stood an aged, bearded man, apparently Saint Joseph; he wore a cap, a light blue beret. These symbols—the giant mouse and the blue beret—represented hypocrisy and fraud according to art historians. Also significant was the virgin's strange image composed of three elements: the face of a woman, the hair and arms depicted as branches of a tree, and the lower body the shape and texture of a reptile or fish.

Gazing at this Holy Family, Dolores questioned Gisela; she wasn't only questioning her granddaughter but also herself. What child would choose to belong to such a family, she asked? Also, who would be willing to embark on such a journey riding a rat? More importantly—as it related to her own heartbreaking experience of the past—who would accept this devil as mother? Dolores was now on the verge of insanity. Gisela, the smart young woman who so badly wished to become an illusionist one day, contemplated, her mouth agape, the images before her.

Dolores pointed out that the giant mouse was covered by a red cloth, only its face and front limbs visible. Lower in the picture, in a pond, an armless child appeared with a small bowl hovering over its head. The bowl was filled with something. Could it be food? A spoon was at its side. The child symbolized the orphans that the poor used to place in the major churches to elicit pity and donations from compassionate passersby. The child's chest was like a dove's, suggesting innocence.

Now turning to the orphan's image, which in fact could be a symbol for Gisela, Dolores once again asked her granddaughter the question that she had searched for in the past. Why wasn't there in the vast tableau a reference to a girl raped by her own mother? The picture didn't show in that unholy family the figurative example of a blighted vagina.

Perhaps, Dolores replied half-aloud to her own query, the answer could be found in the Christian theology the painting represents. Bosch was a medieval surrealistic painter, a male, and he depicted an immaculate virgin devoid of original sin. The virgin's sexual organ—she is a virgin and mother—are forever absent, silenced.

The perversion of Dolores's life was now in front of her own eyes for Gisela to contemplate.

Dolores now indicated that the triptych illustrated not only the four traditional elements—heaven, earth, water, and fire—but a fifth one, light. The light here was that of twilight, made up of shadows that floated above human beings, as if indicating the path of hardship that lay ahead. This light could be interpreted, Dolores uttered again half-aloud, as the antechamber of knowledge.

Gisela noticed the figure next to the rat. It had the legs of a horse and a body shaped like an elongated cylinder made of clay. The cylinder's mouth is the horse's behind. These clay containers, albeit smaller, are traditionally used to carry water in Portugal. The animal bore an armored mount, a sort of clown whose torso was made of feathers. The face was filled with spikes and no eyes were visible. Gisela asked Dolores what she thought was inside the clay cylinder.

Poisonous weeds, *ervas daninhas,* Dolores replied as in a cry. Dolores had discovered the perfect retaliation with which to toast Uncle Rudolf and Aunt Frieda. And she intended to involve Gisela in the revenge by asking her granddaughter to ruthlessly make use of the portal keys she had so cleverly devised for her imaginary professor's journey by train.

A further step in strengthening the already close bond between grandmother and granddaughter.

The Blood of Others

Edgar was born in a small, remote, and obscure village in northeastern Portugal, Trás-os-Montes. Here the territory is rough and its inhabitants robust. The land is capricious, hardly worth tending due to an extreme climate; the winters are tremendously cold, the summers burning hot. Not without reason the region of Trás-os-Montes is referred to as "Behind-the-Mountains." Edgar's father was a primary school teacher, his mother a housekeeper: hardworking, honest, and resourceful folk. The small farm where Edgar grew up, not far from the provincial city of Bragança, provided the essentials for the family's sustenance: potatoes, cabbage, turnip tops, olives, and onions as well as pigs, chickens, and rabbits. A small vineyard produced a thick red wine, the kind that goes well with wild game. Boar and bison are common to the area, a reminder that men and beasts share similar fruits of nature. Legend has it that the region's temperamental people and its corpulent animals mingle rather well. The populace is said to enjoy the feeling of having *uma alma limpa*, a clear conscience. And that they wash it, when necessary, with their own blood.

Or the blood of others.

Edgar's parents dreamed of a better life for their only son, a life better than they had had, which meant a passport for Edgar out of their stifling, restricting environment. Like so many others in the past, emigration was a possibility. Many emigrants had returned to build modern houses with all the amenities in nearby villages. However, what Edgar's father had always envisioned for his son was different. It was a life in the country's capital. Horizons were broad in Lisbon, the city provided room to maneuver.

Under the circumstances, a college degree was the crystal-clear path for success. Constantly following his parents' advice and persistently applying himself to get high grades, Edgar excelled in his studies. Thus, he ended up in Coimbra, a prestigious university town, to study law as an undergraduate. With an unyielding belief that their sacrifices on Edgar's behalf would eventually pay off, his parents sent him a monthly allowance. Generally speaking, Edgar wasn't crazy about legal issues; he was, nevertheless, diligent and attentive. Above all, Edgar preferred corporate law. He dreamed about becoming a legal consultant for a large firm, a respected expert, a valued friend of his corporation.

Edgar rented a room in a large apartment located in Rua de Todas as Esperanças, the Street of All Hopes. Here, the household helper was a hardworking, beautiful country girl named Diana. And it was in Diana that the young Edgar found the passion that filled his heart. When she cleaned his room on Thursdays, Edgar stayed chained to his desk, book opened, pretending to study. Above all else, he yearned to see Diana's bottom move around while she handled the vacuum cleaner. Only in this vision did he find the enthusiasm that gave meaning to his studies. By lunchtime, Edgar could again attack the law's voluminous tomes.

On Saturdays, Edgar usually persuaded his friends to visit him around eleven p.m. Diana also lived in the apartment, and the young men would spy on her as she undressed, exposing themselves to considerable danger as they hung from a window to get a peek. The street where the apartment was located, All Hopes, symbolized this highlight of the week. Edgar didn't seem to perceive the contradiction of sharing his object of desire with his friends; their company only added to his pleasure. Edgar rationalized that it was better to enjoy the moment; his parents would never accept him marrying down. From birth, greater plans had been designed for him.

The family counted on the support, in due time, of Dos Passos, an attorney whose wife owned the Trás-os-Montes village's only manor house. Dos Passos had a prominent practice in Lisbon, and if Edgar succeeded in his studies, his mother planned to seek Dos Passos's patronage. Perpétua had been in charge of the manor house's keys for many years. Following a long-established ritual, she opened and closed its doors when the distinguished family and their friends arrived for holidays.

Edgar had been a regular guest at the manor house as Dos

Passos had two sons close to his age, but a little younger. During the summer the three boys were inseparable. Familiar with every inch of the surrounding terrain, Edgar led adventures through the fields. Besides being a teacher, Edgar's father was an accomplished hunter and he had always brought his son out with him during the hunting season. Over time, Edgar had developed his own specialty: he enjoyed maiming birds with a slingshot, a sadistic pleasure that very much amused the city youngsters on vacation. Executing perfectly aimed shots at the tiny legs of birds perched on bushes or trees wasn't a Lisbon amusement. The fact that Edgar indulged in the country sport for hours on end during the sizzling summer afternoons was indicative of his determination. Aiming mercilessly at the creatures, Edgar managed to break their tiny legs.

During the holidays at the manor house, Dos Passos took an interest in young Edgar. Not merely because his sons raved about their friend's skills, but because he saw in the boy an enormous will to thrive, to carve his own way. After a long lunch, Dos Passos would send for Edgar's mother to join him in the parlor. After settling the previous months' accounting with Perpétua—he was in charge of bookkeeping despite his wife's ownership of the house—the attorney would inquire about her son's studies. Showing trust in the boy's future, the attorney would add a generous present for Edgar following the report.

During the summer in which Edgar finished his law degree, Perpétua approached Dos Passos. Edgar could have done it himself, but placing his mother as intermediary showed respect for Dos Passos's social standing. After all, she had been trusted with valuable possessions; sending Edgar on his own for such a delicate conversation might appear offensive. If she got a green light, Edgar would talk to Dos Passos himself. It was one thing for Edgar to enjoy time with the children of his mother's boss but altogether a different one to ask for an internship at the law office of such a reputable attorney.

Dos Passos indicated a seat to Perpétua when she arrived in his presence, and she sat uncomfortably on the edge of her chair.

"Dr. Dos Passos," Perpétua said, addressing the attorney in the expected manner, as if he were a medical doctor, "once again thank you for the trust your family has placed in my hands over the years. Today, if I may, I would like to attend to a matter concerning my son Edgar."

"Go on," Dos Passos said in a pleased tone of voice.

"As you know, by the mercy of God my Edgar already finished

his law degree in Coimbra." Perpétua continued gathering the necessary strength. "I must inquire now about your kindness in providing my son with an internship in Lisbon. I can vouch that perseverance and determination are among his best qualities."

Dos Passos had been waiting for the request for years. He, therefore, replied amicably.

"We've invited Edgar over the years so that I could form an opinion on his character. And I can assure you that your son has passed the test with flying colors. I'll be happy to give Edgar a first chance in life."

Tears of joy came to Perpétua's eyes.

"However, I must explain to you," Dos Passos continued. "My law firm is a busy enterprise, it's not a place for lazy bones. I work on average ten to twelve hours a day. Even fourteen, if necessary."

Perpétua only nodded; she knew this already.

"Some professionals are unable to handle the pace. Lisbon's legal work is often overwhelming. I demand from my subordinates the same amount of work I do on my job. Will Edgar be up to the task?"

When Perpétua nodded yes again, the attorney stated the difference between an internship and permanent employment. He added that Edgar reminded him of himself when he was young. He offered Edgar a small stipend, adding that many interns in his office weren't paid at all. Ending the conversation, he told Perpétua to send Edgar over to talk to him that same afternoon.

And this is how Edgar arrived in Lisbon with the opportunity to work in a well-known law firm. He was to work under Dos Passos exclusively so that the senior attorney could supervise his progress in detail. The veteran attorney planned to engage Edgar in broad legal matters. In time, he could introduce him to friends at major corporations because he knew Edgar enjoyed corporate law. Being given the chance of a lifetime, Edgar had better prove his worth. According to Dos Passos, it was one thing to earn a five-year law degree from Coimbra, another to handle the grueling legal affairs of a well-established Lisbon office. The firm had several partners, as well as trainees, secretaries, and receptionists.

Edgar arrived at the end of the summer and hoped that his childhood friends, Dos Passos's sons, would introduce him to their circle of friends. They belonged to a cosmopolitan world with added exciting opportunities. Diana, the old college heartthrob he had not dared to date in order to spare his parents a situation they would never accept, was now a distant memory.

During the first few weeks of Edgar's work, Dos Passos confirmed that he had an ambitious young man under his tutelage. Edgar displayed an uncommon feature in the new generation: he was willing to work the number of hours his boss demanded. Day after day, nonstop. The workload was ample: a trial to attend at the start of the day, following long hours of preparation the evening before; a complex will to read to heirs who hated each other; a business sale's contract to discuss with antagonistic parties. The demands never stopped. Edgar worked without batting an eye for more than ten hours a day. He was determined, focused, and always had a smile on his face.

Dos Passos was past sixty, but he still went to the office every Saturday morning, a habit dating from the firm's opening. No matter how much Alma, his wife, begged, she had never managed to change his schedule. Only Sunday was a day of rest in the attorney's eyes. He refused to accompany Alma to midday mass, and indulged in a sumptuous lunch followed by another feast at dinnertime. Frequently the attorney didn't even bother to change out of his pajamas.

The couple had disagreed over Dos Passos's work schedule for many years, and Alma knew that she had lost the battle. In her mind, her husband's professional efforts were unquestionably excessive. It wasn't for money that he worked so hard. In addition to his lucrative practice, she herself had family money. Nor was it ambition that drove him; often he had even confessed to hating many aspects of his job.

Alma believed that her husband's never-ending legal commitments were the only way he knew how to live. She thought his drive a form of drunkenness, a mechanical way to numb his secret inner feelings. For her, her husband's nonstop pace seemed an escape from reality, a substitute for living a full life. She found comfort in the thought that, at least, he hadn't erred in the way of some of her friends' influential husbands. He hadn't yet disappeared into an amorous reverie. That being the case, her husband's professional endeavors must be commended.

When Dos Passos pressed the combination to open his office's front door around ten o'clock in the morning on Saturdays, he felt like a king entering his palace. An observer couldn't fail to notice, either, his satisfaction at finding Edgar already immersed in his work. Aware of his boss's routine, Edgar was the only intern who showed up on Saturdays as the city was barely waking up from the excesses of Friday evenings. When working on a complex case, Dos Passos summoned Edgar to think out loud with him. And the two discussed for hours this or that peculiar legal feature, this or that legal statement by an eminent authority. When the discussion ended, Dos Passos gazed, animatedly, at the statuette that held a prime position in his office. It was of the Justitia Virtutum Regina, the Roman goddess.

It was evident that Edgar wanted to please and, luckily, he had talent galore. Moreover, he didn't intend to disappoint anyone—not himself, not his parents, nor his benefactor. If any of the other trainees or one of the secretaries got sick, Edgar invariably lent a hand. The office employees shared a large room for work; if necessary Edgar answered the phones or replied to emails. At lunch break he often ran errands to the notary public office, usually eating lunch standing up at the counter of the coffee shop across the street. After seven in the evening, when clients stopped coming to the office, Edgar took the time—just like he did during the peace and quiet of Saturday mornings—to organize Dos Passos's folders.

If during the first months of work the friendship between Dos Passos and Edgar tightened, the same couldn't be said about Edgar's relationship to the attorney's sons. Although Edgar had been invited a few times to have dinner at his boss's home in Lisbon, his friendship with the former playmates didn't develop. The young men were used to spending their time with privileged friends. Theirs was a world in which the family name and its social connections meant more than individual talent. Both boys were studying medicine, an ambition shaped by their mother's side of the family.

Before visiting his parents for a couple of days at Christmas, Edgar gained proof of his boss's satisfaction with his work. Dos Passos handed him a nice bonus check to celebrate the holidays. The gesture stood in sharp contrast to the way the boss treated the other interns or even the secretaries. Edgar knew that Dos Passos didn't mince words and didn't treat his subordinates well. He wanted the work to be done expediently and professionally; that was all. He enjoyed repeating his life axiom: what he imposed on himself, he imposed on others as well.

On the train back to Lisbon after the holidays, Edgar had rare leisure time to reflect on his boss's attitude. Disconcerted, he thought that something about it wasn't right. An inner voice began to nag at him that Dos Passos was exploiting his staff. And therefore the same applied to him as well. He felt a silent warning, something he had trouble putting into words. The slow realization of his work conditions raised a degree of cynicism. To continue the outstanding performance, Edgar needed to develop some emotional distance now.

The need to stay put was evident. Every now and then Edgar spoke on the phone with his friends from Coimbra and few had found jobs comparable to his. In just a few more months of uninterrupted effort, he would know with certainty what professional opportunities lay open. The corporate world continued to be his dream and he had been able to develop a few contacts in that milieu. That winter Edgar bought a new suit, silk ties and brand-name shirts that required ironing. He sought to appear in the affluent style of his Lisbon contacts.

As the winter and spring months went by, Dos Passos started delegating more and more responsibility to his protégé. Noticing that her husband was less overworked, Alma shared with her friends that it seemed the Virgin Mary had heard her prayers in Fátima, the Catholic shrine.

On the first of May—a national holiday on which both Dos Passos and Edgar were working—the attorney called him to his office. Dos Passos had decided to reward the efforts of his trainee on this symbolic day and invited him to remain in the firm after the internship. He offered a proper remuneration and considered the possibility of paying for Edgar's specialization in corporate law. Edgar knew now that his dream was within reach. His first Worker's Day in Lisbon had been crucial. And his hard work, in fact a dog's life, was paying off.

The following summer Edgar had practically no holidays and his mother complained about this state of affairs. But Edgar explained to Perpétua that she should be proud of the trust Dos Passos had placed on his shoulders. Alma had managed to reach her goal: the couple and their sons were finally going on a Mediterranean cruise. The summer months normally had less work, and Edgar had been placed in charge of Dos Passos's clients during his absence with a power of attorney prepared for the purpose.

Edgar took the opportunity, then, to move out of his single room to a new place. He could now afford his own apartment and rented a small, dimly lit ground floor. It didn't matter; he was only home to sleep.

At the beginning of September, a trainee in the firm invited Edgar to his wedding. This became, coincidentally, the day that

Edgar's life took yet another turn. One of the guests at the wedding was a young attorney named Paula. Busy with work, Edgar had almost forgotten that sex existed. But Paula found him handsome and started flirting while dancing. She was a couple of years older, divorced, and the mother of a four-year old boy. A romantic relationship ensued between Edgar and Paula. Thus, if the working days at the office were just as busy as before, at least some of Edgar's nights were spent in enjoyable intimacy.

One of the things that Edgar first noticed about Paula was her perfume. Unable to identify the smell, Edgar thought of Diana, the object of his long-ago infatuation. She had also emanated a special scent that had been sweet and lingering. This made Edgar yearn to be back in the fields of his childhood. Diana had smelled of the linseed oil used to polish furniture, a wax resulting from the mixture of honey and lemon. And with Paula it was exactly the same: she had the natural scent of a working woman, of someone whose day wasn't over at seven in the evening. It was comforting that her clothes emitted the same scent as Diana.

Edgar immediately took to Vitor, Paula's son. Vitor was cute, displaying a mischievous smile. His mother picked him up from the kindergarten after a day of work. Back at home, she had to oversee his shower, other activities, and prepare their dinner. It was evident that Paula's day didn't have enough hours to address her own needs.

Paula's life wasn't easy. Edgar noticed that her schedule was just as problematic as his. And that was exactly what had captivated him from the start. He couldn't even decide which of their two lives was tougher. Edgar worked for Dos Passos on average ten to twelve hours a day; for Paula it was exactly the same if her professional and personal tasks were combined. Her parents lived far away and weren't available to help their daughter. Vitor's father was unemployed, but even when he had work he was always late in paying the child's support. Paula had considered the possibility of sending Vitor to live with her parents. But her son gave her such joy that she was not willing to let him go. She also wanted to oversee Vitor's education with loving attention.

Paula enjoyed a stable professional situation. In order to be available to Vitor, she worked for a solicitor instead of a high-powered attorney. Many of her tasks were more bureaucratic than she had envisioned, but it was a job she could perform without major logistical problems. She wrote rental contracts, tax-related receipts, and dealt with similar matters. Every once in a while she took care of issues she enjoyed: workers' dismissals without due or just cause or corporations' lack of safety measures at the workplace. When Vitor got sick, Paula worked from home; her boss always allowed her the flexibility to tend to her son. Edgar admired Paula for being a good mother.

Being slightly older than Edgar and more seasoned, Paula gave her boyfriend some sage advice after their lovemaking.

"Yes, Edgar, I work hard. But part of my job includes taking care of Vitor. As you see, he is mine alone."

"I know," Edgar replied.

"When is your workload going to get lighter?"

"Maybe one day." Edgar was vague on purpose.

"Dos Passos is exploitative."

"I'm grateful that he gave me a first chance in life," Edgar insisted.

"The price you pay is not worth it. Moreover, he doesn't pay you enough."

"With time, he might." Edgar was afraid to expose to Paula his inner feelings.

"Fat chance! You work on workers' legislation once in a while but seem unaware of progress since the Industrial Revolution."

Edgar remained silent.

"No 'decent' remuneration equals the slavery you are subjected to."

With Edgar seemingly distant, Paula continued. "If Dos Passos enjoys working so many hours, it's his own problem. Not yours."

"I know you want the best for me," Edgar said, caressing Paula's hair.

"Mark my words, Dos Passos forcing you to submit to his pace is hideous."

"You know I want to advance professionally, don't you? Dos Passos is my entrance door."

Laughing tenderly, Paula asked Edgar if he was aware of *semana inglesa,* the Portuguese equivalent of free weekends. When he answered he didn't know what she was talking about, she blew a kiss at him.

On Sundays, Edgar, Paula, and Vitor spent time together in Campo Grande, a large garden in Lisbon. While Edgar and Vitor played ball, Paula ran to the supermarket to get the grocery shopping done for the week. Edgar wished more and more to have Saturday mornings free to spend time with what seemed to be his new family. Asking Dos Passos for the time off, however, was out of the question; he feared the consequences.

One day, the three went out early on Saturday morning because Edgar planned to go to the office around ten o'clock. However, while Paula was grocery shopping, Vitor had an accident. Some older boys had showed up and wanted to join the soccer game with Edgar and Vitor. Frightened, Vitor tripped and fell over a wooden beam studded with rusty nails. Edgar took Vitor to the closest pharmacy but was advised to go to the nearest hospital. The cut was deep and might need stitches.

As a result of the incident, for the first time since he walked through the door of Dos Passos's law office, Edgar didn't do what he was supposed to do: he didn't show up at the office and he didn't call his boss. What excuse would he give? He had never mentioned either Paula or Vitor.

The following Monday at work Dos Passos asked Edgar if he had taken care of a particular pending case. Edgar replied that he hadn't yet but that he would during the day. Because Dos Passos didn't ask the reason for his absence on Saturday, Edgar didn't provide one. Mondays were usually very busy, and Dos Passos seemed irritated. When he asked a second time if the case had been handled already, Edgar, intimidated, told him a lie for the first time. Yes, he told his boss, the client had been contacted. To him it was a white lie—he knew he would resolve the situation at the first opportunity. Thoroughly trusting Edgar, Dos Passos didn't inquire about the specifics of the solution.

Edgar tried to continue the work to keep up the pace in the office that he had maintained before meeting Paula. He got up at six o'clock in the morning and by half past seven he was in the office. He struggled to complete his office hours on Saturday mornings. But he started to feel adrift, as if in the middle of the ocean, close to drowning but not knowing how to swim. He listened to Paula, but he was most afraid of listening to himself. How great it would be, how well deserved, to have the weekend just for himself, forty-eight hours without thinking of legal tomes! Also, personal matters required his attention at the moment. He was moving from his apartment into Paula's. Not only would he save on rent, but he would also be close to the woman he loved. He wanted to help Paula care for Vitor. Vitor, himself, was ecstatic at the new plan; he was about to have the father he always missed. Edgar delayed telling his parents, they would hate the idea of their son having a relationship with a woman who had already a child. No rush on that front.

After moving in with Paula, Edgar felt ready to consider his innermost feelings. Yes, Dos Passos definitely took advantage of his subordinates and, yes, Paula was right about workers' legal rights. Trying to change jobs, however, wasn't an option. Where would he get a reference letter? Edgar now needed an income more than ever. It had made him happy to buy Vitor a brand-new pair of soccer cleats. He also bought him a television set for his bedroom. On Sunday mornings, he and Paula could stay in bed longer while Vitor watched TV.

Edgar's current situation required the same sort of savvy balancing act he had demonstrated when shooting his slingshots at the birds' tiny legs in the village. He was now constantly concealing from Dos Passos the work he left undone, the accumulated pile from the previous weeks. If the birds managed to still fly with broken legs, so must he. Extreme prudence was needed to conceal his inability to finish tasks on deadline. Was it an art or an adventure? The only thing he knew was that he had started a game that required the utmost secrecy.

Edgar was now cutting corners regularly. He left the office systematically at six p.m. to spend the evening with Paula and Vitor. Weeks went by with work piling up on his desk. And he kept telling Dos Passos that the work had been completed as planned. And Dos Passos himself, busy as ever, believed him. He hadn't even revoked the power of attorney he had granted Edgar when he took the cruise.

All hell broke loose one day in the late morning. A longstanding affluent client called Dos Passos and stated the following:

"My dear friend, something is going on. Unlike the information Edgar conveyed to me, the Setúbal factory I bought recently hasn't been registered within the legal time limit."

"Let me call you back in a few minutes," Dos Passos said, assuming a misunderstanding had occurred. He needed to verify the facts.

After questioning Edgar, Dos Passos called his client back.

"First, let me apologize," he said. "The required registration has indeed been delayed." Then he gave an excuse. "We're implementing a new computer filing system, a few mistakes occurred. But do not worry, we'll take care of the matter today."

"This situation places both you and me in a very delicate position," the client said hurriedly. "Since the Setúbal factory is not registered, and the legal time limit for registration has passed, the factory doesn't belong to me."

"I'm well aware of that. But I promise you this matter will be solved today." Dos Passos sounded matter-of-fact.

"Today is too late," the client answered, out of his mind. "I found out the tax administration issued a notification already. The previous owner didn't pay his employees' social contributions to the state; he owed outstanding taxes. You know how it is in these cases. The tax bureau asked immediately for the factory's confiscation."

"What?" asked an incredulous Dos Passos.

"Why wasn't this matter taken care of months ago?" The firm's client was shouting now.

Dos Passos remained silent. Edgar's oversight had been astounding—and it had happened right under his nose. The client had paid the full asking price for the Setúbal factory, and now it wasn't his anymore.

"I'm outraged," the client stated. "May I ask how you intend to resolve this matter?"

Dos Passos made up another excuse and said he would call right back. He needed to get his act together, find a solution. What else might have Edgar left undone without his knowledge?

Suddenly, as in a flashback, he remembered the power of attorney he had granted Edgar during his vacation.

The attorney headed for the workroom that Edgar shared with others at the firm. Red with anger and yelling as loud as he could in front of everyone, Dos Passos told Edgar what had happened. He stated that professional integrity was a key element when practicing law in his firm. Throwing the document with his power of attorney at Edgar's feet, he then slapped him full force in the face. Edgar was a fraud. And he was fired.

Then, Dos Passos told Edgar to collect his personal belongings and leave the firm immediately. He was going to make a couple of calls, then leave for lunch; Edgar had better be gone by the time he returned. Oddly enough, the attorney's old reliance on Edgar barred him from sensing the obvious danger of this hurried decision.

Edgar listened in silence, his right hand covering the place where the harsh slap had landed. He headed to the toilet and called Paula from his mobile. He asked her if she could manage to get away from work and meet him soon. When she showed surprise, he said he would explain what had happened when they met.

Then Edgar returned to the workroom to find that everybody had vanished. Under the circumstances, colleagues had taken off for lunch earlier than usual. Filled with never-ending determination, Edgar made one last gesture at the Dos Passos law firm. The room had several computers. Edgar rapidly worked on each and every one of them, deliberately deleting all the information pertaining to the firm's clients.

Then he crossed the corridor—dead silence seemed to rule the place—and entered Dos Passos' office. The computer was turned off. Edgar headed back to the door, but his eyes caught the sight of Justitia Virtutum Regina, his boss's beloved statue. Here was the legal system's moral force. The sword of truth now seemed an elongated and mediocre hairpin; the cloth covering the eyes, standing for exemption, had been transformed into a head and neck scarf; and the scale representing the balance of justice was now the buckle of some belt.

Empowered with the might the Trás-os-Montes beasts of his childhood possessed, Edgar grabbed the statuette and threw it at the window. With a thundering crash, both window and sculpture shattered in a thousand pieces.

Only then did Edgar pick up his jacket and leave the office. He was now at peace.

My Bones

Abroad and homesick, I once had an idea: to build a family tree using old forgotten photographs from my antique chest of drawers. The best picture is that of my grandparents. They sit side by side along a garden wall decorated with a single grapevine. Their outfits are black with a dash of white; their lips display fulfilled smiles. My Grandma Emília is wearing a long-sleeved black dress with a V-neck. The material on the left gathers to the waist giving her pose a touch of class. She wears a gold pin surrounded by small pearls. Grandpa Augusto wears a suit and tie, his suspenders hardly visible through the well-cut jacket. His right hand holds the mandolin he played all his life.

The photo unleashed treasured childhood memories. In particular I recalled the Sunday visits to my grandparents' third-floor apartment in Lisbon on São Bento Street: a long, steep, and winding *rua* on a busy trolley car route. My father led the way up the narrow, wooden stairway into a charming residence; it was cozy, ordered, and spotless. As we came in, my grandparents beamed with sheer delight. There was a sense of poise in the atmosphere. Grandma Emília always wanted me to sit close to her on the sofa. She enjoyed holding my hand and, once in a while, beatifically caressed my face. Midway into the visit, grandma gave me something previously hidden in the ornate cabinet nearby. She asked me to close my eyes and then gently placed a round object in the center of my palm.

It was the now defunct five escudos coin!

Monday afternoons felt magical. After school, I exchanged the escudos into centavos and bought multicolored lollipops, one at a time, all weeklong. These were the so-called *chupa-chupas.* I was in no way a spoiled eight-year-old girl, so the five escudos were a fortune to me. With the candy, I more easily endured the nuns at school, the senseless homework, and my division tables—always eagerly awaiting my next visit to Rua de São Bento.

Decades later, in what seemed a tribute to those memories, my father left the family a burial chamber in the Lisbon Alto de São João Cemetery. The cemetery is dedicated to São João who is, like São Bento, a Catholic martyr. The documents relating to this bequeathed vault arrived in a black-leather folder that contained a key, the original drawings for the memorial, and various identifying papers. I thus discovered, to my surprise, that Grandma Emília had built the vault to honor her husband. The drawings, carefully folded, bore Grandpa Augusto's engraved name on top. They specified that the exquisite Vila Viçosa marble should be used as building material. Grandma had intended that her husband lie at rest with the same quiet dignity she herself had exuded all her life. The gift obviously showed that he was the love of her life for all eternity.

When property divisions took place in my generation, my relatives—without consulting me from afar and surely believing that the relic wasn't worth much—made sure I got the tomb.

Little did I know.

One blazing summer afternoon while vacationing in Portugal, many years after the bequest, I drove from Arrábida to Lisbon to visit my burial chamber. Not that I was inclined to keep company with the deceased that day. I drove to the Alto de São João Cemetery for a far less noble reason: I needed cash. And I needed cash badly. The thought of selling the family crypt had therefore been in my mind for longer than I dare to confess. Somewhat horrified by my objective, I arrived at the cemetery oblivious to the airless, roasting afternoon heat.

This was the start of my adventures with Simplex, the national program in Portugal designed to simplify bureaucratic affairs for the average citizen.

At the cemetery's headquarters, I found a middle-aged public servant staring intently in my direction as I passed through the office's entrance. He seemed hungry for prey, as if the deceased buried around weren't enough to satisfy a vampire's lust. My first order of business was to locate the tomb. The task, I felt, meant appeasing the man behind the counter. I must speak in a low tone of voice, display a needy expression, and convey apprehension.

With a modest demeanor, I handed him the vault's ownership certificate. It was a copy of the old title, not the real thing.

After taking his time to examine the document that bore my grandparents' name, the number of the crypt, the cemetery's street location, and the name of the funerary agency that had handled the burials, the fellow turned it over. Slowly, he inspected its back. Gazing into my eyes, he asked for the original record.

As I lied stating that the original was in his hands, the man replied that it wasn't. Did I detect, momentarily, a note of enthusiasm in his voice? The clerk proceeded to ask who had erected the vault. When I replied that my grandmother had, the clerk displayed an unquestionably satisfied smile. He then slowly asserted that I could have stolen the certificate.

That statement I was unable to contradict.

"You've a problem on your hands," he added.

That much I had already figured out.

My inquisitor continued our exchange by stating that the only possible way to locate the vault was through proof of its tenure, which, obviously, I didn't seem to possess. Thus, he couldn't help me. An unfortunate situation, he avowed. I seemed to have a vault that, for all practical purposes, I didn't own.

I acknowledged that the original title might have been lost in the labyrinth of time. He nodded.

Suddenly remembering the rusty key in the leather folder, I placed the ancient trophy on the counter, loudly, for effect. My tormentor didn't lose his composure. A bloodthirsty smile emerged from his mouth when he referred to the magnitude of my dilemma. He responded circumspectly. My key could, indeed, open the tomb. But I must weigh my actions carefully, lest I end up in prison. I could be arrested for trying to open my crypt; the cemetery had spies on watch. Observing my utter bewilderment, he explained that the law forbade people without legal titles from opening burial chambers. I could be charged with infringement and summarily locked up. He compared the situation to a person trying to enter a house using someone else's key. Justice might follow in due course, not to mention the souls of those resting underground.

"Gosh," I replied.

Trying to get the fellow on my side, I asked if he was willing to look into the registrar's books that lined the wall behind him. The huge centenary tomes were covered with a white, dreary dust similar to the residue of decomposed bodies. I had noticed other clerks picking up the books periodically, but not without a major effort due to their size. Certainly, these volumes revealed significant details.

"Ah, the books," the clerk alleged, "Yes, we can look at them."

As he turned his back, I saw his gray face turn fleetingly yellow in the sunlight that streamed through the small window next to the bookshelf. With the dirty nail of his index finger, he searched the digits displayed on the spines. I marveled how the long row of books looked as gray as his face. A friend had once commented to me how people tended to become similar to the objects they touched every day. I was witnessing such a case.

Soon the man pulled out one of the books, having found the correct range of numbers. As he placed the book on the counter, he opened it right in front of my eyes.

The clerk's gestures were slow; time didn't seem to matter inside these walls. The pages had red lines from top to bottom and in the top areas formed a *quadrícula,* small squares. Licking his middle finger, which displayed a nail that had not been cleaned or trimmed in a long time, the official turned page after page. But that was of minor concern. I could see the public servant enjoyed feeling that he was in command, so once again I tried to win him over. As he leaned over the book, my eyes followed the digits indicated by the dirt under his nail.

As in a thriller, he didn't tell me what I was about to see.

And I didn't dare to ask.

After a prolonged silence, the official pointed out the names of my corpses, easily deciphering the old handwriting. Each name bore a number inscribed in a metal piece; and the metal piece, by the coffin, identified the cadaver by number. As I leaned over, the clerk volunteered the information that my bodies had been exhumed. Only bones, not flesh, remained in the crypt.

Entrances had been registered with the dates of birth and death carefully recorded. The chamber had five small coffins. The first entrant was Grandpa Augusto, followed by Grandma Emília; later, her two younger sisters had arrived, and, lastly, a distant cousin.

The reading aloud of my ancestor's names had the unexpected power of subduing me, as if I were hearing my grandma's voice again. I immediately recalled the day she had passionately recounted how she had met grandpa. Her father, a musician she remembered in adoring terms, had introduced her to a younger fellow instrumentalist. His name was Augusto. Great-grandpa had played music with sentiment all his life and in particular during the months preceding his death from tuberculosis. Fulfilling his dream, his eldest daughter, Emília, had married a musician. His mission in life, thus, had been accomplished.

Maybe the low-level bureaucrat noticed me drifting away, for he now described hurriedly the steps I must take to legally possess the vault. Since there were countless departments scattered throughout the city, he jotted down the specific City Hall address I should go to. There, the clerk said, I must obtain a *segunda via*, an authenticated copy of the vault's title bearing my name as owner. I needed to get a *senha*, a ticket, upon entering the building and then wait patiently in line until my number was called. Public servants were busy in these offices, he warned. I should plan a few hours for my visit. He further advised me that it was imperative to bring along the informal credential in my possession.

The possibility of getting a title of ownership was small, the clerk continued. People in the tomb were a generation removed; they had died in the previous century. Maybe my father should claim the vault, he advised. Had the crypt ever been under his name? The reply that my father was deceased and buried somewhere else was considered a major family oversight.

When I asked for a photocopy of the page we had examined, I didn't get an answer. Perhaps the Xerox machine was not working that day or the tomes were so ancient that photocopying might damage them.

My last question concerned how long it might take to get an original certificate. This time my tormenter reframed my question forcefully. If lucky, I would get a notarized second copy claiming ownership. The difference escaped me, but he explained. Because I didn't possess it, the one-and-only original couldn't be obtained; it no longer existed. Therefore, my City Hall visit was most important.

And how long might it take to get the *segunda via*? The answer was uncertain. Each case being unique, sometimes it took weeks, sometimes months, and in some cases years. Further along the way, he warned, I might be asked to establish legal blood ties with those resting in my crypt.

I fully understood now the task that lay ahead.

Following the interchange, I said good-bye in a hurry. And for a bit of relief, I took a handkerchief from my pocket and wiped my perspiring forehead. Exiting the building, I turned left, pretending I was leaving the cemetery grounds in case the clerk might be able to see me through the small window. Then I ran into the side alley bordered by the cemetery's black iron fence. I had visited the burial chamber with my father many years ago. Surely I could find it. In a frenzy, I followed the numbered tombs leading to my own.

I had the entrance key: thus, what could go wrong? What cemetery official in his or her right mind would be spying on me in such broiling heat? I passed hundreds of *gavetões*, drawers containing corpses; they formed an area called the *columbário.* The name evokes a space where doves, the symbol of peace, live together. My only company was the nauseating smell of cadavers combined with the odor of adorning fading flowers. As I sped along, large droplets of sweat streamed down my face.

A few burial chambers were worth admiring along the way. Some were miniature Portuguese houses just like those inhabited by the living, only smaller. One looked like a small country estate in Minho, the northern part of the country. It had organza-trimmed curtains on the windows, fresh flowers on the iron windowsills, and the vault's number displayed at the entrance door. I peeped through the glass doors of a few vaults. Framed pictures and vases with plastic flowers were on display, as well as crucifixes, rosaries, and images of Jesus, the Virgin Mary, and patron saints.

Contradictory feelings flooded my heart as I walked along the fence. How utterly callous to want to exchange my grandparents' crypt for cash. No life event, however traumatic, could justify my actions; those bones contained my own DNA. I felt inclined to call the divine and say a prayer as an apology for my intentions.

For now, however, I needed to keep my thoughts on practical matters. If I had the right key, my family bequest would be open in a few minutes. I had to be careful while trying the lock in case one of the spies, emerging like a phantom from the scorching afternoon heat, asked for the vault's papers. Checking left and right, I confirmed that only the dead populated my environs.

Minutes later, there it was: the Vila Viçosa marble vault I still remembered from the earlier visit with my father. The opaque glass door was enclosed by thin brass trim. Grandpa Augusto's name was inscribed on the top of the tomb: Augusto Luís Góis da Silva. I saw the lock on the right side of the door. Once again, my handkerchief came in handy, for I needed a steady hand to turn the rusty key. With delicacy, I inserted it into the lock and tried to turn it: once, twice, three times. I persisted: ten, fifteen, twenty times. Slowly-thirty, forty, fifty times. But the key inexorably refused to budge. If it bent or broke in my hand, I would have another challenge. Professional help might be necessary, and where would I find a willing accomplice? After all, I was breaking into my own estate.

"I should have brought oil, just in case," I reproached myself aloud.

I drove back to Arrábida exhausted from the day's emotions. The moon was out that evening and I sat on my terrace admiring the twilight by the sea. It was one of those nights redolent of jasmine and flowering vines and shrubs, nights when nightingales and frogs are heard in distant ponds. Relaxing in my chair, I absorbed the sounds of the cosmos hearing, as one, the rhythm of my own heart. The universe contained both living and dead as if they were one single entity keeping me company in my distress.

Then I went to bed. And as often happens in Latin American novels of magical realism, a vision appeared to me. It wasn't a dream; it was an apparition. Soon after a period of deep sleep—I'm under the impression I even snored—I suddenly awoke as if disturbed by someone entering my bedroom. In the penumbra, I distinctly saw a young man sitting on the corner of my bed. His face looked familiar, as if he were a relative I had allowed to enter my private quarters. He looked superb, dressed in an attractive black suit with a white shirt and gray silk tie. His features were elongated with dark eyes and a long nose. His skin seemed transparent.

The figure was staring at me, intently, a half smile on his face. I didn't get flustered, perhaps because the veiled smile was a personal introduction. I didn't dare move; my lovely apparition might disappear into thin air. At first, I had concentrated on the young man's face, but now, pensive, I turned my attention to his chest. In amazement, I saw that he carried a mandolin like the one grandpa had in his picture. A string instrument with a body shaped like a half pear, the back rounded and made of strips of wood from which emerged a long fingerboard. I have sufficient musical knowledge to know this to be a Neapolitan mandolin. Staggered, I saw the arms and the hands of the young man adjusting the mandolin as if readying to play. Virtually unable to breathe, I saw him carefully adjust the pick between his thumb and first finger of the eight-string fingerboard. He played a few chords as if tuning the instrument. Then, suddenly, he was playing a solo only for me, his eyes focused on the four pairs of strings grouped together.

Incredibly, the musician knew my taste, for these were eighteen-century tunes typical of the Enlightenment. The music was pleasing to the ear, light, airy, and graceful. My musician played excerpts from three or four sonatas. It was as if I sat in a concert hall, the only difference being that there was no applause, only a brief interval between the melodies. I felt suspended, half on earth, half in heaven. A kindred spirit had found me and the feeling of comfort was indescribable. When I fell asleep again, my musician was still playing.

I woke up rejuvenated, as images of Grandpa Augusto dashed through my mind. A feeling of pride was palpable in one of those: Grandpa standing among a group of musicians in their twenties, each one holding a string instrument. The picture had been taken in the São Bento apartment.

In the following days I chatted with elder relatives and asked details of Grandpa's musical background. Uncle Raul, already in his nineties, told me that Grandpa Augusto had practiced classical music with simplicity but great virtuosity. He detailed how the mandolin was a popular instrument in some Lisbon quarters in Grandpa's youth. My uncle recalled Grandpa acknowledging how his soul filled with joy when he played. I had discovered why.

I didn't share my night vision with Uncle Raul; he would think I was out of my mind.

Comforted by recollections, it was time once again to redirect my attention to the possibility of selling the vault. I therefore paid a visit to City Hall a few days later. Equipped with newfound wisdom, I chose a cool day for my trip; public buildings in old Lisbon don't usually have air conditioning. After I sat for more than an hour with a *senha* sticking in my hand, a young red-haired woman shouted my number. She handed me a sheet of paper that listed the *requerimentos,* the required paperwork, which I needed in order to acquire legal ownership of the possession I risked losing.

I rolled my eyes reading the Herculean list of instructions. The clerk seemed amused by my reaction as she touched her reddish curls with her agile fingers. She told me that I wouldn't be exiting the building without a photocopy of the list. I replied that I lived abroad and wasn't used to so much red tape. Then I frowned while asking, "Tell me, how is Simplex working for the Portuguese public at large?" My query amused the woman further. She said that the part of the program dealing with the dead was naturally taking forever to implement. As I left the building, my only hope was that God's mercy would grant me the pleasure of hearing my young musician play the mandolin again. Only for me, by my bedside.

It is hard to describe what made me pursue my quest in the following months. Above all loomed my desperate need for cash. As the weeks went by, various matters required my attention. I must figure out what to do with my bones if indeed I could sell and must empty the tomb. Once I returned to the cemetery grounds for advice. The public servant on duty told me that in her official capacity she must abstain from counseling *munícipes*, the citizens of the municipality, on how to dispose of remains. The woman's perfume stayed with me all day long; it reminded me of the depths of *inferno*. When I insisted on my quest, she told me to leave her alone.

Little by little, firsthand knowledge about the business of dying came to dominate my life. Stores catering to death proliferated near the cemetery and grabbed my attention. A few shops sold fresh flowers and elaborately shaped crowns to embellish funerals. Fair enough. Other shops displayed mortuary items on shelves along the walls: miniature coffins in various types of wood, ceramic pots for ashes, crosses big and small, and ribbons in shades of purple. For sale there were also *santinhos*, petite pictures of Jesus, *terços*, rosaries, and *medalhinhas*, small medals bearing the effigy of a martyr. A shop owner confided that it would have been lucrative to engage in the traffic of souls—as if trafficking in drugs—but he feared offending the dead.

"I need to ponder these words," I heard myself expressing.

Cremation had become a big deal and the choice of containers was plentiful. Some cremation pots didn't disintegrate; they remained intact as if brand new. There was something for everyone: pots decorated in the deceased's favorite colors; pots shaped like elves; disposable pots that could be thrown in the sea for the fish to eat. For people who enjoyed displaying loved ones on the mantelpiece, there were pots designed to adorn a living room.

I got to know other professionals besides the shopkeepers. The ones in charge of the *crematório* confided they had to get used to the smell of burned flesh while cremation was under way. I met *coveiros*, the gravediggers, who buried and unburied bodies. During exhumations, these specialists separated decomposed brain from hair and muscle from bone. Talking once to one of these fellows, I noticed that one of his eyes was green and the other brown. Not only that, the eyes looked in opposite directions. How could one live like that, let alone handle such a job, I wondered. Assuming this man had an idea on how I could dispose of my bones, I called him later. To my amazement, his voice mail played *The Godfather* soundtrack. In an accent mimicking Italian, the message stated that he, the local mafia leader, was currently unavailable. Sharp hoarse guffaws could be heard in the background. Then came the end of the message: "I'll return your call; if alive I'm sure you will answer."

"I'll never contact this guy again," I murmured, alarmed.

I met the construction workers, a long list of authorized dealers in charge of building, repairing, and cleaning the burial chambers. They built crypts and sepulchers, carved angels, and sculpted saints according to a client's taste. They used so-called precious stones such as *granito,* granite, in gorgeous dark tones, and milky marble in off-white and pale pink. Many of these builders made good money as intermediaries in the sale of vaults. The bribes they undoubtedly had to pay city officials in order to get or renew their licenses must have been high. In reality, these were the cemetery's real estate agents; they not only gave advice on best plots and prices but also on good deals in carving stone.

There were also bus drivers in charge of transporting people back and forth from the main entrance to the gravesites. Gardeners and street sweepers used witches' brooms to clean the grounds while security guards kept the cemetery under surveillance after the gates closed for the night. These groups joked together all the time, turning somber only when another funeral car entered the gates carrying a fresh corpse. Apparently, there had been quite a bit of vandalism at night in previous years. Hooligans enjoyed breaking into the cemetery and stealing keys from the headquarters. They opened crypts and removed corpses; only God knew their macabre intentions.

I couldn't help but notice that the business of dying was modernizing. Some of the up-to-date practices included placing cadavers in large drawers with open holes allowing air to circulate. Apparently fresh air facilitates decomposition. Notwithstanding the horrible smell involved, I liked the idea. It was more hygienic than a cadaver closed in a container for posterity. At one point, the state bureaucracy was so inefficient that the municipal government was thinking of turning cemeteries into private-public enterprises. However, progress in that direction was impeded by the fear of widespread corruption, including an array of new bribes.

My mission was accomplished months later when I carried a suitcase—a suitcase not a bag—of documents to the City Hall. I had visited several archives and spent considerable sums for official seals. But a task started is a task that needs completion. Upon depositing the thick file, I inquired about the lapse of time to obtain my *averbamento,* my vault's registered ownership.

The answer was vague.

With luck, as well as with the support of those souls watching over me, my papers wouldn't get lost on their way to the cemetery's department in charge of codifying the burial certificates. This procedure completed, the head of management would send out a signed final verdict. The decision was of a public nature because, although the vault was private, it was located in a public space. Once released, the verdict needed to be published in the *Buletim Municipal*—a daily publication that all *munícipes,* all citizens of the municipality, could read at leisure. Only after these steps would the verdict be final.

I decided to take it easy after the long ordeal. In fact, there was plenty of time to figure out what to do with my bones.

A handful of possibilities was emerging. One was to have the bones cremated and the ashes spread in the cemetery's designated location, O Jardim das Cinzas, The Ash Garden. But since I was dealing with the bones of people deceased long ago, the waiting list for cremation was not months but years. I had the option of immediately removing the bones to a less expensive cemetery where they would be placed in rented drawers. Burial drawers are public, not private dwellings, with the fees requiring only the renewal of state licenses at specific intervals. The transportation procedure, however, was comparable to a second funeral for each set of bones and required the use of several funeral cars that would cost a small fortune.

As I debated these options, I had succeeded in opening my tomb. One day, as if by miracle, the oil I had carefully brought along in a tiny green jar did its work. I stood at the vault's threshold as if entering the São Bento apartment. Grandma Emília's imprint was at once noticeable. Each coffin was covered with a white embroidered linen cloth, still impeccably ironed after decades. Each had a mother-of-pearl rosary lying on its lid. The light of day breaking through the entrance conjured up Dante's *The Divine Comedy.* Circle 4, Canto 7 of *The Inferno* refers to the differences between avarice and prodigality and how the goddess Fortuna delights in changing man's circumstances.

My last undertaking was a stop at the building for burial codification. It was located in Alcântara, near the Tejo River. Since I was leaving the country for a few months once again—my chilling quests and cemetery digressions would soon become a distant recollection—I must be sure my dossier had arrived. After a few minutes' discussion, the head of the department went inside to look for the file. Later, he emerged to say that my records were judiciously stacked together with hundreds of others. No, there was no chance the procedure could be sped up in the next week. But the size of my dossier suggested that the formalities had been met. One day, he was certain, I was going to receive a registered letter with the much sought-after signature and stamp.

Near the stairway I noticed a few armchairs in a circle, perhaps placed there for people in my circumstances. I plunked down in one of the chairs to rest for a while. "The unbearable summer heat is getting to me again," I whispered while sipping some water.

Looking around, I noticed hanging on the walls several huge black-and-white photographs of angels carved in stone. The colossal figures gazed towards the heavens with nurturing smiles and wings opened like protective cloaks. A few captions were under the pictures. One of them suggested that cremation had been reintroduced in Portugal after the 1974 Carnation Revolution. Cremation was promoted as practical since space in the nation's cemeteries had become scarce. A string of zeroes flashed through my head: if terrain was limited, then the current value of vaults, including mine, must be high. Grandma's tenderness came to mind, and like a supplicant, I asked for insight in my hour of trouble.

That afternoon I decided to cremate my bones, regardless of the number of years my name might linger in the maze of the cemetery's waiting list.

Back home in Arrábida for the evening, I once again sat admiring the twilight from my terrace. As night drew over the sky a few constellations emerged, compelling me to match their forms with names I had memorized in school. It was enthralling to look up and see bright light in organized forms, showing me that the world made sense after all.

This was the night my apparition took hold of me for the second time. Again, the young man appeared at the end of my bed. Once more, breathless, I woke up with the sensation of a relative entering my bedroom. As before, I wasn't frightened by the supernatural intrusion. I had lived through the previous marvel; I only wished for the music to be as thrilling as before. Moving my eyes from the young face to the mandolin, I noticed that my musician wore suspenders. He delicately positioned the instrument against his chest, away from his neck. Then he placed the pick between his right fingers and strummed a few chords to check the tuning.

The compositions I heard that night were, again, deliriously enjoyable, radiant, and playful. Scarlatti had created them for string instruments, which displayed his Iberian magnificence. He was called *Escarlate* in Portuguese, Scarlet, the most flaming of reds. Very appropriate. Lying in bed and enjoying the music, I observed my young man vigorously stirring his fingers backward and forward. The fingers were as palpable as this page, moving fast between the four pairs of strings and changing constantly to alter the pitch of the notes. The tremolos were bright and affirmative, as if from another planet. It was the realm of the divine, of contemplation and of reassurance.

As happened the first time, my instrumentalist took a brief pause between pieces, and then he started playing again. He serenaded me for quite a while, and just before I fell asleep, I heard a few compositions that had a different tone. They were more melancholic, lyrical, and even sad. My musician was playing Carlos Seixas, the eighteen-century Portuguese composer. During his years in Lisbon, Scarlatti had met the Portuguese virtuoso, the latter being credited with introducing the great master to his characteristic southern European style.

Transfixed by the Carlos Seixas compositions, I was forced to accept the presence of death in my own life.

Eventually, I did receive the title to my burial chamber by mail. By sheer coincidence I was back in Arrábida. From start to finish the process had taken several years, and I had worked hard to earn the deed. I read the letter with a modicum of anxiety. The text was as terrifying as the whole business itself. The first line read in a characteristically archaic language: *Bearing in mind the resolution dated of August…engraved in procedure number nineteen thousand and twenty-three, slash…* The text continued in this vein for half a page. But, at the end, there it was: the petitioner was entitled to the crypt's property.

"This is a moment worth recalling," I said.

After the event, I went back to headquarters and placed my bones on the cemetery's waiting list for cremation. I bought white cloth bags for the bones' transportation and chose urns for the ashes.

The clerk whom I had originally talked to informed me that, as he had suspected all along but didn't disclose, I needed to get the so-called *certidão de teor*, or Parentage Certificate, from City Hall. If I wanted to sell the tomb and remove the ashes from the cemetery's grounds after cremation, it was mandatory that I establish blood lineage with my deceased relatives. A fresh Ariadne thread complicated my progress. If the voluminous, dusty books stated that the corpses had been placed in *perpétuo lugar*, perpetual residence, then the ashes couldn't be removed from their grounds. Therefore, their everlasting residence couldn't be altered at my whim.

Home or abroad, my ancestors and I are thus joined in unexpected ways. The tie is permanent; it will endure for all my days on earth. I can either accept this fact or prepare for annihilation. No doubt, I must exercise a certain degree of temperance. "Such solitude!" I'm starting to whisper once in a while.

But will my nocturnal apparition continue to keep me company? If unable to sell the vault, at least I can have my nights brightened by music. Instead of classical melodies, I'm ready for Neapolitan songs, tunes traditionally played in the streets of southern Italy in times of celebration. I cannot say, for sure, that I will be able to recognize the young face of my visions. Grandpa Augusto was already over sixty when I was born. But this musician is someone who loves me despite my frailties. How sublime! A spirit appearing in my sleep to play enchanting music for me alone when I need it most.

I often think how I wish I had heard Grandpa Augusto playing the mandolin during his lifetime. If only once. I regret not knowing that side of him. I often contemplate the smiles in my grandparents' photograph and sense their depth of feeling for each other. The smile is the same on both lips, and those lips show a form of intimacy I need to discover. But I am certain of one thing: Grandma Emília heard Grandpa Augusto practice the mandolin. And those were melodies of love, submission, and admiration.

I need to settle down with those memories.

A Perfect Common-Law Marriage

Maria and Patricia are childhood friends who live in Oporto by the Douro River. They were born, raised, and educated there. Both have grown children and are now divorced. Maria has a past of alcoholism, a problem that seems at present under control. The women are returning home by car after visiting friends in Lisbon for a long weekend. The break was fun, it cheered them up. The trip back home is the perfect time to catch up, to discuss private matters, the kind of thing they've been doing for as long as they can remember. The two friends decide to take a detour on the way back to Oporto to spend a couple of days at Patricia's parents' manor house near the Spanish border.

Patricia's son, António, will soon be married here and Patricia's mother has been supervising the preparations on-site. The village is typical of the Beira Baixa region: the small houses are made of granite, there is a charming fountain close to the main road, and a church embellishes the main square. In the past as now, the houses of the aristocratic families continue to be a source of local employment.

Today, the landed gentry has moved either to Oporto or Lisbon, but the families continue to be intimately linked to the estates and their servants. They often visit during Christmas and Easter and spend the long summer months here. Like António's wedding, these celebrations consume endless months of concerted efforts and provide a further source of jobs for locals. Affectionate ties reduce the gap between city and country due to a web of long-term relationships. It is a world of mutual help and intimate friendships in which the rural and urban worlds form one entity. If willing, the hard-working and diligent village women are employed by the rich families in their city dwellings to serve as maids, housekeepers, and seamstresses.

Maria and Patricia hope to reach their destination before dark and agree to stop for lunch in Abrantes. Happy with the prolonged journey, Maria welcomes the opportunity to talk about her personal affairs, to discuss once again *her* Duarte. Duarte is the man she lived with after her divorce, the man with whom she bought and shared an apartment, and the man who died recently leaving her exposed, unprotected.

After his death, Maria discovered that her relationship with Duarte hadn't been as stable as she had thought. The use of the possessive adjective, *her* Duarte, is thus merely subjective. Was Duarte, really, *her* man? Maria feels a sorrow she seems unable to shake off. As an art lover, she carries in her purse a book entitled *Black Paintings* by the Spanish painter Goya. A somewhat morbid private accessory, it reflects the paralyzing doubts that continually assault her spirit. Alone again, Maria struggles with recent events, the main fear being that the Oporto court might force her to abandon the apartment she bought and shared with Duarte.

Maria and Duarte never got married because she was afraid that if she died before Duarte, her two daughters would not inherit all of her possessions. Maria contends that Duarte's desire for a share of her estate exhibited an inexplicable and irrational attitude. Duarte had a good job as marketing director at a prosperous Oporto enterprise, owned real estate of his own, and enjoyed many highly placed connections. She acknowledges that he had been a pillar of support with her drinking problem in the aftermath of her divorce. As a result of this, she thought of Duarte as the man of her life. Even though unable to tie the knot again, buying an apartment together had been an easy decision.

Maria continues to attend AA meetings regularly because she wants to avoid slipping into former habits. It has been hard for her to accept the fact that she has had a drinking problem. Everybody drinks in this country, she had said back then. That Duarte had accompanied her to the first AA sessions had been a crucial step in her recovery.

Maria now faces a more fundamental battle than alcohol. Duarte's former wife and daughter have a joint court case to evict Maria and force the sale of the apartment she shared with Duarte. She currently lives there by herself. If she had cash available, she would solve the issue by buying Duarte's share.

With Patricia behind the Audi's wheel heading north on the highway, Maria says:

"My court case is scheduled to resume again next September. The judge wants to hear more witnesses. You recall you are one of them, right?"

"How could I forget that I'm going to testify on your behalf?" Patricia replies, always a positive influence in Maria's life.

"Duarte's ex-wife and daughter, a grown woman, almost twenty-five, want to eat me alive."

"They're horrible people." Patricia has heard about the women many times before. "But you must stop looking at Goya's *Black Paintings*; they put ghastly thoughts in your mind."

"Those two cannibals are ready to devour me." After a pause she says, "When I read the accusation I could only think of getting a drink, a long, soothing one."

"You mustn't!" Patricia almost shouts.

"Duarte's ex-wife and daughter have sworn that Duarte visited their home frequently. And a bunch of witnesses can vouch for them."

"It's normal to stop by even when a marriage ends. Duarte wanted to see his daughter."

"That's not what they say. Brígida says Duarte came by because he wanted to be with her, his ex-wife. And Anabela could have seen her father somewhere else."

"She can say whatever she wants, the question is whether it's true or not."

"Precisely, and I'm hysterical with suspicions. Why did Duarte hide the fact that he visited Brígida and his daughter so often?"

"If he did, he hid it to spare your feelings."

"Sometimes I feel on the verge of madness."

"You must stop looking at Goya's paintings, remove them from your purse. Calm is essential for your success."

"Anabela immediately wants her father's fifty percent share of the apartment. As an alternative, she insists I pay her rent equivalent to that amount."

"She must be disturbed by her father's sudden death."

"What about me?" Maria utters a bizarre cry and continues. "Just imagine if the judge grants Brígida what she wants and recognizes that Duarte had, after the divorce, 'the perfect common-law marriage with her.'"

"Horrifying circumstances for you, I agree."

As they approach a service station of the "new Portugal"—meaning convenient and impersonal—Maria suggests stopping for a coffee.

"What was I supposed to do when Duarte entered the ER in a coma, except call Anabela?" Maria says as they sit down at a table.

"You did the right thing!"

"See where it got me. From then on Anabela and Brígida stationed themselves at Duarte's side at all times." Tears flood Maria's eyes now. "And they prevented me from ever seeing him again."

"Life isn't always fair," Patricia says, placing a tender hand on her friend's arm.

"I asked the doctors," Maria continues amid tears. "But since Duarte was in a coma, only his daughter could see him. And she demanded her mother at her side. My status of companion wasn't recognized."

"Such violence imposed on you."

"Anabela acted like an exorcist. She said that her father didn't want to see me!"

"I wasn't aware people could talk in a coma." Patricia smiles wryly.

Maria doesn't acknowledge Patricia's irony and says, "Anabela told me that if I entered her father's room, she would call the police."

"Jeez! Why didn't you kick her ass?"

"I felt cornered."

"It was bad luck I was traveling and couldn't be at your side." Patricia doesn't want to say that during her calls from abroad, Maria didn't seem entirely sober. "You could have threatened Anabela. After all her mother sells steroids illegally. She gets them for her pharmacy and sells them on the black market for high profit."

"What if Duarte came out of the coma—like Jesus resurrected—and she accused me of spreading lies about her?"

"Never forget the Portuguese saying, "*Aquele que poupa o seu inimigo, às mãos lhe vem a morrer*. He who spares his enemy will surely die at his hands." Patricia is concerned about her friend's frame of mind. "At least you would have kissed Duarte goodbye." Then trying to brighten up the conversation, she says playfully, "Now you'll have to wait for eternity!"

"It's my fault," Maria complains. "Duarte proposed, but I didn't want to marry him."

"You did the right thing. Duarte was a nice person but unpredictable. And he was as vain as they come." Patricia glances at her watch and smiles at her friend, "How about we get going? I'm dying to see Abrantes again."

Back in the car, they reach the town in less than two hours. Patricia heads to the castle and parks near the fortress; she wants to enjoy the beauty of the ancient stone wall. From there, the two friends stroll in the public garden. Patricia has visited the area countless times en route with her family, but she wants to give it a quick glimpse again.

The garden has a small pond with two or three miniature bridges that lead to tiny houses located at its center. The houses still shelter ducks and swans as they did when Patricia was a child. The scenery is dreamy: playful, sensuous, and charming. The garden is a bit unruly in the typical Portuguese manner. The flowerbeds, a mixture of marigolds, poppies, and tulips, are so small that they seem more fitting for the decoration of the windowsills of a dollhouse rather than a public garden. A mixture of lavender and raspberry scents perfumes the air.

After the visit, the women head to a nearby restaurant. During the meal Patricia tells Maria, "Rosa, your housekeeper, is grotesque. Thinking of her bothers me. As I told you before, it was a mistake to hire her."

"You're right, but Duarte insisted on her working for us when we moved in together. Rosa had worked for him and Brígida for many years, and she worked for him during the time he lived alone. She had even worked for Duarte's mother-in-law. You know how it is in this country: servants might be employed by one family their entire lives. They are patronized and they patronize back. Rosa knew how to iron Duarte's shirts, cook his favorite dishes, and polish his shoes. You know I'm lazy!"

"Rosa should never have entered your home. She worked for Anabela and Brígida at the same time as she worked for you. It was inevitable, with time, that she would become a go-between."

"Duarte always got what he wanted from me. And Rosa seemed an easy solution," Maria replies.

"The man lived for bodybuilding, to cultivate his image!" Patricia wants Maria to see things for what they were.

"Duarte enjoyed looking good. As you know he went to the gym every day." And then out comes the secret. "Did you know that he used women's face moisturizer and waxed his chest?

"How can a demi-God die so quickly?" Patricia was still astounded at Duarte's sudden death.

"I wonder if the steroids killed him," Maria replies. "I've told you before, he bought them from his ex-wife. Then, to complement his fat income, he sold them to his friends."

"Not so honest of him," Patricia interjects.

"Brígida's pharmacy makes quite a profit on the illegal sale of steroids alone," Maria continues.

"See how you could have denounced her when she didn't let you see Duarte?" Patricia reasons for effect.

"Well, as a matter of fact, I also sold them," Maria had never told her friend this detail. "The money came in handy when my oldest was studying in Paris. I was involved with organized crime!"

"Another mistake," states Patricia sternly.

"I wonder what Rosa will testify in court," Maria says after a pause.

"We don't have to wait long," exclaims Patricia. "I find her shady, irrational."

When dessert was served—a mixture of eggs, almonds and cinnamon that the waiter said a nearby monastery had been making for centuries—Maria asks, "Changing subjects, how is your mother?"

"She's thrilled about António wanting his wedding at the family house and has placed Josefa, our old housekeeper, in charge of arrangements."

"I bet," Maria says.

"Can't wait to see Josefa; I love the woman to pieces."

"I still recall your story about Josefa with you on her lap and the two of you looking at the crackling fire in the kitchen's gigantic chimney."

"It's one of my best recollections, us enjoying the fire together," Patricia adds.

"That must be why you place such commitment, so much blaze, in everything you do." The image matches perfectly her friend's character.

"I will never forget the logs burning under our three-legged iron pots and pans when I was a child. The legs of the utensils made the cooking slow, preventing the food from burning."

"Your description is so comforting."

"Josefa is utterly ethical, and she never liked priests or masses," Patricia says. "She moved in with us as an adolescent and her salary supported her invalid mother."

"Remember when Josefa grounded you, but she ended up crying more than you did?"

"She wants me to be a role model to everybody, like a torch, a flame."

"And you are!"

"Josefa taught me to have principles."

"What would she say of my situation?" Maria asks. "I'm divorced, a mother, and I shared a bed with a man without wanting to marry him."

"For sure she wouldn't be as condemning as Anabela and Brígida," Patricia says, once again trying to cheer up Maria.

As soon as they pay the bill, the two women are back on the road expecting to reach Patricia's estate in a couple of hours. The family's manor house has an ivy-covered façade with several balconies on the second floor adorned by iron railings that rusted long ago. Pot-bellied flowerpots burst with red and white geraniums from the bars, creating a bright, cheerful contrast. Old-fashioned lace curtains cover the windows. Each side of the house offers stone benches with large armrests for relaxing. An iron bell exhibiting the patina of time flanks the main entrance. Upon arrival, Patricia's mother answers the doorbell and greets the women with visible pleasure.

After two hours of conversation during dinner, the women's eyes are closing. A bedroom has been prepared in advance and the two friends head there to spend the night.

Once in bed, Maria can't resist one last rumination: "Do you think it's possible that I find out in court that Duarte and Brígida were involved in a relationship? That Duarte was sleeping with both of us at the same time?"

"I never knew steroids increased sexual prowess!" Patricia jokes once again.

"Don't make fun!" Maria is exasperated at the comment. "I'm scared of the court's possible findings."

"My testimony alone will be worth ten of the other side's witnesses!"

"It's essential that my attorney proves my common-law marriage with Duarte. Otherwise I cannot enjoy the five years the law gives me to remain in the apartment without paying Anabela."

"Your attorney is experienced, I trust her. Moreover, she has a reputation for winning difficult cases."

"Both Brígida and I will be using the same argument. She says the common-law marriage was with her, that Duarte and she became really close after their divorce!"

"Brígida is evil. But don't forget that she has to prove that she also maintained a domestic relationship with him."

"What if she manages to do it?" Maria is tossing and turning in her bed. "What if Duarte was leading a double life that I have only just discovered?"

"You did often complain about Duarte getting home late." Patricia says, careful not to alarm Maria. "Besides, I think that Rosa's testimony will be crucial."

Maria asks Patricia earnestly now, "Do you think the woman is as heartless as some of Goya's individuals?"

"Unfortunately, I do. And we know where her loyalties stand."

"She's so treacherous. She let Anabela into our apartment one of the afternoons I was at the hospital trying to see Duarte."

"That's unbelievable!"

"After she let Anabela in, it was easy for Anabela to search the living-room drawers. I'll never know what she took, but I did find an empty drawer. I suspect her mother ordered the visit."

"Those two are witches."

"I fired Rosa the next day, but it was a day too late."

"For sure, she is the most dangerous witness against you."

"Let's see whom the judge believes. I must produce evidence that it was me, not Brígida, that had a common-law marriage with Duarte."

"Hard to take, really," Patricia acquiesces.

"Brígida kept Duarte's family name after the divorce. She also took care of his real-estate dealings. She's already presented all the supporting documents in court."

"She's eager to prove her relationship with him."

"A romantic relationship, that is, not only a domestic or a business one." Maria doesn't want Patricia to miss the detail.

"Well, my dear, let's go to sleep now. You're under such pressure. I must confess I feel you're on the right track, you haven't started drinking heavily again."

"I've managed with the friendship of people like you."

"Brígida masquerades as a human being, most terrifying." Patricia gets up from her bed to embrace her friend goodnight.

"At the end of this struggle there might be nothing left for me, not even one good memory of Duarte." Maria smiles sadly when saying this. "This is why some of Goya's bizarre faces are so comforting to me."

The next morning after breakfast Patricia spends time alone with Josefa, and the two walk around the farm talking intimately.

Later, sitting by the side of an old mill, Josefa makes the usual recommendations before Patricia's departure: the need to uphold one's values, to maintain ethical positions at all times, and to pursue ideals for the common good.

Back in Oporto, Patricia and Maria agree the long weekend has been fulfilling.

With September comes the trial in Oporto's Family and Juvenile Court, the same building that handles marital and children's cases. Maria looks her best, the way Duarte always liked her. But she is anxious. Both of her daughters are to testify. After greeting her attorney and her witnesses at the court's entrance, the group heads to a small amphitheater inside. The disputing parties sit on opposite sides of the room. Rosa is next to Brígida and Anabela, a threesome that looks like an unruly mob. Rosa's large round face and cavernous eyes give her the appearance of a worn-out peasant.

As soon as the judge calls the court to order, the registrar presses a button to record the testimonies.

Maria is the first witness to testify. She feels vulnerable, but she wants to show her relationship with Duarte was solid.

With the intention of clarifying a few points regarding Maria Sacadura and Duarte Rebelo's relationship, the judge begins to ask delicate questions.

"Did you sleep and engage in sexual relations regularly with Duarte Rebelo?" he asks in a polite voice.

"Yes," Maria answers simply.

"Did Duarte Rebelo have all his meals at home?" the judge proceeds.

"Not all," answers Maria. "Several times a week only."

"But often and repeatedly?"

"Yes."

"Were you aware that Duarte Rebelo had regular meals at his ex-wife's home?"

"No, I wasn't." Maria adds in a clear tone that she wasn't in the habit of questioning her partner.

Afterward the judge questions Maria's two daughters and they confirm that Duarte and her mother had shared the apartment where she now lives alone.

Maria's attorney tries to demonstrate the common-law relationship between her client and Duarte. She asks similar questions of different witnesses. Can they testify to a continuous companionship between Maria and Duarte? Did Maria and Duarte share a home? Do they know, by chance, if Maria and Duarte shared the same bed? Did Maria and Duarte spend their holidays together?

Maria's attorney calls Rosa to the stand now. The record indicates that Rosa is an illiterate single mother of two teenage boys. She has been employed by Brígida and her mother, at various addresses, her entire life.

Maria's attorney has a hard time interrogating Rosa. The housekeeper either pleads lack of memory or mixes up dates. For the common-law bond to be legal, the court must ascertain that the relationship existed for at least two years and one day. But Rosa can't seem to give a straight answer to establish cohabitation between Maria and Duarte.

Rosa manages to incorporate in her statements the gratitude she had for the deceased. She admired how the former boss, a mature man, took such good care of himself. He dressed elegantly, exercised every day on the bicycle he had at home. When living alone, he always enjoyed the company of fine ladies. Many times, she had found women's underwear in his bedroom. She simply washed it and placed it back in the master bedroom. Working for Duarte was much more entertaining than watching television.

A few times the judge interrupts Rosa to remind her to stick to the questions. She stops, seemingly well schooled on how to behave in court.

When asked if she received the same salary in both households, Rosa answers affirmatively at first. But when the amount of weekly hours is specified for both households, it is obvious that Rosa earned much more working at Brígida's. To explain the difference, which, apparently, she hadn't noticed, Rose explains that Brígida always paid her according to her financial needs. Some months she received much more than her standard salary.

As to the inquiry whether Rosa had seen her boss in the months prior to his untimely death, the answer is clear. She saw him at both homes: she saw him with Ms. Maria and she saw him with Ms. Brígida.

"Did Ms. Maria Sacadura and Mr. Duarte Rebelo share the same bed?" asks Maria's attorney.

Rosa states she can't say. What she can say—because God has given her two eyes!—is that Maria and Duarte didn't get along well. They fought constantly.

"What did Mr. Duarte Rebelo and Ms. Maria Sacadura argue about?" the attorney inquires.

Rosa replies that she worked in their apartment on Saturdays and that they were frequently at home. She states the two fought over the way Maria dressed. Her boss liked to see Maria in skirts, but she insisted on wearing jeans. Duarte didn't like cleavage, but Maria displayed hers. Duarte was often in the living room reading the newspaper while Maria spoke on the phone with her friends, and calls were expensive.

Moreover, the boss visited the cellar often and got upset over the number of bottles of liquor that were disappearing week after week. Duarte, Rosa stated, was getting exasperated with Maria's recurring drinking habit.

Rosa adds that she has seen Maria, on several occasions, under the influence of alcohol.

After pausing to collect her thoughts, Rosa proceeds with her version of events. She had also seen Duarte at Brígida's home on innumerous occasions prior to his death. She worked there every weekday, and he came by regularly.

"Did Mr. Duarte Rebelo have dinner with Ms. Brígida Rebelo?"

Rosa can't answer; she left before dinner started. But she always cooked and laid table settings for three people: Ms. Brígida, Mr. Rebelo and Anabela.

Upon arrival, the boss sat on his favorite couch and acted as if at home. He poured himself a whisky, took off his shoes and switched on the television. When she left at day's end, he always said goodbye in the same manner: *See you tomorrow!*

Maria's attorney turns at present to the relationship between Rosa and Brígida. Rosa's answers clearly demonstrate her allegiance. Ms. Brígida Rebelo has been a constant friend, someone who has helped her in the past and at present. She has promised to get a job for Rosa's older son, who had a serious motorcycle accident a couple of years ago. She also managed to enroll the younger in Casa Pia, a fine public institution for boys, in her opinion. Rosa can never forget such generosity.

There is yet another reason for Rosa's affection for Ms. Brígida. She saw—again with these two eyes that God had given her!—that the lady lived with a broken heart, as if stabbed straight through. She knew this was related to the divorce.

"Who paid your salary at each work place?" the attorney wants to know.

Brígida paid her monthly; she took the money from her wallet and gave it to her when she came home from the pharmacy. At Maria's home, sometimes it was Maria, sometimes it was Duarte who paid her. Maybe without realizing it, Rosa was confirming the existence of a common domestic economy between Maria and Duarte.

"Why had Rosa allowed Ms. Anabela to enter Ms. Maria Sacadura's apartment when she wasn't present and Mr. Duarte Rebelo was in a coma in the hospital?"

"What was wrong with that?" Rosa answers as quickly as lightning. Ms. Anabela was not a stranger; she had known her since she was a baby. It was normal for her to enter her dad's apartment. She had asked for coffee as soon as she arrived and Rosa had gone to the kitchen to prepare it.

"Are you aware that Ms. Anabela emptied a living-room drawer?" The attorney is slipping into areas she hopes Rosa hasn't been instructed how to answer.

"No. And those issues don't concern me, I'm only a maid doing my job." Rosa proceeds to state that Anabela seemed very disturbed that day. She had brought the coffee on a tray with a small lace napkin to cheer Anabela up.

Rosa then states that she wants the court to know a detail. Ms. Maria Sacadura fired her without "just cause" soon after her boss's death. Feeling entitled to financial compensation, she has already filed a complaint with the maids' union.

The next witness to be called to the stand is Brígida Rebelo. For years Brígida has dyed her hair a platinum blond, which gives her a cheap *femme fatale* look. She has rather large breasts and wears a green skirt with a sleeveless black top. Maria's attorney asks Duarte's ex-wife if she can describe the type of relationship she had with her ex-husband after their divorce. Her reply is that the couple had maintained a relationship despite living separately. The relationship had multiple components, she continues. The couple's assets remained in common after the divorce; she handled his real estate holdings and received the monthly rents with his consent; she also paid his annual taxes.

More relevant than the business connection, Brígida adds theatrically, was the tenderness the couple had exchanged since being divorced. It was based on the high esteem and the love they felt for each other. This explains why her ex-husband visited so often.

"What was the purpose of your ex-husband's visits to your home?" asks Maria's attorney.

"Our home, not my home; excuse me for correcting you," asserts Brígida. She adds further, "Duarte visited me because he enjoyed my company," replied Brígida. And she continues, "Our bond was never as strong as during the weeks preceding my beloved passing away."

Like a hydrogen bomb spreading through the amphitheater, Brígida brings in one more factor to her case, "As the documents I filled with the court show, Duarte Rebelo's common-law marriage was to me, his ex-wife." And as if filled with newfound strength she continues, "The relationship of my dear Duarte with Maria was ending. The fact that they bought an apartment together meant nothing. Duarte always placed his money in real estate ventures. The loving relationship, the daily, domestic one, was with me."

When stating this, Brígida looks Maria's attorney straight in the eyes, and repeats loudly, "With me, his ex-wife!"

The judge feels presently the need to intervene and says, "Ms. Brígida, can you specify what leads you to such a statement?"

"The intimate nature of our relationship," she replies. "The reason my ex-husband didn't stay the entire night at home with me was that he felt sick during the last months of his life. He feared doctors terribly. He also was disillusioned with Maria and her repeated alcohol abuse. This deterred him from leaving her abruptly; he felt sorry for her."

The judge turns now his eyes from Brígida to Maria, trying to scrutinize her reaction. Brígida adds loudly as if to interrupt the judge's thoughts, "After my Duarte left our home and we got divorced, our communication improved tremendously. May God rest his soul in peace. Our second honeymoon was on-going until his death."

"Did you and your ex-husband have intercourse?" The judge feels it the proper moment to ask the intimate question.

"Of course we did." Brígida proudly provides details. "I can't explain it, the secrecy of our relationship after the divorce brought on a new spice, something that turned us on."

The judge takes a few minutes to jot down something but Brígida doesn't stop here. She faces her daughter and declares in a high-pitched voice, "My daughter knows these facts well. Your Honor, I ask you to question her," Brígida tells the judge as if he were a puppet in her hands.

Then Brígida confronts her daughter, seemingly incredulous, across the room. She says grimly, "Why are you looking at me with that creepy half-open mouth?"

When the judge admonishes Brígida that she can't address her daughter without his consent, the woman tosses back her blond hair in a scathing manner. She seems an airplane ready to take off. As she raises both elbows in a dramatic gesture intended to let in some fresh air through her armpits, it becomes evident to all that she never shaved under her arms.

The judge momentarily turns to Anabela and sees the young woman as pale as alabaster. Glancing at his watch, he orders a fifteen-minute recess. He leaves the room in a solemn, hurried, and unfriendly manner. Several people from both parties leave the amphitheater during the interval, but Patricia stays glued to her seat. She doesn't think the legal procedures are heading in Maria's favor. If Brígida is speaking the truth, then Duarte hadn't died as she had thought, from successive overdoses of steroids. He could have died from an unprecedented level of stress: the lie beneath his two romantic involvements.

When the judge returns, Patricia sees his bewildered expression, as if he is unable to find a thread that gives the case a final resolution. He then orders Maria's attorney to continue questioning the witnesses. Patricia shows inordinate composure when called to the stand. She speaks of the many weekends with Maria and Duarte, shows photos she had saved. She states that Duarte and Maria got along well; Duarte often brought her flowers.

The judge's final interpellation that day in the amphitheatre is unusual but not inconceivable due to the mystery involving the lives under scrutiny.

Can Patricia say anything, as insignificant as it might seem, that might shed further light on the relationship between Maria and Duarte?

Patricia takes a deep breath and asks the judge if she can address Anabela from the stand. The prosecution doesn't object. It is as if Patricia can taste an old fire in her mouth, the same that Josefa had crackling in the ancient kitchen while holding her as a child on her lap. Those had been defining moments; she had always returned to them for solace when searching for a reality she felt unable to define.

Choosing her words carefully, Patricia addresses Brígida's daughter by her first name, "Anabela, you must be careful of the influence your mother has over you. You may get married and have a daughter one day. I imagine that you don't want a daughter of yours to be mistreated."

Keeping composed in order to protect her childhood friend, Patricia adds, "Anabela, don't damage another woman on purpose. I know you are pressured by your mother, but your behavior may backfire." After pausing, Patricia continues, "I want you to realize that I was a friend of your father for many years."

Patricia stops herself for a few seconds and then says in a deliberate tone of voice, "You are Duarte's only child. As you see, your mother is damaging your father's reputation. Please, please, do not let that happen. Be principled. We are in a court of law and you'll soon testify under oath. Please tell the judge the truth about your parents' relationship. Your mother is lying, isn't she?"

Anabela stares indomitably at Patricia. With a stiff body and cold eyes, Anabela looks as solid as rock, as immovable as the rock in *Fantastic Vision* so dear to Maria in Goya's *Black Paintings.*

La Belle

In her old age, Leonor has frequent memories of her mother. The lady's name was Georgette. But her closest friends used the *petit-nom,* La Belle, imagining this nickname designated who she really was.

When Leonor was a child, everybody talked about her mother's beauty, which was indeed stunning. An oil portrait in the Lisbon house once took the spotlight above the fireplace, overpowering the entire living room. At that time La Belle was already thirty-four years old, and Leonor—who was the last of her three children—had not yet been born. La Belle had been immortalized in her prime. Back then, in the 1950s, people said that a woman reached her peak shortly before marriage, when all about her was still expectant, like a kindling fire.

The assertion is far from accurate. La Belle had been portrayed through the eyes of a professional artist who possessed a Rubenesque flair. As the owner of a famous studio in the stylish area of Chiado in central Lisbon, the painter had signed his French surname in the lower right corner. Leonor's mother appeared in partial profile from the waist up. She was wearing a stylish black cocktail outfit that displayed the elegance of the times. Black was then as fashionable as ever, and the fabric had light strokes of dark pink here and there. Although her entire figure was not visible, Georgette was obviously wearing a matching skirt. At that time, high-society women who had money and status didn't wear pant-suits. The picture's background was ethereal with a creamy quality that rendered it eerie and foreboding.

A spectacular diamond pendant, a present from Georgette's husband—Leonor's father—adorned La Belle's ensemble. In those days Lisbon women enjoyed wearing opulent ornaments. They used to display them either at home, on festive occasions, or at ceremonies such as baptisms, weddings, and funerals of people of equal social standing. As an adult, Leonor often reflected on this lavish piece of jewelry her mother possessed. Sometimes she even entertained the idea of one day owning it. However, it wasn't an ornament she herself wanted to wear; it was the craftsmanship she admired. Moreover, the gift preserved a moment of family affection. The jewel had an arched upper frame and cascading filaments; it glittered from afar. Leonor always recalled that when her mother wore this jewel, the several pendants stirred lightly at the top of her bosom, a suggestive medallion of her most secret triumphs.

An ostentatious fur stole dominated the painting. It emerged from La Belle's right shoulder and draped her delicate body to the left. Leonor never saw anything similar for sale in the Lisbon of her own times, though she wasn't paying attention to such luxuries. The stole framed Georgette's figure below the jewel, seemingly ready to embrace her.

La Belle's face mirrored the portrait's overall ambience, her veiled smile reminiscent of La Gioconda. Ironically, Leonor had thought back then, enigmatic smiles were the most revealing. The nose exhibited a perfect profile and sustained the curve outlined by the stole. The brown curl emerging from Georgette's forehead was tasteful. If it were not, Leonor would have been the first to disapprove of it. Of the siblings—she had older twin sisters—she was always the most outspoken. The curl was small, the color a shimmering light brown. Leonor's mother didn't need to dye her hair; her natural hair color was, for a while, one of the favorites in the L'Oreal catalog. There was something luxurious about the way it surrounded her face like a soft gilded frame.

A key detail in the painting was a hat with feathers. Were there many or was it just one? Leonor can't remember now. The feathers were proportionate to the hat. They stood up like the glorious tiara of a queen belonging to European aristocracy. Leonor wishes she could recall the kind of feathers, but with age her memory plays disconcerting tricks. It is as if her eyes, barely able to see the passing of days, prevent the discerning of old memories. Even so, she still recalls that the feathers' contours suggested ostriches or peacocks haughtily announcing: I'm here.

The many elements described might suggest a sense of grandiosity in the portrait. Nothing would be further from the truth. The portrait above the fireplace, feathers and diamonds notwithstanding, remained contained, subtle, refined. The ominous background, however, inadvertently suggested family issues that were about to emerge in due time, as if the aristocratic figure with the sphinxlike smile was getting ready to close in on her prey.

In her adolescence, Leonor had ripped La Belle's painting from the wall and slammed it to the floor. Then she stomped on it, trampling it beyond repair. A family heirloom was gone forever, and Leonor was punished for its annihilation. For three months, she was forced to stay at home, grounded for the entire summer vacation.

Leonor's rage stemmed from her long-simmering friction with her mother dating back to the beginning of her existence. Leonor had assumed that outer and inner beauty were interconnected. But, as strange as it may seem, she could still visualize her mother's irritation when breastfeeding her. Georgette was incapable of taking care of herself, let alone her three daughters. As an adult, Leonor wondered whether human beings were ultimately responsible for their own deeds. And the predictable "yes" answer from the psychologist left Leonor breathless; it wasn't the reply she was ready to accept. In order to ease her own pain, Leonor was genuinely looking for an excuse for her mother's behavior.

Georgette died a centenarian. Since then, Leonor's waking thought has been this: how can someone so utterly wicked be rewarded with the privilege of a life spanning several generations? Portugal has a saying, *a maldade dá saúde*—iniquity brings health.

How can this be true?

Leonor had witnessed often how La Belle's character created quagmires that resulted in far-reaching insecurities for the family. Rarely in attendance at family meals at the dining-room table, La Belle had a tray brought to her shaded bedroom. She was unable to start and complete a task, to have a set schedule. Leonor despised her mother's mental disorganization, her incapacity to walk a straight line. The burden of being the daughter of such a mother felt too heavy, the price paid too high.

Undoubtedly La Belle was a clinical case, probably manic-depressive, something that should have been properly addressed. A woman who screamed for hours on end, sometimes all day long, should have been institutionalized.

La Belle had indeed been confined to a mental health clinic on several occasions in a place exclusively for women located on the outskirts of Lisbon. The institution had several floors, and the upper windows, Leonor recalls, had bars resembling a prison. Perhaps the management feared that patients would succeed in throwing themselves out. A visitor would enter the facility through the side door of a low building located on a narrow, winding road. The door accessed a spacious entrance hall. Leonor still remembers that the floors had a geometrical design made of black, white, and brown tiles. As if to bless the visitors, on the left wall stood the portrait of the founder of the religious order. His hair was white, and he held a black crucifix on both hands.

Leonor's maternal grandmother saved the family from despair by moving into their home during those difficult times. Her hair was white with shades of grayish blue caught up in a refined chignon that left visible her neck. She was distinguished-looking, a proper lady who dressed with matching purses and shoes according to season. The graceful woman sat across from her son-in-law for dinners at their polished table, and Leonor enjoyed sitting next to her grandma. Leonor's twin sisters, who were very close, sometimes invited friends to share the meal. Leonor's father, an admirer of the opposite sex, always said his mother-in-law resembled Ava Gardner; an assertion that made her beam with sheer delight.

Leonor's father, a solicitous businessman, had trouble dealing with the emotional chaos around him. His life outside the home was clearly more satisfying than inside, his work providing a major escape. And because civil courts could not dissolve Catholic marriages at that time, Georgette's husband felt entitled to flirt with whomever he pleased. Spanish women were in high demand in the Lisbon nightclubs; *salero,* the Spanish word for spicy, fun entertainment, characterized such diversions.

This trait of female beauty in the family genes is the reason Leonor has, to this day, many mirrors in her own house. She follows the tradition of her spectacular ancestors on her mother's side, women who enjoyed seeing their image reflected, duplicated. Though not a great beauty herself, Leonor nevertheless enjoyed preserving the family's custom. She recalls the large mirrors at her grandma's house were used during carnival time when Leonor and her sisters dressed in costumes and made funny faces before departing for the Lisbon coliseum in search of a national prize for best outfit. Typically, the twins dressed identically as fairies, or witches, or fish vendors with elongated *cabazes*, baskets, on their heads. Leonor enjoyed dressing as a clown. During those festivities, she believed it was possible to shed her skin and belong to a brand-new family.

Leonor is still able to recall her winter weekends at the family house in Cascais, a small port and beach thirty minutes from Lisbon. Cascais was very picturesque with fishing boats dazzling in the winter sunlight, the docks crowded with fishermen wearing dark woolen caps and flannel plaid shirts. The boats bore sentimental names like *Luar de Janeiro,* Moonlight in January, *Estrela do Norte,* North Star, *or Senhora da Guia,* Leading Lady.

While the twins usually played together outdoors, Leonor enjoyed a favorite porcelain doll in the house. Regrettably, the toys were located in a damp wing of the house where the strong north wind blew in from the sea. The playroom smelled of mold, and the floor was made of *laje,* flagstones artistically arranged to form large squares. Several wooden tables lined the room, and piled on the tables were dirty, smelly toys from many generations. There were bits and pieces of every conceivable plaything: dolls of various sizes and shapes, little cradles, an assortment of doll houses, diverse miniature furniture, a battery-operated radio, tin boxes containing pencils and coloring books, even a knight's sword. Spiderwebs and dust covered everything.

The porcelain doll, Lili, attracted and repelled Leonor. The doll had experienced many hands and had long since lost all her clothing. Her hair needed combing and she had only one eye, blue glass and as cold as the room. Leonor always thought that with a bit of searching she might find Lili's remaining eye. She would have to look in the tiny drawers of a miniature dresser or dig under the spiderwebs. But did she want her fingers to touch that sticky mess? While Leonor cringed at the prospect of searching for the doll's eye in such a messy place, she nevertheless longed to have a doll without glaring flaws. For Leonor believed that Lili herself felt handicapped. Only finding the second eye and inserting it into Lili's ocular globe would make the doll whole again, give her a new life.

One morning, Leonor's play with Lili consumed her. She turned the doll's naked little body back and forth, upside down. For sure, Lili needed the same nurturing her grandma gave Leonor when she stayed at the house. Suddenly, someone called her name for lunch and, surprised at the yell, Leonor made an abrupt gesture; at once, Lili dropped from her hands and fell on the flagstone.

Lili was now on the floor shattered in a thousand pieces. The single blue eye had rolled quickly into a corner of the room. And from that ugly corner, Lili's glass eye looked Leonor straight in the eyes.

Leonor stood still, silent, vulnerable. Torn apart inside, identifying with the eye, she saw it as the image of herself. A child can, she thought, have intuitions of this nature. And from that moment on Leonor started seeing Georgette as the doll's cold, glaring eye—observant, taking mental notes. Even today, so many years later, Leonor can still hear her own sobs from the past.

La Belle's love of playing cards dated back many years; life was apparently a deck she handled with pleasure. She loved manipulating her three daughters' affection against each other. The twins were lucky for they didn't easily succumb to her mother's preying game; they formed a united front and had each other for reassurance. When they got married and Georgette acquired sons-in-law, the new relatives were added to her deck. To better rule, Georgette destroyed the relationships between her children whenever possible. She adored, for instance, giving a present to one sibling when another had expressed a longing for it. This kind of manipulation required skill, clever maneuvering, and continuous broadening of her predatory sphere of influence. It demanded, also, an ever-widening scope as, over time, it involved the next generation, the grandchildren.

The recurring pivotal conflicts were money, the family's estate, various pieces of art, even old photos. There was always a lawyer at hand, someone in need of extra cash whose wise opinions backed her up; someone willing to tell Georgette that her intentions were good, her ideas the best. Hence, the family lived like a carousel at carnival time with all members on board for the ride.

Over the course of her life, Leonor had known people who knew how to attack at precisely the right moment, like lions on the lurk. Georgette, however, threw her darts in all directions, aimlessly. She knew that by shuffling the cards of affection she could best exercise her power. Scheming was as vital to her as the air she breathed.

It is easy for Leonor to recall how card-playing served La Belle's ends. Well dressed at charity events, she dazzled everyone with clothing, jewelry, and good manners. She literally enjoyed serving the deck; she played with fervor, excelled at devising strategies, and visualized herself as the winner of choice. During the summer she organized Canasta championships at one of Cascais's secluded club; she enjoyed distributing the players by table, allotting scorebooks, and handing out fancy pens. At home, the twins had a superb strategy for handling their mother's card playing. When they played together, they let her win, the best way to make their progenitor shine with supremacy.

Georgette's behavior with her three daughters was rather different. The twins always used their closeness as a front to tolerate their mother, as if mothering each other. When they became women on their own—studied, held jobs, married and became mothers—the dethroned queen was just that, a dethroned queen. They were both as beautiful as La Belle, as resplendent as the destroyed portrait. For Leonor it was different. She wasn't as beautiful and, as the youngest, she rejected outright the assigned role of knight-errant, her mother's caretaker. Leonor was, thus, the easiest target. Isolated from her siblings she managed, somehow, to refuse the prescribed role. But for her mother this was a form of rebellion well worth punishing; she couldn't tolerate the idea that Leonor had a will of her own.

La Belle needed maturity to accept Leonor's wish for independence. But maturity implied empathy, and empathy required a love that she didn't possess.

Leonor grew up aware of La Belle's two faces: one that only the family knew, imperceptible to outsiders, and another, the socialite who dazzled her friends. It is possible this was the reason Georgette enjoyed inviting friends to her home. Fausta, a member of a prominent family, came by for tea with her daughters on Saturday afternoons. She imposed a sense of respect. Fausta was a heavy lady, wore German high-heel shoes, and showed off noisy jewelry. Her hair was rather short with little waves framing her round, fat face. Leonor's fuzzy remembrance still conjures up Fausta always dressed in purple, like a cardinal in the Papal Curia in Rome. Her oldest daughter willingly ate scrambled eggs mixed with cow's brains, a disgusting recipe but considered invigorating for children, if bribed by Fausta with a promise to visit La Belle within 24 hours. While the ladies chatted in the living room, the girls enjoyed rumble-tumble and played Monopoly or Go Fish.

Once in a while neighborhood *freiras,* nuns who sold elaborate pieces of embroidery, visited La Belle to have tea while showing their merchandise. The family used the diminutive, endearing form for nuns, *freirinhas.* Georgette loved the distraction of the visits, and Leonor knew her mother would dress up for the occasion. Those were splendid afternoons. La Belle sat in the living room and had a maid serve tea, tiny elaborate round cakes, and homemade cookies. The Renaissance-style silver tea set, freshly polished the night before, came off the shelf to impress them. The *freirinhas* always showed up in pairs and stayed for hours displaying the workmanship of their novitiates. As they unloaded their wares from two small, thin, brown suitcases, Leonor was captivated by the way they carefully unfolded the delicate works. It was magical to watch piece after piece of exquisite embroidery and lacework woven onto linen and chambray emerge from the battered luggage. La Belle liked to buy "*napperons,*" miniature tablecloths adorned with bobbin lace to display at half-moon tables, or small bags in cross-stitch to hold napkins at the dinner table, or fine cotton stocking holders threaded with blue or pink garland ribbons. Conversation was marked by religious subjects in which allusions to Santa Maria Goretti, a model of virtue, abounded.

La Belle's favorite discussion with the nuns was her husband's infidelities with the spicy Spanish women. Leonor loved sitting on the thick brocade sofa to admire the silver tea set and listen in on racy family details. She wondered about the kind of erotic, sexual images the *freirinhas* formed in their minds. They exhibited only restraint and forbearance because a child was present. As the *freirinhas'* scent was so utterly different from her mother's, Leonor wondered if they washed with pumice stones and the blue soap used to clean kitchen tiles. In Leonor's maze of faraway recollections, the nun's garments are worth recalling. They wore high, white helmets that left only the face showing; not even a strand of hair escaped the seal around the head. From the neck emerged a white starched and carefully ironed bib; from its middle hung a crucifix. The black outfit had pleated skirts that touched the floor. A brown rope belt with intertwined knots, possibly to remind sinners of Jesus' ordeal on the cross, completed their attire.

The afternoon concluded by all reciting the rosary, the children as well as the maid who had served the tea all gathered around the chaste women. La Belle finished the occasion with a special prayer to Our Lady of Fátima, asking that her strayed husband convert to Catholicism. With a father who was agnostic, this would have been a miracle which Leonor thought, against all the odds, might take place the following day.

The rosary, the home shrine, the daily prayers didn't slacken, however, Georgette's thirst for scheming. As conductor of an insane orchestra, La Belle held fast to her machinations, and her need to divide and conquer remained supreme. La Belle's constant shuffling of her cards, so to speak, explains why she changed her will so many times.

Georgette's mental health was a secret that the family carried with distress. The sisters, whether they expressed it or not, feared their mother's anger. After the father died, no one wanted to ignite a battle by confining La Belle to the mental institution again. Perhaps such a measure wasn't even necessary any more. The worst conflicts belonged to the past since the girls had grown up and the widow La Belle had fewer obligations now.

Leonor still remembers the mental health clinic Georgette stayed in for several months at a time. Visitors came in through an enormous glass door that separated the entrance hall from a long tunnel-like corridor. A soft monastic light entered the area through large circular windows. Large white benches stood on each side of the room. Between the benches sat round enameled vases, also white.

Families came to this space and sat on the benches waiting to speak with patients. Leonor can still summon up the first visit she and her sisters made to her mother with the Ava Gardner grandmother. La Belle appeared in the corridor looking as white as the benches where her daughters were waiting. She was as white as the ray of light coming through the windows. The shine in her eyes was gone: they were empty, absent, locked in time. Her complexion was plain, ghostly white. Any comparison to the magnificent living room portrait was mere coincidence.

There was white, white, and white everywhere. Georgette's smile had turned white, too.

Silence ruled the place as if people were phantoms. Relatives and patients whispered, as if unable to speak in a normal tone of voice. La Belle's lack of interest in her own family was visible. In that first visit, not even the twins could capture her attention.

As a result of electroshock treatments and sleeping medication, La Belle had seemed destroyed. Nevertheless, the family could still be considered fortunate. The only Nobel Prize holder for Medicine in Portugal, Egas Moniz, came to this institution frequently—a separate building held male patients—to perform lobotomies. Women, however, were spared the new treatment.

During those periods when *La Belle* was committed, life at home was quiet and rather nice. Long ago, weren't respectable ladies locked up in a back room at the end of narrow, dark corridors to embroider their entire lives away? And weren't some queens, deemed insane by royal families, held in cages and fed only bread and water? Weren't some nuns placed in underground convent cells and deprived of sunshine until death came to the rescue?

Leonor now wondered why La Belle had not shared a similar fate.

While searching for the answer while her mother was still alive, Leonor one day decided that enough was enough. Her mother had refused to come to her aid when she was going through life-altering circumstances. On the spot, Leonor resolved to desert Georgette. She did it as the soldier who, in order to protect his own sanity, walks away from the battlefield. That same day, Leonor saw Lili's blue glass eye staring at her again: protect yourself, there is still time. Leonor couldn't stand to have a mother whose grasping moves only amplified her own unsettling circumstances.

An ominous dream brought her clarity, like a laser beam penetrating crystal. In the dream Leonor faced a wall made of the heaviest conceivable metal, dark but slightly shiny. Was it steel? Iron? Zinc? Whatever it was, it seemed an insurmountable barrier, impossible for a mere human to cross. Filled with anguish, Leonor wanted to know what was on the other side; what, truly, separated her from her own self.

The dream provided the answer. Leonor suddenly realized that by the side of the wall stood a small, delicate, golden hammer. The finding was transformative. The wall now appeared like a vertical chess game with squares placed on top of each other. Leonor noticed a significant detail. In the top row of the upper part of the wall some squares were already missing. They were now piled up on the floor next to the wall.

A fabulous allegoric event unfolded. Leonor realized that if she could cross the wall her anguish would vanish. She only needed to use the delicate golden hammer and knock down the squares, a block at a time. The path was open, feasible.

Leonor started her journey with that dream. She had found the key to the most secret palace, the most hidden of gardens. A titanic task awaited her but the first steps had been taken. Delicacy, not force, was the journey's escort. And one day, not really recalling how long it took, Leonor had knocked down the entire wall.

The leap was astonishing. As with any little girl, Leonor had loved her mother. As a teenager, even in her rebellious stage, she had sought La Belle's support. As an adult, she had believed she could, perhaps, help her, a woman clearly in distress. Leonor had always tried to keep her own sanity, to downplay her mother's games. However, there had only been room for La Belle's frailty, and Leonor had been prevented from expressing her own spirit.

Aging and feeling engulfed in the mist that announces the eve of death, Leonor still wants to solve some remaining enigmas. Is she drifting away, roaming the long-lost corridors of memories? If she walks to her mother's mirror in her entrance hall, what will she see? Or if she looks in her grandma's mirror in her own living room, what will it convey?

And what if in a moment of sudden audacity, Leonor were to walk to the mirror in her own bedroom? The one she bought herself and has used her entire life? As tarnished as it is, could it still give her news of herself, something that she still needs to unfold or decipher? How will Leonor feel if beyond her reflection she happens to perceive Georgette approaching her in the mirror's background? And how will she respond if her mother displays that peculiar white smile, the same one she saw as a child at the mental health clinic?

Will Leonor be able to respond with compassion now? Or will she reveal the same old detachment?

Khristen

A Dutch woman, Khristen is like a Barbie. And she isn't the real thing because she's from the Netherlands, not America. But for a Portuguese man that doesn't make any difference; nationality isn't the issue. Khristen is a foreigner in Portugal: a foreign woman, that's what matters. Not only is she blonde, she's also tall and slim. Men here have a hard time resisting her physique. Khristen is the vision of a Hollywood star, a paragon of beauty. She has wheat-colored hair, blue eyes and fair skin, and a well-rounded colossal bosom like Anita Ekberg's. Men are dazzled as if by car headlights when looking at her breasts.

Khristen decided to remain in Portugal after her divorce to a Portuguese man. She had met her former husband in Amsterdam while he was on several months' training for his computer company. Zé was handsome, taller than Khristen, with dark skin and black eyes suggesting depth. Smitten, Khristen decided to move with him to Portugal when his training was over. Despite being madly in love, she said she wouldn't share an apartment with him unless married. She wasn't moving just to enjoy a new experience in a foreign country. Khristen, a Catholic, believed in the covenant of marriage as an established way to share life. When Zé replied with a wedding proposal, she willingly accepted. Zé knew that he would never build a future for himself in a foreign country. He enjoyed immensely the sunshine and the sandy beaches in Oeiras, just outside of Lisbon, where he lived.

Khristen loved Amsterdam, but she was open-minded about leaving because of catastrophic events in the preceding months.

Unfortunately, she had been walking down the street at the exact moment that the filmmaker Theo van Gogh was assassinated by an extremist Muslim while pedaling his bike to work. The episode had shocked her profoundly and the damage to her spirit lingered. Like the other witnesses, Khristen had heard and seen the shots, the blasts to Theo's head as if directed at her own. She had also witnessed the cuts on Van Gogh's throat that had left him virtually beheaded. Van Gogh had been murdered in broad daylight and, in a macabre gesture, the assassin's five-page message pinned to his chest with a kitchen knife. During the long police interrogations that Khristen and other spectators were subjected to after the murder, Khristen suffered from post-traumatic shock and needed psychological help. She didn't have anorexia, lack of appetite or similar symptoms. She would just vomit every time she had to testify about the murder. Unable to stop retching, she had been hospitalized several times and put on IV fluids to restore her health.

Khristen inherited her Catholicism from her family, who were originally from the Rhine region in Western Germany. So it was no surprise that she was pleased to move to a country predominantly of her own faith. The couple married in a church and Khristen, dressed in white, made a beautiful bride. Most of her family traveled from Amsterdam for the big event. Khristen was more than ready to fulfill her dream of marrying a dashing Latino, who would one day become the father of her children.

A page turned. Khristen had left behind the traumatic days of police cross-examinations and hospital beds. A new, promising future had begun in an exotic southern European locale, a place where people seemed most welcoming. Although Khristen had a double major in history and psychology, she had pursued a career in the same field as her husband, computers. She knew that finding a job in Portugal wouldn't be easy, but she had savings that would last for more than two years. Khristen didn't want to be financially dependent on her husband, even though Zé made enough money for both of them to create a new life together. She pondered therefore the idea of opening a computer store, a place to sell and repair tech ware and give clients technical assistance.

Zé felt elated, looking forward to a married life and thrilled with his stunning blonde trophy wife. Optimistically, he assumed Khristen's traumatic episodes had been left behind in the Netherlands.

By the end of the first year of marriage, Khristen had learned

Portuguese rather well. She was fascinated with the history of the country. The mixture of races coming from former Portuguese colonies like Angola, Mozambique or the Cape Verde Islands had shaped a diverse population. Fortunately, the country was peaceful with no signs of terrorist activity. She came up with fun ideas. Once the couple spent a week visiting all the country's Moorish castles. A lover of history, Khristen relished seeing the variety of architectural and cultural influences throughout Portugal and learning how peoples lived centuries ago. The North African Moors, Arabs who had established themselves in Portugal, were especially intriguing to her.

The couple moved into Zé's apartment in Oeiras; the place actually belonged to his parents. Consequently, Khristen was spared all the complications of furnishing a new home in an unfamiliar setting. However, she did upgrade the kitchen's furnishings, in particular adding a table for meals. She also bought several different sized woks, similar to the ones she had in Amsterdam. One of her first changes was to move Zé's set of knives from the counter into the cabinets; she didn't like to look at them while sipping tea at the table. She sought to avoid certain devastating memories.

Khristen and Zé enjoyed a busy social life with his colleagues and family. They went to upscale restaurants and danced in many of Lisbon's chic nightspots. The couple's sex life was getting better and better, a source of satisfaction to both partners. Zé was a bit jealous, sometimes even uncomfortable, with the stares his wife's beauty provoked everywhere they turned. His friends, however, advised him to get used to the harsh facts of life.

While finding a job was Khristen's biggest concern, other problems started gradually to emerge. Some had already been discussed while the couple was dating, but they were now acquiring new dimensions. Khristen wanted to have children immediately; Zé, on the other hand, was completely opposed to the idea so early after marriage. Then, Kristen wanted to buy a piece of land to build a little country house by the Atlantic Ocean; Zé thought the idea stupid, the apartment his parents had provided was perfectly fine. Finally, Khristen wanted to hire a weekly cleaner; Zé wanted his mother, now retired, to do the work and save them money.

After much soul-searching, Khristen decided that it was time to open her dream computer shop. She craved more independence, and she knew she could handle the workload and still have time for family and friends. Eventually she settled in a small store in Oeiras's major shopping mall. Her natural beauty, sophisticated simplicity, and good manners soon attracted a steady clientele. Zé wasn't too happy with the public exposure of his gorgeous wife. He realized, nevertheless, that there was no way he could convince Khristen to remain at home. A modern young woman, she was determined to have her own life, fulfilling work, and a steady income. It wasn't long before Khristen's talent for business led to the need for an assistant.

One day, Zé asked her to take a look at one of his personal computers. Something was wrong with his downloaded files and he needed them manually scanned for viruses. It was a time-consuming process, but, having hired Rute, Khristen now had free time to help her husband. As she started the scan, Khristen noticed that a default file kept popping up on the screen. The folder was entitled Almada, the name of a small town on the other side of the Tejo River, south of Lisbon.

Without a second thought, Khristen opened the file.

To her surprise, she discovered a string of emails between her husband and a woman who invariably ended her emails by signing, "Your childhood sweetheart, Yolanda." There were email messages between the two almost every day since Khristen's marriage. It was a sexual dialogue with intimate body parts named, erotic scents recalled, and imaginary orgies evoked. The exchange revealed that this woman was also married and without children. Yolanda described in graphic detail her sexual life with her husband, and Zé did the same.

After reading the emails, Khristen abruptly shut down the computer. She felt dizzy, as if the floor beneath her feet was going to vanish. She now faced a huge dilemma: should she forget what she had seen? Should she delete the file? Or should she confront Zé? The file exposed not only her husband's intimacy but also her own.

Deep in thought, Khristen decided it was imperative to discuss the matter with Zé that same evening. The afternoon dragged on while she considered various possible approaches. During those hours, she noticed with dismay that her symptoms from the past had returned. Her nausea was constant, clearly the result of deep stress. Khristen's marital situation demanded prompt clarification. Once this was done, she felt confident that the signs of distress would disappear. Khristen decided she would take the time to print the Almada file just in case Zé had the nerve to deny its existence. In the end, she had amassed some fifty pages.

Zé had had a grueling day. When he arrived home that evening, he went straight to the kitchen and cut himself a few slices of bread. Khristen approached him and said in a serious tone of voice that they needed to talk. Zé was surprised by her manner and joined her in the living room shortly afterward.

"While cleaning up your computer today—remember you asked me to help you out—I found something very disturbing," Khristen introduced the topic.

"What?" Zé replied. But as soon as he asked the question his expression changed. He knew immediately what Khristen was addressing.

"I found the Almada file," Khristen replied evenly.

"I'm so sorry. I forgot to delete it before I gave you the computer," Zé said with a concerned expression.

"Psychologists say that people do things in certain ways when they want to get caught. I feel terribly hurt and confused," Khristen continued somberly. Then she asked, "What's going on between you and Yolanda?"

"Absolutely nothing," Zé answered as if everything was normal. He made a motion to move closer to Khristen, but she stopped him.

"That's not possible," Khristen said.

"I recognize the file contains unsavory stuff but nothing that I can't explain."

"Go on," Khristen replied.

"There's zilch you should worry about. Yolanda doesn't place our marriage at risk." After a pause, Zé added, "I realize I owe you an explanation; the correspondence can be easily misunderstood."

"Please continue," Khristen said.

"Those emails are a tease with the purpose of sexual stimulation; they're fantasies with no consequences. Yolanda or I bring to each partner at night the sexy content of the emails exchanged during the day."

"What?" Khristen was astounded.

"Aren't our nights of love getting better and better?" Zé asked. "Well, yes, and that's the reason!" Then he proudly admitted to liking that kind of email contact. "What's wrong with it?" he further inquired.

"I feel insulted you are sharing my intimacy with someone else," Khristen said, on the verge of tears.

"You must understand that passion can easily die if left unattended," Zé said. He then paused to add, "The emails with Yolanda are a sort of love's reverie."

"Did you ever sleep with Yolanda?" Khristen's question demanded a clear-cut answer.

"Never," Zé answered promptly, conclusively.

Khristen interrupted Zé's denial by rushing off to the kitchen; her stomach had turned upside down. At the door, she tried to reach the garbage can, but unfortunately she saw the bread knife Zé had left on the counter. Repulsed, she threw up on the floor the little she had eaten during the day.

A sleepless night ensued for Khristen in the small guest room, a night in which Zé did not get much sleep either. It was evident that his wife had not accepted his reasoning.

The following morning after a shower and no breakfast, Khristen said goodbye to Zé as if heading off to work. But, armed with the printed emails, she drove instead to Almada. Heading south, she crossed the Ponte Vinte Cinco de Abril, the Lisbon central bridge, while noting that the magnificent scenery never lost its impact no matter what time of day. From the emails she knew where Yolanda worked, and she intended to verify Zé's story by comparing it to Yolanda's. A photo in one of the emails, showing a woman in a rather compromising sexual position, made the face identifiable. With time to spare before Yolanda's lunch break, Khristen toured Almada, a major Arabic military stronghold conquered by the crusaders during the twelfth century. A few minutes before noon she was standing at the front door of Yolanda's office. She was sure Zé's friend would show up.

And she did. Yolanda couldn't believe it when she heard her name coming from the mouth of the stunning blonde by the door. She knew immediately it was Khristen. When Khristen stated they needed to talk, Yolanda quickly discerned the reason.

"Tell me, Yolanda, is it better to speak in English or Portuguese?" Khristen asked Yolanda when they started to walk. "I can speak both, even though my Portuguese isn't perfect. I want to make sure you understand the questions I need to ask you."

"Portuguese is easier for me," Yolanda said, subdued.

"Can we go to a restaurant and sit down?" Khristen asked.

Yolanda led the way to a snack-bar close by and the two women settled at a table by the corner. The place was filled with smoke, something Khristen hated. Once settled, Yolanda ordered a *bitoque*, a steak with a fried egg, along with French fries. Khristen ordered only tea.

Searching her handbag, Khristen took out the printed emails without disclosing to Yolanda that she had discussed them with

Zé. Then, showing them to Yolanda, she asked sternly, "May I ask what's this all about?"

Yolanda looked at her plate and remained silent.

"You'd better answer me." Khristen wasn't mincing her words. "If you don't, I'm going from here to show them to your husband. I know where to find him."

Yolanda turned red.

"It'll be easy to throw these pages at your husband's face." Khristen didn't feel any commiseration for Yolanda. "So either you talk, or I'll do just that."

"Those emails might seem compromising to you, but they're innocuous," Yolanda started.

"What?" Khristen flipped the pages and read aloud, at random, one of them.

"I state again, they're totally innocuous," Yolanda replied.

"Yolanda, I want the truth. I didn't come here to get excuses or apologies." As she said this Khristen coughed, smoke clogging her throat.

"It's that simple. Zé and I went to school together, we're close." Yolanda felt like she was on the crest of a wave. "The emails might appear odd to someone from a different culture. But they're only entertainment."

"Portugal is a Catholic country." Kristen read another email aloud. "And you call this entertainment?"

"Yes!" Yolanda replied disarmingly. "You see, mimicking sex through an email with a third party is incredibly satisfying. It's as if there are three people together in bed at night, instead of two. If Zé asked me to perform what Bill Clinton's intern became famous for at the White House, I'll be able to satisfy my husband doubly."

And Yolanda continued, "With Zé's emails I warm up all day, so to speak, until the time comes to have fun with my husband."

Khristen listened in silence, as if stuck.

"These practices are common everywhere; or wherever the Internet is part of society." Yolanda asked Khristen directly now, "I know you're a computer expert. Haven't these vast possibilities reached you?"

Khristen felt embarrassed by the question. And her expression gave Yolanda a chance to continue.

"Here's something I advise you to take advantage of. Share your sexual fantasies with someone willing to add new dimensions."

Khristen was dumbfounded as Yolanda persisted. "People in the Netherlands don't do this? Or it's you who refuses such practices?"

"I'm just not interested," Khristen said.

"This could explain why I read in *Correio da Manhã* that your country has a high suicide rate." Yolanda seemed content with her own conclusion.

Khristen turned her eyes to Yolanda's *bitoque* without replying. Yolanda was cutting her last piece of meat and looking at the sharp knife distressed Khristen further. She felt a sting of pain in her abdomen; it was as if Yolanda was cutting her own flesh.

"I swear that I never slept with Zé. I love my husband, I'm faithful to him." Yolanda added that she had married in the Catholic Church. Those emails, she concluded, were only an exciting long-distance game.

Khristen was happy to leave the smoky snack bar soon afterward. She had gotten what she wanted: the facts. She felt in awe; Yolanda's story matched Zé's. Khristen left Almada with one certainty: Yolanda and Zé hadn't gone to bed together.

While driving back to Oeiras, Khristen had plenty of time to think over matters. Catholicism in Portugal was totally hypocritical. People used sacraments like marriage to fulfill their own depraved ends. She didn't feel, however, that she was living in a male-dominated culture. Something unusual was at work here. Yolanda seemed as sexually free as Zé; women here didn't appear subjugated to the wills of men. Moreover, the Internet had certainly opened extraordinary doors. Khristen thought how the world described in *Submission, Part One*—the film about Muslim women directed by Theo van Gogh, the film for which he had paid with his life—was so utterly different.

Flabbergasted by events, Khristen decided that, disappointingly, her marriage was over. What Zé and Yolanda pursued together with such relish was repugnant, disgusting, and inconceivable to her. They were perverts. She felt an ache that started at the tip of her toes, took over her entire digestive system, and ended at the crown of her head. She was not the sole inspiration for the love her husband expressed so tenderly in their physical encounters. Regrettably, it was shared with someone invisible, yet present.

Khristen felt used to the core.

From the road Khristen called Rute to say that she was going straight home. Something was wrong with her stomach; she needed to rest and make an appointment to see a doctor. Khristen also called her parents and informed them of her irreversible decision to divorce Zé. Afraid of alarming them, she mentioned only briefly that she was suffering abdominal pains and once again had trouble retaining food. Concerned, her mother advised her to return to Amsterdam and see her old doctor immediately.

A divorce followed, with Zé forced to sign the papers against his will. He protested that Khristen was overreacting. She contended by saying she didn't leave Amsterdam to abide by sexual practices against her own faith. The issue wasn't relevant to religion, Zé said. There were many forms of Catholicism.

Afterward, Kristen moved temporarily to Rute's apartment. Despite her mother's opinion, she saw no reason to leave sunny Portugal. She still dreamed of buying a piece of land by the sea. Moreover, her computer business was doing fine. Also, she knew that plenty of male clients longed to take her out. She was confident that, with time, she would be able to rebuild her life with another Portuguese man. Someone decent, someone who shared her values.

Months passed and one day, as Khristen expected, a client invited her out for dinner. Sérgio was almost forty, divorced, and a senior manager in a foreign company located in Cascais. Khristen accepted the invitation and decided to wear a dress that showed her alluring bosom.

Khristen and Sérgio had dinner in a restaurant by the so-called *marginal*, the road by the Tejo River that connects Lisbon to Cascais. From their table, the couple could watch the moon's shimmering reflection on the water. The conversation flew easily under the paradisiacal scenery. Sérgio bragged about being a lady's man and hoped Khristen wouldn't be offended by the remark. This was a confession he dared to make only to a foreigner. He added that he intended to settle down and soon rebuild his life. He confessed that he found Khristen stunning and was thrilled that she was a professional woman able to stand on her own feet.

Sérgio spoke openly about his past. Perhaps he was enchanted by Khristen's blonde hair and fair skin; or maybe it was the turquoise décolleté exposing her black bra. When Khristen asked why his marriage had failed, Sérgio went on to divulge that a few months after his wedding he wasn't sexually attracted to his wife anymore. The situation left him confused since passion had been so heated during courtship. Perhaps, Sérgio mused, he had trouble with the lifelong aspect of marriage. He noted that while the majority of his friends had controlling mothers, he himself had experienced the reverse. His mother had abandoned him as a child and, as a result, he feared long-lasting commitments. Love was an enigma, a puzzle he didn't know how to resolve. He could stand only at its door; if he tried to enter he might fall into an abyss.

Sérgio described having a whirlwind of different women, so that he couldn't be abandoned. Khristen appeared mystified. Sérgio added that if Khristen thought that having many women friends was the same as having none, she was mistaken. With variety, there was always someone available to go to the movies late at night, dancing well past midnight, or ready to hop on a plane to accompany him while he traveled on business.

After a brief silence, Khristen asked Sérgio if, since his divorce, any woman had tried to be the only one, the companion for good and bad times. Khristen played with her soup spoon; she still had difficulty holding solid foods despite being under the care of a Lisbon physician. Sérgio stopped eating his lemon-sauced shrimp and revealed that, in fact, there had been someone who had wished to fill that role. But after a few months of living together, he had broken off the relationship because he wasn't in love. Sérgio knew, however, that Elisabete still longed for him. She was a secretary in his company, intellectually limited and without ambition.

Khristen insisted on paying half of the bill, and Sérgio didn't try to lure her to bed that night. The couple parted with Sérgio stating that Khristen had a precious gift of knowing how to listen. Khristen was surprised a Portuguese man had spoken so openly about his private life on a first date.

While undressing at home, Khristen thought of Sérgio as a tormented soul, besieged by unresolved issues. Her knowledge of psychology certainly dictated that she approach him with a modicum of skepticism. He lived in myriad worlds, a no man's land where each woman wanted to be his favorite. Naturally this state of affairs didn't bring any long-lasting satisfaction. When a woman tried to get close to Sérgio, he distanced himself. Khristen was sure that Sérgio, deep down, lacked self-esteem.

And what about the women who were part of his harem, so to speak? Sérgio didn't seem able to protect, respect, or nurture them. Surely, these women had jobs and their own financial independence. Sérgio could, thus, sleep with as many as he wanted and as often as he wanted while remaining irresponsible and free. This didn't seem fair to Khristen. If Sérgio was unable to develop an enduring attachment, these women undoubtedly became vulnerable over time.

Khristen and Sérgio enjoyed each other's company and had quite a few things in common to talk about, professionally and otherwise. Their relationship, however, developed slowly. Khristen had rented a new apartment in the back of the shopping mall where her store was located. Since Sérgio also lived in Oeiras, a few blocks away, the two could easily get together on weekends. Sérgio felt free to practice his English, a language Khristen knew very well. The couple's favorite place to walk was Parque dos Poetas, a garden with numerous sculptures of Portuguese poets.

There wasn't a single weekend, however, in which the couple didn't meet a female friend of Sérgio's. Following the Portuguese manner, the women planted a kiss on his cheek. Worst of all for Khristen was Sérgio's mobile phone that didn't stop ringing. Usually, he didn't answer, a way to avoid explaining who was on the line. If Khristen asked, Sérgio muted the phone. Nevertheless, if they were holding hands or hugging she could feel the phone vibrating. Text messaging was also constant, but Khristen couldn't control those. One Saturday when Sérgio had received messages throughout the day, he told Khristen that one of his friends had had a motorcycle accident. Khristen suspected this might be a lie, but she didn't have the inclination to constantly question him.

A few months into the relationship, the couple decided to take a trip to Casablanca to shop, relax, and visit the Moroccan desert. They had a great time exploring the exotic country; Khristen was happy that Sérgio had left his mobile phone at home. Soon after their return, as if to give her confidence, Sérgio gave Khristen his apartment keys. Khristen followed suit and gave him hers. Thus, the couple got used to sleeping together—sometimes at his place, sometimes at hers. At night, they chatted for long hours in bed. They continued speaking in English as if Sérgio needed a disguise and the foreign language offered it. Over time, Sérgio revealed more and more painful events about his mother's abandonment. After yet another disclosure, Khristen seized her chance to complain that Sérgio wasn't paying enough attention to her feelings. She told him she didn't want to see knives on the kitchen counter and he was careless about this. She was tired of reminding him.

One evening, Sérgio disclosed to Khristen that one of his former girlfriends, Elisabete, the secretary he had dated soon after divorcing, was after him again. Sérgio asserted that his newfound openness had to do with Khristen's empathy, her capacity for dialogue. He added that Elisabete had been, in fact, the true reason for his divorce. Sérgio explained that when the relationship with Elisabete ended they had remained friends. However, she still had expectations of him. Lately the situation was getting more complicated because Elisabete suspected there was someone else in Sérgio's life.

As a matter of fact, the last time he went to Berlin for a few days, she had boarded, unannounced, the same plane. No, they hadn't slept together, but it hadn't been easy to get rid of her.

Sérgio was beginning to feel cornered. His office had a glass wall and if he didn't let Elisabete in, she placed her mouth against the glass and stayed frozen in that pose. Only the red lipstick remained when she finally left. A colleague had noticed him cleaning up the mess and asked questions. During the Berlin trip, Elisabete had confessed that her love was unconditional. Recently, she seemed possessed, crazed. She asserted that she wanted him back—for life.

"Under the circumstances, where do you think the two of us are heading?" Khristen asked Sérgio, her voice expressing concern.

"I talk to you more freely than to anybody else," Sérgio's replied.

"Why is that?" Khristen wanted details.

"I feel you're tolerant, understanding, and mature."

There was a sense of urgency in Khristen's voice when she proceeded, "Was lovemaking to Elisabete gratifying in the past?"

"Yes, it was," Sérgio said.

"I must ask a second time. Did you make love to Elisabete during your trip to Berlin?" As if needing to hear the answer unequivocally, Khristen took in her hand the multicolored ceramic lamp Sérgio had bought in the souk near the old medina wall in Casablanca. She brought it as close as she could to Sérgio's face.

"No, I didn't. I told you already once," Sérgio said, briskly removing the beautiful artifact away from his face.

"Have you made love recently to any other of your friends?"

"No, I haven't." Sérgio's face seemed hidden in shadow now.

"So how do you explain our recent sexual distance?" Khristen still held the Moroccan lamp in her hand.

"I've been feeling quite a bit of pressure lately," Sérgio asserted, seemingly lost.

That night, Khristen and Sérgio fell asleep in each other's arms, face to face. Khristen wanted Sérgio to know that she was there for him.

The following Sunday the couple went for another stroll in Parque dos Poetas. In the car, Sérgio received a text message and answered it as soon as they parked. While the pair strolled the paths, they happened to pass a young, rather disheveled, woman. The stranger gave Khristen an intent look and then let her gaze go to Sérgio with an almost imperceptible wink.

Khristen pretended she didn't see it. Instead she led Sérgio to one of her favorite sculptures, the bust of Florbela Espanca, a renowned Portuguese poet. She had read Espanca's poems; they told the story of unrequited love.

Back home, Khristen couldn't let go of the young woman's wink at Sérgio. Eating his dinner while Khristen sipped her soup, Sérgio acknowledged that the unkempt woman at the park was Elisabete. But Khristen shouldn't be alarmed. Elisabete had promised that if he gave her the opportunity to see Khristen once, she would stop the texting. Sérgio had accepted the pact willingly. Unfortunately, however, Elisabete had not kept her side of the deal. The wink hadn't been agreed upon.

Khristen immediately spotted a glimpse of complicity between the friends. And she wished to lay the cards straight on the table, no hidden agenda. Did Sérgio wish to get involved with Elisabete again? Sérgio's reply was an indisputable no. He added that life wasn't a straight line; things often needed sorting out. Khristen replied that she knew that too well. In fact, as much as she wanted, her health wasn't getting any better.

When the conversation ended, Sérgio got up from the table and kissed Khristen on the lips. Later that night, he brought up the possibility of Khristen moving in permanently. There was no point in her paying rent by herself, he said, were she willing to share his apartment. Khristen saw the proposal as a further attempt to appease her qualms. It wasn't her Catholic faith, though, that stopped her this time around. She needed time to reflect, to dwell on many issues.

For Khristen had an uncanny sense that, despite Sérgio's words, he might be meeting Elisabete outside of work. That peculiar wink! The moment of truth came the following morning after another sleepless night. When Sérgio went into the shower, Khristen grabbed his mobile phone and started to read the text messages. The first was from Elisabete and asked if he had enjoyed the movie; as a man, she said, he might have a different response than she. Wasn't the brunette much more appealing than the blonde? And weren't those lace panties the brunette wore simply exquisite?

Khristen felt lost in a maze; clearly Elisabeth and Sérgio were watching pornographic movies together. Were they, also, having sex? Khristen needed answers. Was she in the midst of another insane adventure? Who were these men—Zé and Sérgio—to whom she had given her love?

In distress Khristen planned a strategy; she must be brave at least for one day more. Hurriedly, she said goodbye to Sérgio for the day as if nothing was wrong. After lunch, she text messaged him saying she was planning to do highlights to her hair at the Oeiras shopping mall in the evening. She suggested a quick dinner at his place and then he could pick her up a couple of hours later. She didn't like to return home, at that hour, alone.

Khristen walked to the shopping mall after a brief meal at Sérgio's apartment. He had cut himself a thick slice of pizza, a favorite of his, while she drank tea. Khristen had a suspicion that in about twenty minutes she would find Elisabete if she returned to Sérgio's place. Deliberately, she walked back as slowly as she could. Easy. Easy. Easy, she kept whispering to herself. She started to breathe in slowly, deeply. Up and down. Slowly. Down and up. Slowly. She must allow the designated time to go by; she couldn't act hastily. The hands on her watch seemed to have stopped in time. But she knew that if she rushed she might lose her chance.

When she reached Sérgio's front door, she opened it hastily.

Right at the entrance Khristen heard noise inside; it was followed by the sound of muffled voices. Something crashed into the floor; it must have been the Casablanca multicolored lamp. Should she run to the kitchen and grab the sharp filet knife Sérgio had used to cut his pizza? Or should she run straight to the living room to catch Sérgio and Elisabete naked on the couch, the love pose interrupted?

Black on White

That's the title for a composition my teacher assigned our class to write during the holidays. I need to prepare; the project isn't going to be easy. In Portuguese, *Black on White* refers to the capacity to speak one's mind. The term has been coined in our language, and we always say *Preto no Branco,* never the other way round, *Branco no Preto*. No gray zone exists between black and white, no middle ground. Things are either one or the other.

I'm fourteen years old, and I was born in Lisbon. My mom read a book by Alice Miller called *The Drama of the Gifted Child,* and says I'm gifted. As soon as I could lay my hands on it, I also read the book. It deals with the tragedy of understanding more, earlier, than most children the same age.

I'm an only child and my parents are both professionals. My mom is a medical doctor, my dad an architect. We live in the center of town and I attend a public school. I want to be a medical doctor like my mom.

I'm white. My family has blue blood, and I have pedigree names on both sides. We inherited a noble title when our ancestors served our monarchy in the former Portuguese colonies. One of my relatives was Viceroy in Goa, India.

I've traveled a lot throughout Europe with my parents. I dislike the new fad in our country of many Portuguese visiting our former colonies, places like Brazil, Cape Verde, or Mozambique. I've not been to any of these territories—and I'm not interested. I enjoy traveling to cities that have cultural activities, places like Madrid, Paris, or London. My dad is very good at explaining art when we visit museums abroad.

Poetry is a passion of mine. I enjoy reading and writing it. Keywords are abundant in the genre and I'm proud to say I can name the most relevant in our language. They are: sea, vessel, voyage, discovery, quest, east, love, empire, longing, god, destiny, and overcast.

These keywords have filled my imagination since I was born. In order to grasp a crucial matter at the core of our Portuguese identity, I say the following: when founded in the twelfth century, our territory was small and inhospitable; we went on VOYAGES, by SEA in VESSELS; our QUEST was to go EAST and DISCOVER with LOVE; as a result we built an EMPIRE; this brought us to faraway lands and left us LONGING; we fulfilled our DESTINY with the help of GOD; the Atlantic ocean was often OVERCAST by fog, the concept making an ever-lasting imprint on the nation's psyche.

These words and their interconnections define our distinctiveness, our way of being. I enjoy using all of them, but I have a favorite one. In Portuguese we use words like *encoberto* (misty), *nublado* (clouded), and *dúbio* (dubious) to translate overcast. I best enjoy playing with these notions.

In history class we learned that the moment of truth in five centuries of Portuguese history was the Carnation Revolution that took place on April 25, 1974. Back then Portugal was the poorest country of Western Europe and had its longest empire. A group of army officers, aware that the Portuguese had lost wars being fought overseas to preserve the empire, thought it wise to end them. The revolution succeeded without bloodshed, and the brave officers were greeted like heroes in the streets of Lisbon.

My mom read a lot about the decolonization process that took place shortly after this historical moment. The Portuguese handed the colonial territories to those—the African Liberation groups—who had been fighting for independence for decades. Civil war followed in many of the new African nations. East Timor (in Portugal we call it simply Timor) in Southeast Asia was taken by Indonesia. At the time, people who wanted to leave and had the means fled the emerging countries and arrived in Portugal with virtually nothing except for the clothing on their backs.

My grandma, my mom, and I were talking about this issue the other day. My grandma still remembers seeing a map of Portugal everywhere in Lisbon in the early seventies that symbolized the ideology of the *Estado Novo*, our government. The map showed the world as a globe and displayed the territories that belonged to our country: the archipelagos of Azores and Madeira in the North Atlantic; Angola, Guinea-Bissau, and the two archipelagos—S. Tomé and Principe and the Cape Verde Islands to the South—in West Africa; Mozambique in East Africa; and lastly, East Timor and Macau in Asia. Because we were the last Europeans to de-colonize, our imperialism was responsible for considerable international isolation.

The Portuguese Empire spread over four continents. The overseas territories were huge when compared to the size of the mainland. Just to give a scale of the empire's dimension, continental Portugal has approximately 92,080 square kilometers (excluding the Azores and Madeira); Angola was more than fourteen times the size of Portugal; Mozambique was seven and a half times the size of Portugal. We started the empire in 1415 by conquering next-door Ceuta in North Africa; we arrived in India in 1498 and in Brazil in 1500. A new book says the Portuguese were the first to enter the shores of Australia. Vasco da Gama's voyage to India took place from 1497 to 1499. Macau, currently part of mainland China, was 6,833 miles away from Portugal. The Portuguese arrived in China in 1513 and in Japan in 1542-43. It took us close to 120 years to reach Japan.

To let go of such extensive territories took a considerable amount of time. History books show how Brazil seceding in 1822 was a major blow to the Portuguese. Later and elsewhere, political boundaries were established to grant the Portuguese legal sovereignty of the lands occupied. The task involved major negotiations and conflict with other European colonial powers. In the decades following the 1885 Berlin conference, Portugal's borders were set. The empire embraced vast territories, which roughly coincided with those my grandma referred to on the 1970s map and far surpassed the former coastal enclaves where the Portuguese had traditionally engaged in commerce and trading.

As my grandma explained, the map exhibited in the streets of Lisbon showed the worldwide dimension of the territories under

Portuguese rule. Since we were at war on several fronts of the empire, the government exhibited the map to increase the population's pride in Portuguese history. It was a way to acknowledge that we weren't ready to let go.

I'm only establishing the facts to write my composition. I've heard my mom and dad arguing about these matters since I can remember. The 25th of April is a national holiday; I enjoy staying home from school, reading my poetry, and doing my homework. Besides this holiday—and the distinguished career of my ancestor in India forever praised in family circles—my connection to the former Portuguese colonies is zilch.

My dad says we are an old nation, and the Portuguese inaugurated the era of "discoveries." According to him, the Portuguese played a key role in globalization as we know it today. He says that our huge coastline, about 586 miles, naturally brought the sea to us. This led the Portuguese, in his views, to discover "The Other." Given our Catholicism, Western knowledge, and written language, he claims we took upon ourselves the mission of civilizing "Him/Her."

My mom disagrees with my dad. She replies that "The Other" existed well before we got to those distant lands. It wasn't our "discovering" them that gave these populations either existence or identity.

My dad then adds that, in his view, the Portuguese civilizing mission was unique. We established trading posts and built fortifications on Africa's west coast in the late fifteenth century. This initiative was a universal embrace filled with enchanting moments. He cites Pero Vaz de Caminha's letter upon arrival in Brazil and describes the sense of excitement the Portuguese had upon landing on its shores in Portuguese *caravelas*. At the time, our *caravelas* were the most modern of vessels at sea.

My dad cites Gylberto Freire, the Brazilian author of *Luso-Tropicalismo,* Lusotropicalism. An anthropologist, Freire was paid by the Portuguese government to visit the colonies in the early fifties. In 1953 he wrote a book about the specificity of the Portuguese Empire. For Freire, the Portuguese are southern Europeans who, due to the Moorish conquests of Portugal and Spain in the eighth century—later designated as the Califate of the Iberian

Peninsula—adopted different lifestyles from other Europeans. In his own words, these lifestyles *prendem os sentidos*, "blend the senses." Such an attitude had a major historical consequence: due to the lack of European women in the lands conquered, the Portuguese increased the population by copulating with native women. Thus, we adopted and fully enjoyed polygamy. According to Freire, Portuguese men loved the exoticism of the Venus *fosca*—the woman of color—but, being Christians willing to expand the faith, were aware of the sin of adultery. In order "to exorcise" this behavior, Portuguese men usually treated well the women they mated with and the children they bore in faraway lands. In general, the Portuguese are darker than northern Europeans. As they were used to warmer climates, adaptation to life in the tropics was, therefore, congenial.

For my dad, the easy mingling of the Portuguese with those conquered allowed them not only to help populate the new lands but also to expand Catholicism without major obstacles.

Being gifted, I understand what my dad is saying when he quotes Freire. From here derives a theory of racial harmony that tries to establish the lack of racism in the so-called Portuguese world. According to this theory, instead of colonizing by force, the Portuguese connected to tropical peoples, cultures, and climates by affinity. They brought in new blood by reproduction. As colonizers, the Portuguese were colonized as well; they intermingled, fraternized, and interrelated with others.

As a consequence, a new civilization ensued.

Part of the interchange was, necessarily, language. Children born of local women were often adopted and educated in the Portuguese language and in Western ways. Christianized by baptism, the children learned the catechism in Portuguese and were often remembered in bequests and last wills. Sexual intercourse thus explained, at least in part, an idiosyncratic form of colonization by the Portuguese. The result was miscegenation, i.e., the racial mixing of peoples over time. Many biracial unions were blessed by the Catholic Church—starting with members of the clergy themselves who, despite their own vows of celibacy, abundantly took to the cohabitating practice.

The Portuguese exercised a form of imperialism centered in a distinctive lifestyle; a system that was neither exclusively, nor merely, based on economic advantage and/or political domination. As a consequence, the Portuguese became pluri-racial and pluri-continental.

My mom quarrels fiercely with my dad over these issues. She says that our enterprise at sea was far from noble. It's true that we went to distant lands, settled down, and reproduced. Yes, we traded in spices, fruit trees, medicinal plants, precious stones, tobacco, cereals, rubber, coffee, cocoa, sugarcane, and cotton. We disseminated a wide variety of fauna, including elephants, rhinoceros, and rare birds; and domesticated many animals. Surely, we brought in Western attitudes, our own culture, and our language. However—and my mom says the Portuguese don't like to admit this openly—a major trade was the slave trade. Keywords in our poetry miss the fundamental concept of our involvement in the dirty business.

The Portuguese participated heavily in the enterprise of transporting human cargo by sea. Stretching from the territories around the Gulf of Guinea—as far as from current Guinea-Bissau to current Equatorial Guinea—to Brazil, there was no end to the number of blacks the Portuguese dislocated from Africa. In Brazil alone, slavery accounted for the highest number of workers in cotton, sugar plantations, and gold mines.

According to my mom, we try to ignore and cover up historical facts, a clear attempt at clouding future generations.

She enjoys quoting Charles Boxer, a British historian. Boxer states that a nation that was a leader in placing men and women in chains across the Atlantic Ocean did not share the ideal of racial harmony. For Boxer, the slave trade was based on the notion of racial supremacy. Moreover, it had a clear financial goal, to increase the work force in our largest and most prosperous colony, Brazil. The slave trade brought considerable and substantial revenues to the Portuguese crown. Lisbon was, at one point, one of the most affluent, if not the most affluent, of European capitals.

In Boxer's opinion, the Portuguese clearly discriminated according to color as much or more than other colonial powers. Few blacks or *mestiços* were in positions of power in the state, the military, or the church hierarchy throughout the empire. The exceptions only confirm the rule. Moreover, there was a generalized and widespread feeling that the Portuguese born in the colonies were *portugueses de segunda,* second-class citizens. Exceptions included those considered "assimilated": those who had adopted the European lifestyle and values. In addition, the creation of secondary schools and universities was always a major deficit of our colonization.

If one wants to learn about history, my mom says, the facts are readily accessible.

My dad gets tired of my mom's arguments, and when not busy, he takes me to the movies to see a comedy, his favorite pastime. If he feels like it, he replies that Boxer was a British historian who didn't understand the Portuguese psyche. What we did, the why, the how.

These issues are currently at the center of a fierce national debate, arguments that instinctively have the power to divide instead of uniting our people. The debate is about the Portuguese language and the so-called recently devised Spelling Agreement; we use the *sigla* AO to designate the *Acordo Ortográfico.*

The remarkable poet Fernando Pessoa is now raised to the level of national hero. *Mensagem,* his only book that was published during his lifetime, in 1934, has a great nationalist/imperialist poem titled "O Quinto Império," "The Fifth Empire." Following authors such as Camões and António Vieira, Pessoa, a firm believer in the power and efficiency of myth, exhorts the Portuguese to follow suit with their historical past.

"The Fifth Empire" starts by saying how sad those are who live happily only at home; they do not dream; their end in sight is only death. Then, he adds, to be a man, to be fully human, is to be discontent; the soul needs a vision. Therefore, the earth must be the theater of a clear day, a day in which a new empire will emerge to revitalize the earth.

In translation the poem ends:
Greece, Rome, Christianity,
Europe—the four go
to where all age goes.
Who wants to live the truth
For which Don Sebastian has died?

"The Fifth Empire," according to Pessoa, is still to come. And it will be ours, it will be Portuguese. If our King Sebastian died for the quest of expanding the empire in North Africa in the battle of El-Ksar el-Kebir against the Moors in 1578, it's still not too late to pursue the dream now.

I find this exhortation utterly unconvincing. D. Sebastião is known by history books as *O Encoberto.* The best translation of *O Encoberto* might be, I think, "The Hidden One" or "The Concealed." Since the king's body was never found in El-Ksar el-Kebir, the patriotic legend is one of hope. D. Sebastião might return, alive, early one morning enveloped in fog. Then, at last, the nation's epic destiny will be accomplished. Today, as I write this, we continue to long for D. Sebastião in our collective psyche.

My dad claims that we must maintain our sense of identity and evoke the grandiosity of our past by quoting uplifting poems like "The Fifth Empire."

My mom disagrees once again. She points out that Pessoa's *Mensagem* has far better poems to describe the country's golden age of maritime supremacy. She mentions poems such as "The Stone Pillar," "The Sea Monster," or "Portuguese Sea." She gets energized by the quality of some of the descriptions: the fear of sailors at sea, the women crying in despair at the beach for the safe return of their men, the prevailing and dangerous notion that the world ended at the Cape of Storms in the southernmost tip of Africa (later renamed Cape of Good Hope because it opened the route to the Indian Ocean to the East).

My dad replies that the Portuguese nowadays need a concept that encompasses not only the present but our magnificent past as well. He gives as an example the Commonwealth of English-speaking countries that emerged from the British Empire. Similarly, he holds dear the notion of *Lusofonia,* The Lusophone Countries or The Lusophone World. This designation involves The Community of Portuguese-Speaking Countries.

I must explain.

There are currently eight countries in which the official language is Portuguese. Except for Macau, which was returned to China in 1999—the United Kingdom returned Hong Kong in 1997—all the countries that my grandma saw on the map in Lisbon in the early seventies are considered part of *Lusofonia* now.

The notion of *Lusofonia,* according to my dad, reaches far beyond the dictionary definition of "Portuguese-speaking," for it extends to countries that are historically and culturally linked to Portugal. Our politicians enjoy the notion of a strategic block operating on the basis of a common language, the Portuguese language. The block is created by countries that are rather diverse and spread over four continents. Some are rich, some are poor; some are small, some are large; and all enjoy very different degrees of social, economic, and technological development. Notwithstanding, this doesn't seem to constitute a problem for the successive Portuguese governments dealing with the topic. To overcome obstacles derived from diversity, my dad adds the keyword *love,* the affection shared between colonizer and colonized.

In my dad's view, the Lusophone World is the most efficient agent in defining our *portugalidade,* our Portuguese identity. My dad says that this block of countries has a determining reason to stick together beyond its historical past. For him, these countries must have a historical future. Many believe that Portugal can be the successful link between them and the European Union. These countries are all independent now and some, like Brazil, are emerging world economies.

To acknowledge this state of affairs, my dad mentions the example of the Community of Portuguese-Speaking Countries formed in 1996, *sigla* CPLP. An old Lisbon palace houses the CPLP headquarters and the institution has an Internet site. The site mentions the chimera of the *Instituto Internacional da Língua Portuguesa,* the International Institute for the Portuguese Language.

My mom is cynical about all this and says our politicians want our language to be the last stronghold of the lost empire, a reminder of our past grandeur. In fact, the Spelling Agreement has become a major point of controversy in Portugal in the media, the academic world, and among linguists. An endless amount of hours have been lost in the debate. Public petitions with thousands of names have been signed and sent to Parliament. My mom and some of her friends have stopped talking to each other over the issue.

The AO dates back to 1990 and has tentatively been implemented in a few CPLP countries. It stands as a clear attempt to unify the Portuguese language, a language spoken worldwide by a population of more than 250 million people. The majority of this population lives in Brazil, an economy whose Portuguese language, written and spoken, is expected to have a significant impact on the international scene in the coming decades.

Any foreigner in his or her right mind will have trouble understanding the complexities of the AO implementation. However, since the AO is now mandatory in all Portuguese schools, it affects me. For instance, should I use it in writing this composition?

My mom enjoys quoting the statement from the Pen Club, Pen Clube Português, from the meetings in Barcelona (June 2012) and Korea (September 2012). It's on the Portuguese site, in English:

The so-called "Orthographic Agreement" for the Portuguese language, signed in 1990 by the seven Portuguese-speaking countries (Portugal, Brazil, Angola, Mozambique, Guinea-Bissau, San Tome and Principe, Cape Verde), has not yet been ratified by all, due to the recognition of basic, structural and specific problems and critical aspects of all kinds.

To speak an "essential unity of Portuguese language," with the same orthographic rules, is the aim of the "Agreement." That is not possible, because syntactic, lexical and semantic differences remain untouched. The linguistic variants of Portuguese language are numerous in all countries. The basic critics stress the inapplicability of such a document because the changes that were introduced were not scientifically correct; they produced an artificial language that can only be implemented through computer programs because it does not follow the natural evolution of the language. The radical changes in the European variant of Portuguese mean a real erasure of so-called "mute" consonants (most "p" and "c," which open the vowels and also display the Greek and Latin common roots and word family), affecting the most used words. A complete chaos is established because different writings and accent variations are accepted.

The so-called second Amendment Protocol of 2004 was ratified in May of 2008 by the Portuguese Parliament, by the majority of the deputies, due to party discipline, against the opinion of language experts and specialists in linguistics and against the language sensibility of a considerable majority of the Portuguese population.

According to that Amendment, it would be enough that only three countries, less than half of the eight countries of Portuguese official language (with East Timor as a new independent country), would be enough to ratify the Agreement in order to enforce it.

Since the beginning of 2012, all official documents of the Portuguese government are supposed to be written in that grapholect, which also affects the school programs and has been adopted by a considerable number of publications and publishing houses.

The Portuguese PEN Board calls upon the support of International PEN to its actions with the goal of implementing the discussion about the measures to be taken, in order to use all legal means to revoke that unhappy treaty, which does not respect the language diversity and autonomy of Euro-Afro Asiatic Portuguese.

The technical discussion involving the AO is too far-fetched to be discussed here, and the above citation mentions the major points under debate. The so-called agreement alters the traditional European spelling of Portuguese by changing the language matrix. Linguists argue that European Portuguese loses the common ground with its Indo-European branch. My mom says that the consequences have been disastrous for the language she learned in school as a child.

My mom wrote an open letter to the Minister of Education saying that the AO is a farce, an unprecedented, irresponsible, and unwise step. She explains that the attempt at language unification is not an agreement because linguists are unable to agree on the rules. In her letter she evokes the rights, liberties, and guarantees promulgated in our constitution, in particular, the right to freedom of expression and the right to linguistic identity. Because I'm a minor and my mom is in charge of my education, she says I'm only allowed to follow the norm of European Portuguese in school. She also forbade me to use the computer programs that convert European Portuguese to the rules of the AO.

As a medical doctor, she adds that the translations of medications and medical equipment from English into European Portuguese using the AO are abhorrent.

Moreover, the AO agreement was ratified by Parliament in 2008, followed by a Resolution of the Council of Ministers in 2011. Resolutions are not laws and therefore cannot be legally implemented. Thus, they do not repeal the previous spelling of Portuguese used in Portugal.

As a form of protest, the best-known writers and journalists in the country now end their writings with the following statement: So and So writes according to the old spelling.

My dad says that it doesn't matter whether the AO is legal or not. Since 2012 it has been implemented in schools, ministries, state banks, and the press. The transition period has been set to end in Portugal in 2016. In Brazil, the country that Portugal seems ready to cater to by emulating its language, implementation was also recently delayed until 2016. The Brazilians signed the agreement, but, of course, the country does what it wants.

Parents and administrators in the school system speak of an Orwellian world with prevailing chaos and confusion in the application of the new rules for spelling. However, if a parent or guardian prevents a child from using it, as my mother does, teachers obliged to use the new spelling might refuse to read or grade the work!

As I write this, not all CPLP countries have signed the AO. The Society of Portuguese Authors, *Sociedade Portuguesa de Autores*, has repudiated it and intellectuals demand a debate in Parliament. Surely new governmental commission will be formed to deal with the matter. Many of these bodies, however, are pointless in Portugal, a major reason being that they do not set a pre-established date to present conclusions.

My mom continues to say that a major reason the AO is useless is that the CPLP countries never spoke or wrote the same Portuguese as we did. In these countries, language has always been a mélange of the language spoken by the colonizer and the various indigenous ways of communicating. As such, the European norm of Portuguese should be maintained. Maintaining European Portuguese doesn't prevent, in my mom's opinion, the blend of European Portuguese with other languages. In the CPLP countries the combination is rather diversified, even creative. But the European matrix of Portuguese should be preserved. In addition, there are as many differences in the Portuguese spoken in East Timor as the Portuguese spoken in Cape Verde or Angola or Mozambique. The Portuguese spoken in the various regions of Brazil is also very diverse.

A case in point is the book *Budapeste* by Chico Buarque de Holanda. My mom says the book is great but adds that the book is written in a language different from the one she learned in school. The phonological, morphological, grammatical, semantic, and lexical differences within our Portuguese matrix are huge. She thinks *Budapeste* is a superb example of how Brazilian evolved from the Portuguese norm.

Brazil is not worried about implementing the AO. And why should it be? Brazilian Portuguese is already the language spoken in most international organizations. Some say that samba is the only language that unifies Brazil. So true, I love samba! Despite its words, the beat of Brazilian music—its erotic, open, soft, and light rhythm—has nothing to do with European Portuguese. For my mom the São Paulo Museum of the Portuguese Language is just for showing off.

Our politicians don't seem to understand what Brazil stands for. This is a country that looks to the United States for inspiration, knowledge, and technology. As a continent, the dialogue in the New World is primarily between north and south, not across the Atlantic Ocean.

For my mom, the attempt to unify European and Brazilian Portuguese came too late. Unfortunately—and my dad agrees on this point—the Portuguese didn't do what Spain and the Latin American countries did over the centuries. These countries always paid close attention to the language matrix, its diversity, and the local differences. The effort can be synthesized as language unification within creative proliferation.

This dynamic has not been the case for Portugal and Brazil, my mom says. We must rely on four hundred years of history. It's remarkable that, for all practical purposes, we continue to understand each other. Moreover, the worldwide use of English is the absolute proof of what my mom says: the language of Shakespeare continues to be the lingua franca of the English-speaking world despite the territorial differences worldwide.

The notion in Lisbon of a "common Portuguese language," spoken at the global level, is most utopian. The dream of Portuguese as one of the United Nations official languages is probably a dream of the past; the organization already has six official languages. To have more would only complicate the bureaucracy with added translations. The imagined Portuguese television channel on the magnitude of Al Jazeera undoubtedly will be in Brazilian Portuguese.

The AO is, thus, an inconsequential fast-forward movement that has impaired European Portuguese by attempting to destroy the Indo-European basis of its matrix.

My dad tells my mom to relax and look at the AO as the interplay of global world interests. The situation is comical and disconcerting at the same time. As an example, he cites the attempts of the citizens of the CPLP countries to enter the Schengen Space. This is a private club formed by the countries of the European Union that have abolished the national frontiers. There is free circulation of peoples and merchandise among them. For my dad, this is why so many CPLP citizens now want to have Portuguese citizenship. If Portuguese citizenship were granted to them, freedom of movement in most European nations would follow.

Failing this aim, the closest step, already addressed, is the establishment of a Lusophone citizenship or a CPLP one.

My mom laughs when my dad says this. And my dad laughs, too.

But my mom adds that there is more. Regrettably, rumors speak of corridors of corruption between the CPLP countries. I'll refrain from mentioning the cases that abound in the press because being white I will be accused of elitism and racism. The fact that mature democracies have in place institutionalized systems of checks and balances will be considered of minor significance. However, the other day, a high-ranking German official said on television that if the Portuguese insist on doing business with the emerging economies they must adhere to transparent practices.

Who can disagree with this statement?

Something is most disturbing, my mom points out. Equatorial Guinea, located in the Gulf of Guinea, now has the status of "Associated Observer" in the CPLP. Keep in mind that this is one of the regions in Africa where the slave trade by the Portuguese was most developed. The official language is Spanish, and French is also spoken. The majority of the population is Catholic. Before Spanish colonization, parts of this territory belonged to Portugal, the Portuguese Fernando Pó being the first to arrive. The country has substantial petroleum resources discovered in 1966; it's a fast-growing economy despite its utter poverty, and it is near the bottom of the UN human development index. According to Human Rights Watch Transparency International, Equatorial Guinea is among the top twelve most corrupt countries in the world. But the ruling dictator in Equatorial Guinea now wants Portuguese to be another one of its official languages despite the fact that no one speaks the language in the country.

Dubious, isn't it, to think that Equatorial Guinea could be a member of CPLP in the future?

I'm young, I'm a minor, and I enjoy my language, European Portuguese. I agree with my mom: the European matrix of the Portuguese language must be preserved. Then anyone, anywhere, can recreate the language as much as he or she wants.

Fernando Gil, the philosopher, has said that Portugal has a problem recognizing its territorial dimension, its smallness. But why? I like small. Small like Holland. Small like Ireland. Small like Denmark.

I finished my class assignment, signed it, and my parents have already read it. My mom says that having a gifted child raises delicate issues for a parent; my dad says he doesn't know what to do with me. I didn't follow the AO in my composition, so my teacher might not read or grade it.

I hear Woody Allen wants to do his next movie in Lisbon. I hope that instead of choosing espionage as he stated in an interview by recalling Casablanca, he opts for a satire based on empire, longing, and the crucial meaning of the keyword "overcast" in the Portuguese language. If he includes the current discussions in Portugal about the Spelling Agreement, hilarious as he is, he will have a masterpiece on his hands.

CPSIA information can be obtained at www.ICGtesting.com
Printed in the USA
BVOW05s0905290514

354694BV00003B/688/P

9 780991 504725